JASON KINDLE

JASON KINDLE

ENGINEER—THE GALAXY

S. A. GEORGE

iUniverse, Inc.
Bloomington

JASON KINDLE
Engineer—The Galaxy

iUniverse books may be ordered through booksellers or by contacting:

iUniverse
1663 Liberty Drive
Bloomington, IN 47403
www.iuniverse.com
1-800-Authors (1-800-288-4677)

ISBN: 978-1-4759-5149-3 (sc)
ISBN: 978-1-4759-5171-4 (ebk)

Printed in the United States of America

iUniverse rev. date: 10/30/2012

TABLE OF CONTENTS

Dedication vii

Epigraph ix

Warships—Earth—Narin...xi

Characters xiii

Chapter I.   Galaxy—Origins 1

Chapter II.   Galaxy—Battalion I 30

Chapter III.   Galaxy—Plot..42

Chapter IV.   Galaxy—AR'TYN..48

Chapter V.   Galaxy—They Came...68

Chapter VI.   Galaxy—Breedlove, The Search..............................90

Chapter VII.   Galaxy—The Executions...95

Chapter VIII.   Galaxy—The Planet Reactivated 98

Chapter IX.   Galaxy—Memory Revisited 109

Chapter X.   Galaxy—What on Earth 125

Chapter XI.   Galaxy—The Children—Jacob 145

Chapter XII.   Galaxy—The Choice..157

Chapter XIII.   Galaxy—The Journey...168

Chapter XIV.   Definitions..193

Credits 205

DEDICATION

To those who study the Heavens and unravel mysteries to the enjoyment of all of us who appreciate the wonders of the universe.

To Kay, thank you for encouragement, friendship and typing this manuscript.

To the creator of the wonders we see from our tiny but remarkable planet.

Thank you Ida and Rodger for being so special and very encouraging.

EPIGRAPH

This book leads the reader through several adventures as experienced by Jason Kindle a young man traveling from Earth to a new world in deep space along with two hundred others. Their ship is called The Galaxy. Jason is training to become a botanist like his parents but an encounter with an alien woman changes all that and be becomes an engineer. He is pressured to grow up quickly and is challenged at every turn. He must make decisions that affect others to protect those he loves, putting himself in harm's way.

The visit to NARIN'MAR is one of the most remarkable journeys in his young life, taken to save the life of the alien woman he has joined with.

WARSHIPS—EARTH—NARIN

HUMAN:

Patrol Cruisers: Laser armament—carry 6 "ION" engine —Warp 6

Long Range Cruisers: Laser armament—carry 20 "ION" engine —Warp 6, 7

Short Range Cruisers: Laser armament—carry 6 "ION" engine —Warp 6, 7

WARSHIPS:

Galaxy (Prototype—deep space):   Laser cannon armament "ION" engine X—Warp 4

Battalion Classes:

I.	ION X—1 Warp 6
II.	ION X—2 Warp 7-8
III.	ION X—3 Warp 7-8

NARIN:

Photon Engines

Matter—Antimatter: These ships are long, oblong with colorful markings on the under-section extending to the nose with small markings on the two wings on either side.

Patrol Cruisers: Laser armament—carry 10 "Photon" engine—Warp 8

Long Range Cruisers: Laser armament—carry 20 "Photon" engine—Warp 8

Short Range Cruisers: Laser armament—carry 10 "Photon" engine—Warp 8

Warships:

Prototype (deep space):   Laser Cannon (largest warship)—"Photon Y" engine—Warp 8, 9

All Warships (deep space):   Laser Cannon—"Photon X" engine—Warp 7, 8

CHARACTERS

Jason Kindle:	Young passenger aboard The Galaxy, married to Myra, becomes a botanist and engineer.
Allison Kindle:	Jason's sister
Bella Kindle:	Jason and Allison's mother married to Jackson, both were botanists.
Jackson Kindle:	Jason and Allison's father married to Bella. The botanist who created the 'toxin'.
VE'AR:	Narin leader, father of Myra, father-in-law to Jason
Myra:	Daughter of VE'AR married to Jason
MY'AR:	Daughter of Jason and Myra
JAS'AR:	Son of Jason and Myra
Colonel Sobel:	Commander of Galaxy Ship
Lieutenant Colonel Benoit:	Colonel Sobel's Second in command
Henry Ferris:	Chief Engineer on Galaxy Ship
Lieutenant John Miller:	In charge of security under Colonel Sobel
Marco Fox:	Friend of Jason Kindle, communications expert
AR'TYN:	Narin scientist, marries Lieutenant Wanda Sykes

Bright Star:	Planet destination for the Galaxy, their new home world
Sanctus:	Planet that became a Narin outpost and also a sanctuary for the human population if attacked on Bright Star
KA'OW:	Mystery planet named by the Narins meaning 'The Ancients'. Home of the Crystal Entities
Galaxy:	Commander Sobel, Colonel and Judge on Galaxy ship, first earth ship to reach the new world
Earth Force Battalion I:	Commander Scott, Lieutenant Colonel on Battalion I first class warship
Earth Force Battalion II:	Commander Neal, Colonel and Judge on Battalion II first class warship
Earth Force Battalion III:	Commander Breedlove, Admiral on Battalion III first class warship
NARIN'MAR:	Narin home world
Dr. Rashid:	Doctor and friend of Jackson family aboard Galaxy
Thomas Bruffel:	Crewmember, master sergeant aboard Battalion 1
Sergeant Blondell:	Part of Battalion II crew, wife of Colonel Neal
Private Forbes:	Part of Battalion II crew
Lieutenant Wanda Sykes:	An officer on Battalion I, wife of AR'TYN
MAR'TYN:	Narin scientist who helped Jason to walk again
Lieutenant Colonel Brandon Wells:	Commander Neal's Second in command
Private Sussman:	Assigned as a new recruit on Battalion II

<u>Chief Master Sergeant Ralph Natinski:</u>	Crewmember on Battalion II
<u>Judge Jonathan Iglesis:</u>	Judge aboard Battalion III
<u>Engineer Ovilla:</u>	Chief Engineer, part of Battalion II crew
<u>Commander Neal:</u>	Colonel, Judge in command of Battalion II
<u>Commander Breedlove:</u>	Admiral, in command of Battalion III, mentor to Colonel Neal
<u>Commander Scott:</u>	Lieutenant Colonel in command of Battalion I
<u>AR'BIN:</u>	Narin who escaped imprisonment for crimes against Narin society
<u>SA'MAR:</u>	Narin astrophysist from NARIN'MAR
<u>Dr. Hanna Sol:</u>	Earth astrophysist
<u>Dr. James Weed:</u>	Earth astrophysist and engineer —creator of the Mechanism
<u>The Mechanism:</u>	Manmade black hole, launched into orbit around Earth's sun
<u>Murphy:</u>	Park security guard on Earth, Washington, D.C.
<u>Evander Kowalski:</u>	Mechanic from the Battalion I
<u>RU'AR:</u>	Narin woman married to Evander Kowalski
<u>Jacob:</u>	Son of Evander and RU'AR
<u>Dr. Planck:</u>	Chief scientist aboard Battalion II, Ethiopian
<u>Lt. Vann:</u>	Communications officer aboard Battalion II
<u>AN'ZAR:</u>	Narin commander and later admiral of prototype warship

<u>Crystal Entity:</u>	Entities on planet KA'OW, looked like Crystals
<u>John Ames:</u>	Minister aboard Galaxy
<u>Lieutenant CH'AR:</u>	Narin lieutenant aboard ship carrying passengers in stasis
<u>Ianis:</u>	Name of constellation and star producing the green spectral light
<u>BEN'ZAR:</u>	Narin scientist on mission to Ianis
<u>AUR'ZIN:</u>	Commander of mission to Ianis (over all four ships)
<u>Dark Matter Entity:</u>	Malcolm, the human miner
<u>Jennifer:</u>	Human, Malcolm's choice
<u>BA'LOL:</u>	A Narin commander
<u>SO'TYN:</u>	A Narin commander
<u>Mark:</u>	Steven and Shirley's son
<u>Dr. Vu:</u>	Entomologist on Bright Star
<u>Jonas Zondervan:</u>	Rabbi in training officiating at a small temple on Bright Star
<u>SETTIS:</u>	Rebel Home World
<u>Jamie Fox:</u>	Daughter of Marco and Allison
<u>JA'LAR:</u>	Narin ice boat competitor
<u>I'SA:</u>	Province on NARIN'MAR
<u>PAL'EO:</u>	Town on NARIN'MAR where Jason lived as Myra was reborn. City of Mar University.

CHAPTER I

GALAXY—ORIGINS

2100 AD Washington D.C.

"The pollution is level ten," a news report said, "limit all outdoor activities for the next several days."

Tragic things were happening on planet Earth, intermittent acid rain and other terrible consequences of global warming. The other planets Mercury, Venus and Mars were experiencing their own climactic problems. There were wars fought between the "First Four" as the planets were called, for fuel. The moons had provided areas for mining as the planets' resources became depleted.

The planetarium had provided a diversion especially to those attending school who couldn't play their sports outdoors on certain days when the pollution was bad. Jason Kindle and his friend Marco Fox attended the planetarium normally on weekends; they could only imagine what space travel would be like.

Jason's father Dr. Kindle was a botanist who was keeping a secret. Several miles away he participated in a project with other scientists to find ways to maintain life while traveling in space and the ability to grow sustaining foods once they reached a habitable planet. Animals could be brought and put in stasis, also the cells of the animals to be cloned would be preserved as well as vegetation, plant and tree seedlings. The project would culminate in the eventual launching of the largest space ship ever for deep space passenger travel and the only one to reach across the Milky Way. Only those chosen as Dr. Kindle, astrophysists, scientists, doctors, people who could contribute to finding and maintaining life on another world, teachers and the accompanying families as well as the Commander, crew and the military would venture out into that realm of deep space to find a new world, a new home. Astrophysicists had selected three possibilities. Ages of the travellers would range from sixty and under in good health; many families would be split forever as some were left behind. Months passed.

A week before, the ship, known as the Galaxy was to launch, those going packed and prepared themselves. All two hundred were now put in stasis, this included the Commander, his crew of twenty-five and twenty of the military. There was a super computer running the ship and making corrections in trajectory as needed while secondary computers performed other tasks.

A small ship after fifty years attached itself to the Galaxy. Something exited the craft and entered the large ship. Looking around, the Presence entered the stasis area after carefully searching the records of each in stasis, stood over one chamber and opened it. The young man inside was fast asleep. The Presence left him knowing he would awaken soon. Hours later he did, his legs were weak and he fell several times. He saw his mother, father and sister among the two hundred still asleep, it frightened him. He was fifteen at the beginning of the trip and hadn't aged in fifty years of stasis. He didn't know how long the ship had been traveling, could he reenter stasis or simply age and die before the others? He continued to walk carefully as he made his way to the smaller galley. He reasoned that this trip to find a habitable planet was worth any risk even the failure of his stasis chamber if it could save mankind.

He began a daily exercise regiment then on to studying plants, he was being schooled as a botanist like his mother and father before stasis and it was to have been continued when everyone awakened. In the meantime he compiled information on how space travel affected plants, lighting, chemicals, growth patterns—the journal would help others even when he was gone. It was important to Jason to make his mother and dad proud of him.

His I-pod became his companion, the music was a mixture of late twentieth and twenty-first century rock and classical. He loved ice cream and randomly made raids on the smaller of four galleys. The basketball court offered no competition but he competed with himself for exercise. The shower, sonic and water relaxed him. The loneliness was overwhelming, sleep was difficult.

A week passed, he was in the galley sitting in a chair with his feet up braced against a table reading. Suddenly, as he was drinking hot coffee, someone entered, he spilled the coffee in his lap and fell backwards onto the floor. He looked up and saw a woman, creamy skin, tall, black short hair, beautiful, wearing a metallic white suit.

"If you're not real, let me imagine a while longer," he said.

She now stood over him, he stood up. She touched his face. "I'm real." She was fascinated with him, he had thick brown hair and grey eyes.

"I'm Jason Kindle." He stood about five ten, she was about as tall. "I'm the son of scientists in stasis. Who are you?"

"I arrived a week ago observing you after freeing you from stasis."

"How did human beings get out this far?" assuming she was human.

"They didn't until your ship." She could tell he didn't understand.

"You've been observing me?"

"You and your kind are aliens to us . . . yes, I've been observing you."

"Oh . . ."

"We can read your thoughts." She turns to him.

"Don't, not now, it's not good what I'm thinking," he said.

She laughed, "You're one of the younger ones."

"I'm fifteen, technically having been taken out of stasis I'm not older biologically but around fifty-five years have passed."

"Only fifty," she replied. "You can call me Myra, a close equivalent of my name and easier to pronounce. The trajectory of your ship has been altered, you and the others are headed into a white sun."

This was startling to Jason, he sat as he listened. "Can the course be altered?"

"It must be if any of you are to survive. My mission was to decide your fates."

"Based on what? You don't know us."

"But I know you, I studied you, reading your thoughts, studying the database of each one in stasis. Thinking mathematical equations won't totally block your thoughts from me Jason. We must begin to prepare you to save your ship. Your body, your brain must be reconfigured to absorb a vast amount of data needed to pilot and maintain this ship. The data will be fed directly into your brain over a period of days so not to cause a stroke or heart failure."

"You've read up on this obviously."

"I've become familiar with human anatomy."

"Why me?"

"Why not?"

"When?"

"We start tomorrow, my ship will aid in the process as you will be aged ten years, that should mature you enough. You have four earth weeks to begin the course changes."

"Tell me who and what you are."

"I will show you what I am, but not just yet."

Jason showed her places on the ship that were special to him including the botany section. "These plants and seedlings are all we have of Earth." She listened, being interested in the problems on Earth and these courageous people who were making the journey to survive. She encouraged him to document what he was about to do with her help. She hoped his sacrifice would be appreciated by those whose lives he saved. He realized that he couldn't reenter stasis and would die before the others awakened.

That night he assisted her in getting a chamber ready to age him. He prepared himself and laid down inside. He was hooked up to a neuro-interface to transmit the data from the Galaxy into his brain as he was matured physically and mentally. He asked one question.

"Have you ever done anything like this?"

"No, but I am confident," she smiled. "Try to stay calm, you might pass out."

The chamber was cold and he was only allowed a sheet for warmth. As the process began he felt as if his body was being pulled apart, he cried out briefly even as he struggled not to, then he passed out.

In three weeks all the pertinent data had been fed into his brain. She had fed him using a food source made up of vitamins and nutrients through a type of I.V. she found on the Galaxy. She awakened him, "It worked Jason, your life signs are good." He sat up as she steadied him, she saw how muscular he was, now taller, mature, she then removed the neuro-interface connections transmitting the data. He walked over to a bed and collapsed, she allowed him to sleep for several hours. "You did good Jason," she said. She stayed with him not believing how brave he had been.

Two days later he was awake. As he studied the changes it was hard to comprehend that physically he was now twenty-five. He had some lingering side effects as headaches and muscle aches as a result of rapid growth mentally and physically.

He found a uniform on the Galaxy, not totally resembling the uniforms of the crew but was appropriate for addressing the ship's log. He got a haircut by a robotic pair of hands in the barber shop, shaved, then addressed the crew documenting everything pertinent, what he was going to do to put the Galaxy back on the correct trajectory with the help of an alien entity.

Myra took her ship and nudged the Galaxy then the course changes made by Jason and Myra kicked in and would take the Galaxy to the intended planet still within the Milky Way Galaxy avoiding the sun and its gravitational death grip on the ship now traveling at Warp 4. Jason again explained that the trajectory had been altered probably by a passing ion storm even showing by diagram the new course. Myra was standing by him for a few moments as he addressed the ship's log. ["I am documenting the changes because I can't reenter stasis and will not be around to explain our actions. Ship's log out, Jason Kindle acting in the Commander's absence. Good luck on the new world."] The logs were also sent to Earth as well even though hundreds of years would have passed.

Myra was going to leave the ship and Jason but she now had feelings for him. She read his thoughts one evening as he was looking through the data base at people he knew, he didn't want to die and certainly not before experiencing loving someone; he had developed feelings for Myra but couldn't see how she would feel the same.

One evening she asked to stay with him on the Galaxy, she had been reading about human sexuality. They went to his parent's compartment.

"I want to join with you."

He seemed surprised. "I have feelings for you Myra but I don't expect you to reciprocate."

In a while she attempted to join herself to him. "I did research on this."

He was emotionally still a boy trying to respond as a man. "I've never done this so I'm very awkward." He was frustrated at himself.

"We should keep trying," she said.

"You'll be leaving me."

"I want to join with you, to get to know you, I didn't say I would leave you."

"You didn't have to . . . to stay with me and see me die outside of stasis."

Finally they were able to join. They kissed, he was filled with emotions he had never felt before. She was feeling bonded to him now, she didn't understand these feelings but wanted to.

He slept. She required far less sleep than a human being, she watched him most of the night wondering if she could save him, touching his face, she kissed him then slept.

Jason urged her to leave and not see him die. "You've fulfilled me."

"Let's work on the stasis problem," she said pretending she didn't hear him. They did, on his chamber on the Galaxy then on hers aboard her ship, to no avail. His frustration was evident even as he tried to mask it, he wanted to live and be with her.

They sat in an observation area watching the stars. He treated her to ice cream. "How are you breathing our atmosphere?"

She showed him three pills. "I have only three left, each will provide a source of air for twenty-four of your hours. I will then be forced to leave in three days." She looked at him not wanting to leave.

The next evening they would say their goodbyes and celebrate their collaboration and friendship. Each presented food and drink from their two cultures. He brought her flowers from the botany lab. They talked, he played music from his iPod, she did as she played sounds emanating from a crystal banwith, an instrument which made music when spectral light hit it. They made love for the last time. As she is joined to him she revealed herself as she really was—she didn't want to thinking he couldn't handle it. When he saw the brightness of her form, who she was, he took a deep breath as if startled and closed his eyes for a moment.

"Are you all right Jason?" She asked.

"I will be, it's a bit overwhelming . . . I could get used to it." He now loved her more at that moment.

She knew without reading his mind that he wouldn't survive the loneliness when she left him which she did the next day.

As time went on his thoughts turned, his uniform was exchanged for very casual clothes, the Galaxy was sterile without anyone to talk to—he now knew engineering and other things about the Galaxy. His hair had grown longer and was now in a braid, he had a goatee and smaller moustache. Periodically he would check the new course on the main computer and was very capable now of piloting this huge ship when and if it became necessary. He also checked the botany lab and made reports. Sleep was sporadic and he slept in the piloting section, the noise of the instruments and main computers seemed to fill the loneliness at times. He contemplated what his life had come to and what would never be. He prepared himself for an eventual death. Jason dreamed about his new world and what awaited all two hundred travellers. Myra was there, he was holding her hand on that new world.

Two months passed. There was a voice that called to him. "Jason." He didn't awaken. "Jason." She had returned to him, it seemed longer than two months.

He opened his eyes, "Myra?"

"There is a way you can live, if you're in my stasis chamber."

"You're really back." They embraced.

She kissed him, "We'll make this journey together."

"How? Let me hear it . . . by the way your use of contractions is getting better."

She shows him how it could work and using a chemical she found on "A planet several light years from here, you would call it a type of salt."

"You have given me hope."

"Prepare yourself for the next one hundred and fifty years."

Jason did, haircut, shave; appearing in uniform he addressed the ship's log. ["Jason Kindle acting in the Colonel's absence, I am about to reenter stasis on the alien ship, if it works, alien technology will have saved me. I hope to be there with all of you when the Galaxy arrives home . . . ship's log out."]

He removes his uniform and puts on a stasis outfit. They have planned their strategy. He would sleep in her stasis chamber breathing the vapors from the salt which she would modify through a mask which would preserve him, she would be in with him breathing her own atmosphere and monitoring his life signs for the duration of the trip even as she slept.

The Galaxy stayed true to the new course and arrived in orbit around the planet which was twice the size of Earth circling a white sun with one moon joining two other planets in this small solar system. Rotation was every twenty-eight hours.

Stasis chambers were opened, everyone made it but one, Jason Kindle who apparently had a stasis chamber to malfunction and died one-hundred fifty years earlier. His parents and sister cried as they mourned the loss of their son. The Commander and crew discovered entries to the ship's log documenting course changes saving the Galaxy from being vaporized. The main computer was thrown off, it was surmised, by an intense ion storm. They saw the alien woman credited for helping save the ship and all on board, she appeared standing by Jason. He repeatedly told them that he had been aged ten years to accept the ship's database concerning piloting, engineering and navigation only as the data was fed into his brain, no information other than that he had told them.

The crew noticed there was a large object clinging to the underside of the ship. They found Jason inside; as they opened the stasis chamber a white vapor exited. The atmosphere inside was alien.

"Jason Kindle," the Colonel said as they awakened him. "I hardly recognize you, you are grown." They helped Jason sit up.

"My mind isn't so clear right now."

"Seems you saved our lives and you also give credit to an alien entity."

"Yes Sir, all documented."

"With all the knowledge you now possess I'm prompting you to be part of my crew in engineering."

"I don't feel I deserve it . . . my parents and sister? Did they make it?"

"We all did."

The Colonel looked at his Lieutenant and two soldiers who were very paranoid about the situation and gave signals for them to back off. Jason tried to walk.

"I like the uniform," the Colonel said as he saw it folded neatly in the alien ship.

"If I was addressing the Colonel and crew, I felt I must look my best."

"Where is she, the alien?"

"Around here somewhere, I'm anxious to find her."

He was taken to his parents and sister. They couldn't believe he was alive thinking he had died as a result of an interrupted stasis. His mother cried as she hugged him, everyone hugged him not believing how grown he was.

"Ten years did this?" His father said in disbelief.

"Yes Sir." He hugged them. "My little sister," he laughed, "I am now twenty-five, older than you."

She was hesitant at first to accept him but glad he was alive.

"There is a shortage of ice cream," he said to her.

She smiled. "We could always talk about anything," she said.

"I hope we still can, I know things are different."

Later, Jason was commended, "For saving two-hundred lives and the ship and we'll thank your friend as well."

No one else aboard knew about this commendation except the Colonel who gave it and his executive officers and the Lieutenant of the military and two of his men.

"Thank you Sir and I honestly don't know her whereabouts, she doesn't present a danger."

"How would you know that?" Lieutenant Miller asked him.

"I just know, she kept us from being vaporized."

"And that is well and good, but anyone aboard this ship needs to declare themselves non-hostile," the Colonel said. "Now go to sickbay with the Lieutenant and get checked out."

"Try to find her Jason," the Lieutenant said emphatically as he escorted him to sickbay.

"Yes Sir."

Afterward, Jason left feeling confused like he had been interrogated.

The Lieutenant later talked candidly with the Colonel. "All the information the boy has downloaded in his head presents a danger to us from anyone wanting our technology."

The Colonel then replied, "When you looked at that alien spacecraft, didn't you feel as I did that they didn't, wouldn't need anything from us—creatures so advanced and we're living on their doorstep?"

The Lieutenant didn't reply as he and his men left.

Jason tried to reach Myra but couldn't, even trying telepathically. He then went to his parents' compartment. They felt uneasy, no one knew how to act. Then he spoke.

"If it's all right can I stay here? I realize outwardly I'm different but inside I'm still Jason."

"Of course Jason," his mother said, "you changed so much, we'll get used to it."

"I have no clothes but this outfit."

"Jackson," she called Jason's father, "can you help Jason?"

He did. "Looks like a trip to the store for you son, but try these on, we're both six feet now."

"Thanks."

"Oh, your mother and I read your reports concerning the botany results, fine work . . . now let's eat."

Afterward he took a sonic shower, Myra suddenly came, she kept him from expressing his surprise with a hand over his mouth.

"They are wanting to meet you but it's more like to interrogate you like they did me . . . don't reveal yourself yet Myra, it doesn't feel right."

"All right."

"How long since you've eaten?"

"Several hours while I was still aboard my ship."

"Well you can't go back there, I can't get near it. I'll bring you something if you'll just tell me or better yet I'm through with my shower, let's go." Then, "Mom, Dad, I'll be back soon, going to look at clothes."

He left for the galley instead, Myra remained as a white almost invisible mist communicating with Jason remembering what foods she liked when they shared their respective cultures earlier. He came back to his parent's compartment with a tray of various foods and a pair of new pants; no one saw her as she entered with Jason.

"Still hungry," he said as he went to his room. Myra ate and drank and spent the night with him. She was nervous, he held her.

The next day he attended botany classes. The stares and whispers spoke volumes to him, he tried to ignore it. The next class was mathematics which he easily understood because of his mind being restructured and the data fed into him. He was with students he had known all his life but he felt he didn't belong anymore.

The Colonel summoned him after classes were over.

"I could use you Jason in either engineering or navigation, your choice, your decision, you're twenty-five now."

"But Sir, I'm a botanist."

"Son what do you want to do aboard this ship? If botany is your choice then I respect that, however we could use your new found knowledge to assist us."

"Yes Sir, it would be a privilege, I'd like to discuss this with my parents."

"Certainly, tomorrow then."

"Thank you Sir."

The Colonel decided to see if Jason would fit into this new role and add any input to running the ship and hopefully to keep an eye on him and from possible harm from the Lieutenant who was determined to use any means to make Jason answer all questions and produce the alien.

Jason discussed the Colonel's offer with his parents. They agreed it was a privilege.

"I would earn my degree in engineering and perhaps navigation."

"It sounds too good to be true," his father said, "I think you should do it."

He and Allison went for a walk, he discussed the opportunity with her.

"You'll miss your friends," she said.

"At the moment I don't seem to have any. No one is comfortable with me, even Mom and Dad can't reconcile that I'm truly Jason, they are distant, asking me personal questions to validate me as their son. You don't believe I'm your brother."

"I'm trying to . . . think about it, you're out of the stasis chamber, aged ten years saying an alien entity intercepted the Galaxy and together you both saved the ship from vaporizing."

"Right, why would they believe any of it, no records of this but the personal address to the ship's log, it was never acknowledged publically so . . . but her ship should be proof."

"No one else knows? If there was some way to prove it; only one person could find those records, Marco. Her ship doesn't prove everything, her help or being on our side."

"Don't bother with Marco. So far as anyone knows I'm an aged fifteen year old with navigation, engineering and piloting abilities pumped into my head by an alien woman now hesitant to reveal herself to a nervous military and accommodating Colonel who will have her probed, examined and probably extinguished . . . great."

They got ice cream.

"Jason, somehow this will work out," she said.

"We'll see, my physical for my new job is tomorrow, but there is more to this. Emotionally I'm still fifteen and I don't know if I can handle what's coming."

She touched his hand. "Let's walk . . . where is she?"

"I don't know, I've brought her food, she'll die if she doesn't get away from here . . . the air she's breathing is toxic, our secret."

"Yes, out secret. Do you love her?"

"What a question." Jason didn't answer.

That night Myra visited him. They talked about several things and what he had told Allison.

"How are you breathing this air?"

"The same thing that helped you in stasis, the salt combined with another chemical and combined with the sonic shower as necessary."

"Do I need to . . . ?"

"No, I'm good for several days from what you brought."

"I start in engineering and probably navigation tomorrow, the Colonel wants to keep me close to keep an eye on me. We have to get you to your ship before they find you. I wish I could join you wherever your journey takes you."

They made love quietly.

The next day he reported to the doctor for the examination. He stripped down and laid down on a table. His DNA was tested, x-rays, heart, lungs, his brain was wired and checked. Dr. Rashid was a friend of the Kindle family, Jason didn't know the neurologist who checked his brain patterns. The Lieutenant was observing the examination, Jason wasn't aware he was there.

"All areas are capable of working at once," he said.

Jason was then questioned extensively while wired to a truth monitor.

"Have you had intercourse lately?" Dr. Rashid asked. He didn't ask if he joined with the alien.

"No Sir, what does this have to do with my job?"

"The monitor says differently . . . never mind that, you passed."

He had known the doctor for years and now felt like he was a stranger. He then reported to the Colonel and started to work in engineering.

The Colonel, Doctor and Lieutenant all conversed later about Jason's examination.

"You put him through too much at once," the Colonel said.

"We have to know things about him," the Lieutenant replied.

The Colonel didn't appreciate the treatment Jason was getting but allowed it.

Jason then worked with the Chief Engineer, Henry Ferris who familiarized him with the areas he would be responsible for. After working with Jason for several hours, he asked him what improvements could be made and was impressed with his knowledge. Over a period of two weeks, Jason made several suggestions to improve engine performance and how it would affect the whole ship. He was given credit for several improvements which the Chief Engineer documented for the Colonel. Jason seemed to be fitting into his new role much to the disapproval of the Lieutenant. He was being carefully watched; bringing the food back to his parent's compartment was now under scrutiny.

"How did it go today?" His father asked him, hugging him.

"Good, Chief Engineer Henry and I seem to be making improvements."

"Dinner is almost ready," his mother said as she gave him a hug. "And the Lieutenant stopped by, he wants you to report to sickbay for another exam tomorrow."

"That's ridiculous, I've been for an exam nearly every day for two weeks."

"Now Jason, just placate the man."

"What concerns me, besides these excessive exams is that the Lieutenant would know when you're alone here after all day in the botany lab," Jackson said, "knowing we both would meet with him . . . that guy's got a screw loose. Jason, you should see the doctor."

"Do either of you believe I'm still Jason, your son, even being ten years older?"

They both looked at each other, "The DNA test was inconclusive," his mother said.

"That's impossible."

"We still believe you're Jason; maybe the alien woman did something to change your DNA."

"But she didn't, she aged me and reconfigured my brain to accept a vast amount of data concerning this ship so we could change course and not be vaporized as we headed into a white sun. The Colonel and Lieutenant know this but refuse to give her or me credit for this publically." Allison was out of sight listening.

"If you would just tell the Colonel where she is."

"They would interrogate her and might extinguish her as a presumed threat . . . from seeing their technology aboard her ship, they are more than capable of destroying us if that was their intent." Jason then stood up, "Goodnight," he said. Myra didn't come to Jason that evening, he was very concerned.

The next day he paid a visit to the doctor. He was probed and questioned, his brain waves were monitored. He questioned the results of the DNA test. "Inconclusive," came the reply from the neurologist and the doctor. Jason didn't believe them. He left for engineering, Myra spoke to him, he talked to her as he walked along a busy corridor resisting the temptation to look in her direction which would arouse suspicion.

"Where have you been? Are you all right?"

"For now, but the Lieutenant is planning a destructive end for you and your sister and for me."

"We have to talk," he said.

"Make every effort to appear that things are normal," she replied. "I know things aren't going well for you Jason."

"All I wanted was to be with you."

She touched his shoulder, "We will be together."

He now began to work that day with Henry. Hours passed as evening came and both had worked overtime. Suddenly as Henry and Jason were walking down the corridor, plasma discharges surrounded them. There were others who saw this but couldn't shut the power off. The plasma discharges burned them. "Stay there," Henry told Jason, he called on his ship communicator for help. The Colonel was notified. Henry shouted orders to the others. Finally the power was shut down.

"Are you all right?" the Colonel asked.

"There's no way this happened by accident," Henry told him. "I saw someone leaving quickly before this happened . . . I'm all right, Jason, you ok?"

"Sir, I'm all right, just a burn on my leg."

They were escorted to sickbay.

Later that evening Jason went home, his parents worried about him, were relieved. They ate dinner as he relayed the events of the evening, then a call. "It's the Colonel for you Jason," Allison said.

"Jason, if it's convenient, meet with me in my office, say thirty minutes."

"Yes Sir, I'll be there. I'm to meet with him now."

"We'll see you later son."

Jason left. He knew his parents were pretending to accept him, maybe they would in time. He arrived at the Colonel's office.

"This conversation is totally private between us, no monitoring and not recorded," he told Jason. "Where is the alien woman?"

"I never really know. I do know she didn't cause the plasma disturbance earlier."

"How do you know?"

Jason looked to the floor for a moment thinking, then as he faced the Colonel, "She wouldn't harm me . . . she wants to leave but doesn't want to leave without me. Her people have the technology to destroy us or welcome us as evidenced by that ship of hers. I have been isolated from my family and friends as a punishment for not bringing her to be probed and interrogated as I have. If she doesn't leave soon I fear she will be extinguished. No one aboard this ship knows but you and certain members of your crew and the Lieutenant and his men what this one alien and I did together to save the Galaxy and you acknowledged that to me."

"We haven't released the information because we're doing more research. What does she know about our weapons?"

"I don't think she cares about our weapons, just feeding me data on navigation, engineering and piloting this ship."

"Have you and she . . . ?"

"Yes despite our difficulty at first in doing so." The Colonel didn't pursue this.

"You lied about that to the doctors."

"Yes. In part because the Lieutenant has initiated these interrogations and grueling physicals done on me . . . I believe it's to wear me down and discredit me."

"I'll see if I can do something about it. Will you bring her to us?"

"She'll die." Jason was sincere and was determined to protect her as best he could.

The Colonel changed the subject, "Henry says you're doing well."

"He's a good instructor. I hope his burns weren't serious, we both dodged a bullet."

The Colonel was a good judge of character and he was studying Jason. "Go be with your family and consider today a job well done . . . Henry will be fine, we'll find whoever sabotaged the plasma relays . . . be careful."

"Yes Sir."

The Colonel kept his word and no one knew what was said in their private meeting.

Colonel Sobel had been given the monumental task of being the first to bring two-hundred passengers across the galaxy in a newly designed ship for long range interstellar travel. He knew most of the passengers going and some intimately as Dr. Jackson and his family. Bright Star was the planet chosen of the three possible choices as he and scientists had discussed. It was going to be very challenging, including how he would deal with the citizens of their new found world and a fragile beginning as a new government was formed. How would new life forms be dealt with? He had thought back on these questions and his decisions even now as he scrutinized a relationship between Jason Kindle and an alien entity which he would later regret.

The minister, John Ames who became a passenger on the trip was a last minute replacement for a friend, a minister the Colonel knew personally for several years who died the night before the trip. This devastated him. In the past he had sought his friend for comfort and advice. Minister Ames had preached two Sundays in one of the Galaxy's galleys before everyone was put in stasis. He was asked to bless the trip by the Colonel. Unfortunately he preached a 'do what you want attitude no matter who it hurts', which reflected his attitude. He did say a prayer for the trip which went something like this: "If there is a God, we hope he sees us through this, if not were . . ." Everyone had the same reaction, shock.

"Were did they get this guy?" Jason whispered to his Dad.

"I wish I knew and could send him back."

Bella, Jason's mother whispered, "I heard there have been recent suicides in his congregation."

"He looks and acts very immature," Jackson replied.

Colonel Sobel had a visit with Pastor Ames the evening before stasis. He needed comfort and reassurance but he instead comforted the pastor who seemed very unsure of anything at that moment. He and his Second in command, Lieutenant Benoit, discussed several matters before the journey began. They were friends and had fought together in the Mars-Earth Wars.

Two hundred years had passed when they awoke from stasis. The Colonel, after the initial shock of the missing Jason Kindle whose stasis chamber had opened prematurely, sought out the pastor and took him to an observation window showing the part of the Milky Way they had just crossed.

"If you look out there across the galaxy and the trip we just made, you can't convince me there isn't a God."

Pastor Ames just stood there as he looked out that window at the galaxy saying nothing for a few moments . . . then, "Thanks for being a good navigator and getting us here."

The Colonel then gave a firm pat to his shoulder. "Now we have a new home and you have people who need your encouragement." The Colonel then left to find Jason's remains and comfort the family; he was found alive on the alien ship.

Jason again stopped by the galley and brought home more food, he was followed by two guards who then entered to see who was eating the food. Allison caught on and began eating it.

"The food is for her, she hasn't felt well."

"Not in days," she said.

The guards were satisfied and left.

"Is she here?" Allison asked after taking a bite of the food.

"Thanks for covering for me and I don't know if she is."

Bella and Jackson came home as the guards left.

"They wanted to escort me here after the meeting with the Colonel; he asked questions about the plasma incident—seems Henry and I were meant to . . ." He didn't finish. "Goodnight, I'll be gone most of the day tomorrow." He hugged them wanting to feel loved. To his surprise Myra was there as he showered. They made love. She then ate the rest of the food.

"The salt is running low Jason."

"How long?" he asked.

"Five days is all I have to extract breathable air."

"I've got to get you out of here."

They talked.

The next day he went over the events of last evening studying the plasma relays. Henry found him. "Find anything?"

"Unfortunately no. Hopefully they'll look into it. We were sabotaged . . . why?"

"The inspector will say they found nothing; whoever did this was careful." He looked at Jason, "Let's get to work, you've got a degree to earn."

"Yes Sir."

Hours passed, break time came, Jason went to the closest galley. Marco came over to him and sat at his table.

"Marco, you got what you wanted," Jason said with a tempered smile.

Marco put down his school books. "That's just it, I'm not gloating over this . . . you're actually becoming very popular."

"I miss being in the class with friends my own age, but since I was aged by an alien who actually needed my help to keep the ship from being vaporized, I'm not fitting in. Engineering is using me and my new found knowledge to get my degree . . . why are you here?"

"Allison made me aware of things, the interrogations, the examinations. There has been a conspiracy against you. I've been digging through the ship's records and logs and I've found your entries along with the alien woman."

"That could get you banned or jail time. Be careful Marco, the Lieutenant in charge of security and the military is powerful, he will come for me and anyone who gets close, that might include Allison."

"Everyone thinks I hate your guts."

"You do."

"You wouldn't let me date Allison."

"She's vulnerable and you lied to me about sleeping with her to travel here."

"I would never take advantage, I think I love her . . . I regret the lie."

"Good answer, I won't try to stop you, she does about what she wants anyway."

"Where is the alien?"

"Myra? I don't know, I'm getting concerned, her breathable air supply is gone in five days and I've got to get her to her ship. They want me to turn her over to them. I won't, she isn't a threat."

"I think I can help, hang in there."

"You too." Jason was glad to have an unlikely ally in Marco.

That evening when he got home, two guards were there and took him for an interrogation. His mother and father reluctantly let him go. For four hours Jason was interrogated by the Lieutenant, he could feel his anger as he asked questions demeaning to him, trying to break him down. He didn't understand it, wondering if the Colonel was aware. He was given a physical afterward.

"His heart rate is up, it might be too much all in one session," the doctor said.

"Cut him loose," the Lieutenant replied.

Jason left, he arrived home and walked straight to his room and collapsed on the bed facing the wall and covered himself with a blanket. Allison knocked on his door.

"Jason, dinner."

He couldn't even respond. Allison came in with their father.

"Son?"

Jason turns toward them, "Are you sure? The Lieutenant has convinced the Colonel and everyone that I'm some counterfeit humanoid creature. This is now every day, he's wearing me down."

His father sat on the corner of the bed. "You're my son, I know that."

"You're my brother," Allison said.

"Allison, you believed in me first. When they come for me the last time, my memory will be erased, if they go too far I'll be dead . . . they're paranoid that the knowledge put in my head will somehow be used destructively."

"Jason?" his dad was in disbelief. "I've talked with the Colonel but he wants the alien before stopping the interrogations."

"You know what will happen, then they will come for Allison."

Jackson then stood up leaving Jason and Allison and talked with their mother. "This has to stop," he told her.

"They're just trying to find out . . ."

"They are killing him Bella, do you understand they're purposely wearing him down, our son, he is our son and if you can't see that God help him. He has remained in a fetal position since he got back, weak and tired . . . won't you look in on him?"

"Dinner is ready," she said with a worried look.

"Count us out." He was angry with her.

Allison brought Jason soup, he drank it.

It was later, everyone had gone to bed, his mother came to his room, he was sleeping. "I love you son," she whispered, then stood there a few moments and left. The Lieutenant had come by earlier and threatened her with the loss of one or both children if she acknowledged that Jason was truly her son.

Marco, in the meantime, worked to copy the ship's log entries concerning Jason and Myra, he had two friends helping, he heeded Jason's warning.

When Jason arrived at engineering the next day, Henry knew he had been through something. Jason wouldn't talk about it to protect Henry. The Lieutenant came by and talked privately with him. Henry noticed but couldn't hear the conversation.

The Lieutenant threatened him to produce the alien and threatened his family. "And you have an interrogation this evening."

Jason was so distracted that he was about to make a fatal mistake. Henry saw him about to touch a large relay barehanded. "Stop, don't touch that relay or you're dead," Henry shouted.

Jason for a moment thought it would all be over if he did, then he considered Myra, he moved his hand.

Marco caught up with him at lunch.

"I was threatened by the Lieutenant and my family is in danger. There is another interrogation this evening . . . I don't think I can handle another."

Marco just listened. "I have two others working with me on this, we will get Myra to her ship somehow and a shipwide transmission to everyone. After your interrogation, I'll drop by with the plans . . . you're a strong person Jason, you'll win this . . . see you then."

Jason put on a good front as he returned to work. He told Allison there was another visit with the Lieutenant and the doctors that evening. Reluctantly he made it to the appointment.

"Mr. Kindle, you're still holding out on us," the Lieutenant said.

"I've told you everything."

"You're deceiving us, wearing you down seems the only way to find this dangerous alien."

"She's not dangerous."

"And how would you know that?"

Jason endured another physical exam and a two-hour interrogation. When he arrived home, Marco was there with Allison. He had checked their compartment for listening devices.

"Found one in the kitchen probably when your mother had a visit the other afternoon."

The three discussed plans.

"They're coming for me, not satisfied that I'll turn her in. I'm of no use to them now."

The next morning the Lieutenant's men found him at his parents' and compelled him to go to sickbay. Allison was in class when she heard a voice, it was Myra. "They have Jason, he is having his mind erased now—hurry, get your parents and call Marco." Allison never saw Myra but she heeded the warning as she left class.

Jason was on an operating table covered with a sheet, a shot was given to calm him.

"Don't bring him back," the Lieutenant told the doctor and neurologist. Dr. Rashid protested but obeyed after being threatened.

Electrodes were taped to his head, he was strapped down, a machine monitored his vitals. His parents, Myra, Allison, Marco and two friends arrived quickly—the Lieutenant was gone, the one guard was standing out front. Myra distracted the guard as Jason's father knocked him out. They rushed in and removed the electrodes. Jason's mother cried as she kissed her son, she found a bottle of adrenalin and a syringe.

"I used to be a nurse," she said and gave him a shot.

Marco made a video recording of this as she asked, "Who gave the order?"

The doctor replied, "The Lieutenant."

"Were you going to bring him back?" Jackson asked.

"No, then we were going after Allison," the doctor said.

Marco recorded the scene of Jason being systematically terminated and the doctor's confession. He quickly ran the ship's log of Jason's entries to save the ship and the alien woman standing beside him and to follow was the documentary in sickbay. Everyone was now seeing and hearing the truth.

They helped Jason to dress. "It's over," Allison said, "we're free."

They all helped, fascinated by Myra who they finally met. Allison and Jason walked behind Marco and a friend who carried some duffel bags and a briefcase and the dog.

"Take care of them Myra," Bella said and hugged her.

"I will."

They helped distract a guard at her ship as she changed form and entered. Her ship burrowed into the sand and moved beyond the Galaxy until it could surface several hundred feet away. She waited.

Jason shook Marco's hand, "I'll bring her back to you safe and sound. We appreciate everything you've done."

Marco then hugged Allison and kissed her.

Jason began running for Myra's ship carrying the duffel bags and briefcase. Allison followed carrying Curtis. Suddenly she screamed as she stumbled and fell. Curtis ran away. Jason looked back and dropped the duffel bags and briefcase. He saw the Lieutenant running toward them. He ran toward Allison and attempted to pick her up.

"Stop there," the Lieutenant said.

Jason then sat by her and pulled her closer to protect her.

The Colonel made a decision to save them. "Get out there," he said to one of his men as he was watching the events unfold. "If he tries to harm Jason or Allison, put a bullet in his head." He had repeatedly tried to have the Lieutenant stand down. This was also recorded, played by Marco shipwide.

Allison screamed at the Lieutenant, "Leave us alone." The Lieutenant heard a voice behind him.

"I have this aimed at your head, shoot to kill if you harm either one."

The Lieutenant had made up his mind to at least kill Jason despite the warning. Suddenly the sound of thunder began to emanate from above.

Myra sent a message to Jason, "Look up."

Three ships larger than hers appeared. One used a laser type weapon holding off the Lieutenant and his men, it even slightly burned the edge of his boot as a warning.

"Come Jason, bring Allison," Myra told him telepathically.

He looked back at the Lieutenant then carried Allison to the ship. Another of the three ships used a tractor beam to pull up the duffel bags, briefcase and Curtis.

"Allison, no friends, no iPod, no Mom and Dad . . . you ready for that?"

"I'm going," she said emphatically to Jason.

"Good girl," he said as they entered the ship.

They strapped themselves in and were given devices to have breathable air. Jason made a last transmission to the Galaxy: "Thank you, those who believed in me—Allison and I plan to return when our minds won't be erased. Truth is power, the Colonel is a good man, the Lieutenant is a paranoid who has tried to influence the Colonel with bad ideas for all of us. Out here we need every friend we can get. Jason Kindle out."

After they were airborne, Jason wiped away tears, Myra touched his hand, he held hers for a moment then he played his iPod. Myra asked him to open his mind so she could hear it. He sat back and listened to one of his favorites, "Bitter Sweet Symphony"; as Myra listened, she knew it relaxed him and all the turmoil he'd endured seemed to fade away as they accompanied the three other ships to a new beginning somewhere. He fell asleep.

Three days later all four ships arrived in orbit around a planet. It had no life at all and half an atmosphere. Myra, Jason and Allison arrived there to meet her people. Jason and Allison were still wearing devices to enable them to breathe, they beamed to one of the larger ships to meet with those from Myra's world. The crews and others of all three ships kept a human facade out of respect for the humans aboard. Jason expressed his thanks for the rescue from his people and for Myra's help saving the Galaxy and all aboard.

"My people are afraid and confused at the moment—they are worth saving."

"We are glad we could help," one said. "I am called VE'AR, roughly a human equivalent of my name." He was six feet tall with grey hair almost shaved, clean shaven.

"I'm Jason Kindle, this is Allison, my sister." Jason then sees Curtis. "You rescued our dog!" He and Allison pet Curtis lovingly.

"Nice to meet you Sir," Allison said.

VE'AR shakes their hands. "What are your plans Jason Kindle?"

Jason looks at Myra, "I don't know since some of our people were about to annihilate us."

"I will suggest something, stay here with us, learn about us, we will learn about you and advise you, then do as you will."

"Sounds like a plan . . . Myra? Allison?"

They agreed.

"When did you mate her?" VE'AR asked him. As quickly as he asked Jason, Myra communicated with him to wait on that one. "We appear as you are to make you comfortable as Myra did." He walked over to Myra and communicated telepathically. "You have joined yourself to this one?"

She telepathically answered, "Yes Leader, I mated him."

Raised eyebrows reflected his surprise. He turned to Jason and Allison, "We have a celebration planned, it's all right to bring the small creature, dog?"

"We call him Curtis."

They seemed curious but totally treating both Jason and Allison with respect. They were called Narins and wore white metallic uniforms as she did. The celebration was preceded by a meeting with Jason and four of the males. Myra had joined herself to Jason and he would now be questioned to see if he felt the same as three listened and VE'AR questioned. They didn't want it to be a one-sided love initiated by Myra and not reciprocated by him. Four surrounded him as they sat on an elaborate rug on the floor. VE'AR sat facing him.

"We have never had a joining with another species," he looked at Jason.

"I am young but I can learn."

"Will you hunger for your own upon returning?"

"Not in this way. I love Myra, I accept her as my wife."

"Then you have seen her as she is, as we are?"

"Yes."

VE'AR looked around the room, Myra came and sat by Jason. "Then it is done."

Allison hugged Myra and Jason, "I'm so happy," she said.

They stood up and he kissed her, something VE'AR's people had never done. The celebration began. Two rings, an Earth tradition were made for Jason and Myra.

Jason didn't want his mind read and for the most part it wasn't. He was also presented with the duffel bags and briefcase which had been quickly brought by another friend who helped them escape with Myra. This delighted Jason. Everyone was curious. He gave Allison her iPod. Curtis had made several friends even with a few spots left on the carpet.

They stayed aboard Myra's ship which was large enough for privacy for their joining ritual that evening.

"Who is VE'AR?" I like him.

"Our leader and my father."

"Your father? Was he reading my mind? He asked me about mating you."

"Probably not reading your mind but they want to know your motives and intentions. They respect you Jason and my decision to join with you."

He smiled as he held her, she kept her human form for the time being.

A week had passed. VE'AR ordered the planet to be terra formed and made alive again. It shared the same sun as Bright Star, the human settlers' new home. Jason was fascinated. All four ships were now orbiting above the planet as three of them began to use tractor beams to increase the rotation speed. Various areas were molded into mountains and valleys with the use of sound emanating from each ship. An atmosphere was created as deep probes brought up water. Seeds were also brought from various worlds, some were from Earth; Myra had taken samples of both plant seeds and animal DNA when she visited the Galaxy earlier and these samples would be grown and placed on the planet after the atmosphere had begun to develop.

"I've never seen them do this," Myra said.

"Where are these samples being grown Myra?"

"Look on the horizon in the evening," she said, "you'll see something spectacular that will answer your question."

"Ok." Jason was curious and willing to wait.

Everything would grow faster, then the rotation speed would be slowed to make twenty-eight hour days as humans had on Bright Star.

Two polar caps appeared, two small moons were added borrowed from another system. The planet was named Sanctus by Jason who was given that honor. The air would be breathable for humans for as yet an undisclosed reason while the Narins would have implants to breathe the new atmosphere.

Evening came, Jason, Myra and Allison saw a huge assortment of lights emanating from an enormous dark object which was just now seen coming over the horizon as it was in a low orbit.

"What is that?" he asked.

"Our largest ship in the area, scientific research. You both want to see it?" VE'AR asked.

"My yes," Allison said.

Myra was excited. They beamed aboard the huge ship. Hundreds were at work on various projects. As Jason and VE'AR walked by followed by Myra and Allison each alien changed into a human facade until everyone looked human, out of respect. They had asked Myra earlier how she and Jason copulated, she didn't embarrass easily but advised them not to ask Jason, she told them how.

The planet was VE'AR's plan to save Jason's people if there was an attack by having this planet which was three times the size of Earth as a refuge and as a Narin outpost.

"Who would attack us?" Jason asked.

"There are those coming from Earth in faster ships with destruction on their minds."

"How do you know this?"

"We can feel their anger and intent to harm even over great distances."

"Several hundred years have passed on Earth since we left two-hundred years ago . . . perhaps they'll have restraints on their anger and intent to harm, if they come. Our solar system will have been colonized totally, not just the first four and two moons of Jupiter as they search for fuel. We shouldn't have pushed out this far yet, we weren't ready but Earth had fallen into the greenhouse effect. Some would have survived the interplanetary wars that resulted.

"I hope you're right Jason."

"Where is your home VE'AR?"

"A large planet surrounding a white sun five-hundred-thousand light years away going toward Earth's solar system and beyond the

Milky Way Galaxy is our home world, NARIN'MAR is our origin. We are not located in a galaxy but have spread to other planets in the universe, always in contact. We are peaceful but will defend ourselves if attacked."

"Can you defeat those from Earth if they present a threat?"

"That remains to be seen."

"I wonder if we can? How long before they arrive, if they come here?"

"Perhaps in a year or less . . . if you will allow me to help you use your abilities and feelings you will sense what their intent is and when."

"Does it involve reading my mind?"

"No."

"Then I do and to prepare ourselves for their arrival. They will know about us from a probe that was sent when Myra helped us. Maybe they won't come." Jason was trying to be optimistic. He respected VE'AR and wanted to learn from him. He was amazed at the technology of his people and the terra formed planet now teaming with life.

He and Myra took walks on the planet. The Narins enjoyed doing the same thing. They slept very little to Jason's seven or eight hours a night. They would talk with him asking questions, telling about themselves. Allison had made several friends, some wanted to know about her physically, she also became embarrassed not revealing everything.

Myra told her father weeks later about being with child.

"I wondered when there would be offspring." He hugged her as he had seen Jason do.

"What will they be?" she asked him.

"The best of both worlds I imagine . . . go now, be with him."

"Are you pleased?"

"You are happy, I am pleased and pleased that your decision to intervene saved two-hundred lives."

Jason had to mature quickly, surprised that he would be a father soon. VE'AR had helped by mentoring him as he would face bigger challenges with the arrival of others of his species bent on destruction and discussing Jason's father's role in that coming destruction which he hadn't mentioned yet allowing Jason for the moment to reflect on a positive, that of becoming a father.

"How does this work Myra? Tell me how I can help, what to expect."

She kissed him. "This won't be a normal pregnancy, our child will be special, both of us. Normally the birth happens in four months, little pain, the doctors will help us."

Allison was listening. "I'll help in any way Myra."

Those words were reassuring to Myra.

Four months passed quickly, then a fifth, still no birth. Her true form began to take over, all her energy was diverted to the child inside her. Jason assured her that he had no problems seeing her as she really was.

"You are beautiful whatever form you take," he told her. He wanted her but common sense told him to wait. She was tired. He and a female attendant took her to the bedroom.

Later, he and Allison beamed down for a walk with Curtis while Myra slept.

"This is like a dream Allison. Here on another world, an alien presence, friends, a wife, a child coming . . . you need to be with someone, Marco. I miss our other friends and Mom and Dad."

"I miss them too but right now we have to think only about Myra and the reality that you're going to be a father! We'll see them soon enough."

"Thanks for the encouragement little sister."

They then played with Curtis as they walked. Several Narins were out walking and several had a clone of Curtis with them to walk.

Later, when Jason and Myra are alone, "Where are the Children?" he asked, "I haven't seen any."

"Because there aren't any," she began to cry.

Jason was startled. "Why?" he asked as he held her.

"Ask VE'AR, a germ created and sent out into space made most Narins sterile."

"But you're not."

"I was born on our home world but out here this germ threatens to extinguish us . . . I'll tell you about it, not now."

"What about our child?"

"Being half human, I don't know."

Jason went over to the food replicator trying for pizza, he described it in detail. She nodded yes. They had an evening to talk about everything.

Jason was a good listener but he hadn't talked out his problems that occurred on Bright Star concerning the conspiracy launched against him by the Lieutenant and the mental and physical pain that resulted. He then told Myra about an Earth ship that was coming.

"I felt it as well," she said as she ate the pizza.

CHAPTER II

GALAXY—BATTALION I

Weeks passed, VE'AR felt compelled to now ask Jason about his father. "I would like to meet him."

"You will and my mother."

"What do you remember about him concerning his work?" VE'AR decided to subtly push for the answers.

"Why do you ask?"

"I am interested, we are curious creatures."

"I was very young but I remember the hours he spent working on projects with plants as a botanist. He worked on projects with my mother then gradually began training me as a botanist. Allison wouldn't go in that direction."

"Do you remember if he did various projects for the military?"

"No . . . what is this leading to?"

"I mentioned the ship that is coming, it carries within it destruction on an unlimited scale from work we are certain was initiated by your father."

Jason stood up, "I don't want to hear this, my father is a good person."

"I'm sure he is . . . you asked Myra why there were no children, we know why, a poison sent into space years earlier, hundreds of years earlier from Earth. It was designed to kill any agent dangerous to mankind as they travelled to another world. A brown cloud that has travelled several light years supposed to kill off the competition rendered us sterile, fortunately not on our home world."

"My father didn't, couldn't do this VE'AR. As for what I remember, nothing suspicious."

"Chemicals, names on canisters, conversations held, what you might have seen and heard as a child. Would you allow me to read only the thoughts concerning his work?"

"VE'AR . . ." Jason couldn't finish. He felt an aching in his heart as his friend pressed him for answers, he left.

VE'AR knew he had wounded him, this wasn't his intent.

Jason arrived home to be with Myra. Later he asked Allison if she remembered anything about their father's work.

"I wasn't ever interested in Dad's work, Mom didn't press me to go into the botany profession . . . why?"

"Just curious."

As time passed, Jason and Allison took classes on a range of subjects, VE'AR taught Jason, another, a female taught Allison. Jason and VE'AR had gotten beyond the rift but Jason continued to search for any information on his father and the military.

Two more months had passed, Myra was getting larger, she hadn't lost her sense of humor but was frustrated as she grew; Jason was with her almost constantly. VE'AR knew his concerns about the birth and tried to be reassuring. Then suddenly it happened a week later, not only one but two. Myra had known but didn't tell Jason or her father, a boy and a girl who looked human. Several of the women weren't able to conceive so this was a big celebration for everyone.

"There may be hope after all," Jason said as he looked at VE'AR.

The others were carefully watching the life signs. Jason kissed Myra and held his little girl then handing her to VE'AR, then he held his son. VE'AR seemed very content at that moment.

They talked later. "The children will give us hope," VE'AR remarked.

"Come with us for a visit to Bright Star and talk to our people about possible ways to correct this situation . . . I will talk to my father about what we discussed earlier."

VE'AR gave a firm pat to his shoulder, stood up, "We shall see Jason, I am pleased to have you as her mate."

This caught Jason by surprise. VE'AR didn't normally display emotion, but he realized he meant the compliment.

Four months passed, the children MY'AR and JAS'AR were growing very quickly, normal for Narin children. Jason and Myra looked for the characteristics of both species. They then decided to leave on that visit.

The largest ship remained in orbit around Sanctus. Jason, Myra, Allison and the kids went in Myra's ship. VE'AR and several others including scientists travelled with them in a larger ship flanked by two escort ships. The trip took three days. Jason had mixed feelings about confronting his father, he hadn't told Allison.

Upon arrival a crowd met them. Myra's ship landed on the sandy ground. There were changes since they left, small buildings, fields growing Earth staples, cattle, sheep, goats grown from DNA samples, cloning had been done. As they disembarked they saw the Galaxy, their home for two-hundred years, it was very emotional. VE'AR and several from his ship were with them. Jason's parents and Marco and friends met them outside. Allison and Marco embraced, he and Jason shook hands.

"I told you I'd bring her back to you Marco . . . Mother, Dad," he hugged them as did Myra. "This is Myra's father VE'AR and my parents Dr. Jackson and Bella Kindle;" they greeted each other warmly, "and our children MY'AR and JAS'AR."

His parents couldn't believe children, they were excited.

Colonel Sobel met them outside. "Hello Jason, Myra, Allison and children."

"Sir, this is VE'AR, leader of his people, the Narins and my father-in-law."

"A pleasure to have you Sir on Bright Star."

"The pleasure is mine."

Someone caught Jason's eye, the Lieutenant who was curious but didn't approach him. The sight of him evoked negative emotion, Myra and VE'AR felt it. Her thoughts told VE'AR how Jason was interrogated by the man, humiliated and hurt physically and almost brain wiped for protecting her. Jason and Allison earlier had expressed their thanks to VE'AR and his crew in the three ships for saving them as they escaped with Myra. The Lieutenant looked miserable and now had no authority and Jason didn't acknowledge him. He was greeted now with respect as everyone had seen the ship's log entries due in part to Marco. The visitors were greeted with guarded optimism. The Galaxy had become like a huge city brimming with activity, it wasn't a warship but had weapons. VE'AR didn't detect anything lethal to his people, only questionable substances in small amounts emanating from the botany lab. They went to a restaurant. Myra told the others what she enjoyed of human food.

Later they were introduced to the Studies of Reproduction Laboratory located in a new building some distance from the Galaxy, cloning was done there; Jason had mentioned it even though earlier VE'AR had told him that cloning didn't work on the Narins when he suggested that perhaps science could undo the damage to the Narin's ability to reproduce. Other buildings and businesses were visited by VE'AR, Jason and Myra and others who were curious. Jason couldn't believe the progress made in a year since they left. They saw many things that day.

VE'AR and his entourage retired for the evening aboard their ships. Myra, Jason and the children stayed aboard her ship. Allison stayed at her mother and dad's, Marco was there.

Marco had fallen for Allison years ago and tonight he asked her if she felt the same. "Do you love me?"

"I love you Marco, let's get married."

"Will Jason object?"

"Are you kidding? You believed in him when no one else did. He will never forget that, he's your friend." Marco stayed a while as they talked.

Jason and Marco had lunch the next day.

"I'm glad Marco, you both love each other . . . how have things been around here?"

"Since the Lieutenant was disgraced after we ran the ship's logs, a lot less tense. You know the Colonel sent a sharpshooter to kill him if he harmed you or Allison."

"I didn't until we left and I saw a gun pointed in the Lieutenant's direction."

"What now Jason?"

"We might be here a while, I've missed everyone and Allison and I being the only humans on Sanctus. The Narins gave it an atmosphere as they terra formed it. You'll have to come see it." Jason reflected his excitement. "We had an opportunity to learn from them and hopefully they've learned from us. They are a remarkable people, especially my father-in-law, VE'AR. Our wedding ceremony was special, a celebration of two cultures, it was the happiest I've been in a long time; Myra, simply put, is the only one who could complete me. There is another matter that concerns Dad and experimentation that he did for the military space exploration project two-hundred years ago, this is going to be difficult Marco . . . VE'AR and his people were affected by something my father did. I read about it in their ship's log. I need access to our logs here, but first I'll talk to Dad, don't tell anyone Marco, not yet."

"I won't, if I can, if you need me to, I'll try and get access."

"Thanks, you've already done enough saving my life and reputation . . . oh, I might as well tell you this, there is an Earth warship coming, should be here in two months or less—they are carrying a poison, perhaps created by my Dad."

Marco was stunned. "A warship carrying a toxin created by your Dad will be here in two months?"

"It's not supposed to harm humans but any other life form as the Narins will be harmed by it."

"Life is always complicated in some manner."

Chief Engineer Henry, Jason's supervisor and friend had advised the Colonel to give Jason his engineering and navigation degrees. He did. His piloting degree was almost earned, lacking a few hours.

"I'm even asking him for advice," he laughed.

Jason felt comfortable working with Henry on the cruisers and other craft and teaching his one engineering class five days a week. Myra also taught classes on the sciences and the universe in particular, telling things about her people. Allison was taking classes in the sciences and mathematics.

VE'AR and his people were there to understand and interact with the human race. They had hoped to find a way to bear children again and counteract the poison that threatened to extinguish their race.

Jason kept his promise to VE'AR to question his father, he had but with no results, he would keep trying.

They came as VE'AR had predicted, a year travelling at Warp 7. It had taken the Galaxy two-hundred years at Warp 4 with everyone in stasis.

The hundreds of years that had gone by on Earth and the surrounding solar system hadn't produced the best that mankind could be. They came in one large ship, armed, ready for war, their minds were filled with arrogance and destruction even toward their own people. The ship stayed in orbit a day before they made contact, sizing up the

Narin ships and knew the Galaxy wasn't a threat. As their presence drew a crowd the ship was taken into a low orbit about two-thousand feet above the ground where it remained stationary as several beamed down to the surface. Their Commander was dressed in a dark military type uniform as was his entourage. Colonel Sobel and military personnel, his Second, VE'AR, his attendants, Henry and Jason stood together as they greeted the Commander and his men who were all armed.

"I bring greetings from Earth, I am Commander Scott of the Earthforce Battalion."

"I'm Colonel Sobel of the Galaxy, my Second, Lieutenant Benoit, VE'AR leader of the Narins, Chief Engineer Mr. Ferris and Jason Kindle Chief Assisting Engineer."

"We have come a long way and to meet the Narins at last." He tried to shake hands with VE'AR who wouldn't respond to it but lowered his head as a form of greeting. "We have much to talk about, things concerning Earth . . . why are none of you armed?"

"I assure you our security detail is armed."

"We got two probes sent to us by you Jason and Myra, a Narin."

"She saved our lives," Jason said. The Commander ignored this statement.

"We would like to invite you to dine with us, bring whoever you choose to join you . . . will the atmosphere of our ship be a problem VE'AR?"

"No," he replied. The Narins were earlier retrofitted to breathe the oxygen atmosphere on Sanctus and Bright Star. The Commander was only interested in any information he could gain by asking that question.

"Can we look around?" Commander Scott asked.

"Certainly, and Jason, Lieutenant Benoit, and a detail will accompany you on your tour."

The Commander didn't want any detail keeping watch but he accepted it. They walked through areas that had buildings looking for defense and armament then through the Galaxy. This made everyone uneasy. Myra suddenly appeared with the children after preschool had ended for the day.

Jason hugged her and the kids, "These are our visitors from Earth. Commander Scott, this is Myra, my wife and children, MY'AR and JAS'AR."

"I heard the commotion upon your arrival," she said, "welcome."

The Commander registered negative emotion when Jason said 'my wife', but he pretended otherwise. "Good to meet you Myra and your children."

VE'AR and his entourage were passing by and joined the Commander on his tour. Then the Colonel joined them minutes later.

"I'll see you later Jason, VE'AR," Myra said as she left for home.

"Are there other children of mixed human and Narin?"

"Not to my knowledge," Jason said, "VE'AR?"

"These are the first," he replied.

"Come be with us tonight Colonel, VE'AR, Jason, bring guests, beam up eight o'clock Bright Star time."

"It would be a pleasure," the Colonel said.

No one cared for Commander Scott especially knowing how he regarded the joining of Myra and Jason and his interest in armament, inspecting the buildings and the Galaxy.

"It would be well to join him this evening, see what he's up to," Lieutenant Benoit remarked, "unless he has something against me, being Black and French."

"His ship carries a strong toxin that was created to destroy any and all opposition in space, one we're familiar with," VE'AR said.

Colonel Sobel had heard this from Jason earlier and was made aware of its harmful effects on the Narin race which was very disturbing to him. "We'll try for answers this evening when we meet with him."

"See you there Colonel," VE'AR replied.

"I'll be there with Myra," Jason said.

Commander Scott hatched a plan to befriend Jason and the Colonel and turn them against the Narins. He knew he could turn others if he could turn them and then would destroy the Narins. If that plan didn't work, he felt no guilt in using any means at his disposal to achieve his goals of subduing the human population on Bright Star and enslaving or destroying the Narin entities.

At the dinner hosted by the Commander, Earth was discussed and other planets and moons in the solar system mainly involved in finding new sources of fuel, his mission was also discussed and the duration of the journey aboard the Battalion.

"We have a time frame of five years to find new life and setup stations along the way, manned by say three persons at the most. These stations would monitor activity and report back."

The Colonel then asked a bold question, "Are you looking to preserve life out in space if you find it or to destroy it?"

Everyone seemed surprised at the question including the Commander who was startled by it.

"We'll preserve it of course."

"And then you go back to Earth in five years?"

"Yes."

"Earthforce Battalion is a warship capable of great destruction, yet you say your mission is peaceful," the Colonel continued.

"Of course we mean peace Colonel but also to be prepared for anything."

"How about a tour?" Jason asked.

"Certainly and VE'AR you are welcome to join us, and you Colonel."

The dinner was finished and the tour was begun. The warship was enormous around the size of VE'AR's largest of his warships. Jason discussed the engines among other things with a fellow engineer. He had asked for access to the control room piloting the ship but initially was denied. The Commander then allowed it realizing that Jason had piloted the Galaxy and wouldn't be a security risk. VE'AR knew that the poison that rendered his people sterile was somewhere on the ship. He asked questions about anomalies that they encountered in space on their journey as a distraction to Commander Scott's suspicions. The Commander was feeling very secure thinking he had the advantage over everyone on the planet.

"We did encounter a spider web galaxy three times the size of the Milky Way, then a foursome star cluster each circling one another and a planet bearing only one living grain organism, something we had never seen, as yet unnamed." He was trying to lure Jason into an interest and fascination of the Battalion as a science and discovery ship, not a warship. "Our ship can outperform anything out there and worm holes are now used to cut travel by years." The Commander was baiting VE'AR and both the Colonel and Jason realized that VE'AR was really baiting him. The forty-year-old Commander babbled on as the tour continued and wondered as he studied the Narins why they hadn't succumbed to the poison sent into their atmosphere years ago. He didn't bother asking to see their smaller spacecraft not realizing that there was a mega ship orbiting Sanctus with technology unlike mankind had ever seen. The Narins had hidden Sanctus temporarily by bending light.

Hours later everyone was leaving and praised Commander Scott and his crew for the special evening as they all got acquainted.

"Jason, would you stay for a few minutes?"

He sent Myra home with VE'AR.

There are opportunities aboard this ship for someone like you, heck, you saved the Galaxy from being vaporized."

"But I had help."

"Give yourself the praise you deserve, you saved hundreds . . . you're now an engineer, teaching that to students even as you work. You're young, the probe said you had been aged to accept data to preserve the Galaxy."

"Actually a small amount of data or it would have killed me," Jason said, a lie to the vast amount of data he had actually absorbed.

"Navigation, piloting, engineering?"

"Just enough of these three."

"Come to work for me. How do you regard the Narins?"

"I'm married to one."

"Are you happy Jason?"

". . . Not really, and their ships don't compare to this one." Jason pretended to fall into the hands of this Commander by painting a picture of being dissatisfied.

"How about a change?"

"Let me think about it. What would I be do doing?"

"Working on this ship, learning . . . being happy."

"When would I start?"

"Tomorrow, a few hours after your shift ends at school and your engineering duties aboard the Galaxy."

They shook hands, Jason left.

VE'AR and the Colonel heard from Jason that evening. "I'm in. If I am mentally driven to do things by some means, could it be detected?"

"We can expect the unexpected," the Colonel said, "but a truth monitor probably wouldn't detect what was driving you to do certain things against your will."

"I could detect it," VE'AR said, "Narins have this ability."

"Then let's proceed," Jason said.

Later that night he told Myra. "What I'm going to tell you could put VE'AR and the Colonel in danger as well as myself."

"I won't even think it," she said.

"We have a plan to gain access to the Earthforce Battalion's main computer as I pretend to be dissatisfied with everything and everyone, the Commander has seized on this and is persuading me work for him."

"How dissatisfied?"

"Very. You will pick up on this but I love you and I want to help make things right with the Narins. Things I will say won't be pleasant, don't listen. You know me like no one else ever could." He held her close, she kissed him, they made love.

The next day after Jason taught engineering for his one class and worked as engineer on the Galaxy the next few hours, he was met by Commander Scott as several of his crew were getting familiar with the general population.

"Walk with me Jason, tell me about their ships."

"I have never been allowed near the engine areas; yes I'm married to a Narin but that doesn't allow me access."

"Then get access, we have to know what they're capable of."

"They are a peaceful race, weak, no desire to fight, their ships have no weapons, why pursue them?"

"Because they aren't like us, they aren't us."

"Is space restricted for just our kind?"

"Can I count on you Jason?" the Commander asked ignoring Jason's questions.

"Yes, you can."

"Then do this thing, report to me about their ships."

"Will do."

Jason and the Commander went separate ways. He couldn't ask the Commander about the toxin on board his ship, not yet.

In the days that followed, VE'AR made sure that Jason was allowed aboard the Narin ships as he pretended to investigate for the Commander, reporting back about the engines. Jason was now continually tested by a truth monitor as he was asked questions aboard the Battalion. VE'AR was able to help Jason fool the monitor with his telepathic abilities. The Commander began to believe that the Narins were as weak as Jason had told him and of no threat, but he still hated them and had plans to destroy them.

One evening as Myra and Jason were walking in the park, a recently constructed one, the Lieutenant came toward them.

"Oh no," Jason said as he approached.

"Hear what he has to say Jason," she pleaded.

"They're going to kill us all, not just your Narin friends," the Lieutenant said this with a certainty in his voice.

"How do you know?"

"I hear things, no one thinks I know anything since your broadcast when you left, but I hear things. Humanity from Earth is different . . . be careful of the Commander, he has no soul." The Lieutenant left after this warning.

"Everytime I see him, I can't get past what he tried to do."

"But now you feel sympathy for him."

"Yes. I'm wondering what led him to believe that all of us are in danger?"

That evening Jason's father and mother had invited VE'AR for dinner. Jason and Myra and the children were there as well as two Narin attendants. The food was a cross between Narin and human tastes. VE'AR expressed his thanks for the meal and hospitality. Jason had talked with his father about the toxin he created while on Earth two-hundred years ago for the military space exploration project.

After the meal Jason left VE'AR to talk privately with him, not even the attendants were allowed to hear.

"Dr. Kindle, there is something I must ask you," VE'AR began.

"Please, not so formal, Jackson is fine."

"Jackson, the information we seek as Narins concerns our existence or our demise due to a toxin created by you before you arrived here aboard the Galaxy two-hundred years earlier. What was its intended purpose and how did you create it?"

Jason's father was feeling uncomfortable and guilty. "I am a botanist as you know, a very good one at what I do. It was created from a space microbe, a pathogenic bacterium found on a small moon as a weapon if our offworld expeditions should be met by resistance and self preservation became necessary."

"We had neither attacked any of you or tried to stop your escape from Earth's turmoil, yet your military and scientists sent probes containing this toxin into our areas of space, missing our home world fortunately and sending devastating consequences to our people in the form of brown clouds surging and spreading the poison."

"I didn't know the military would do this, but your people survived."

"It has rendered much of the Narin race sterile, doomed by eventual extinction."

Jackson just sat stunned by what was done with his work. "There is no way to apologize enough for my actions. Jason has confronted me with this but I couldn't believe it, I wouldn't. There is no known antidote; I will work toward finding one VE'AR."

"That Earth ship, Battalion is carrying several tons of the toxin to wipeout any and all competition in space, we pose no threat to any of you."

"The man is misguided, he might wipe us out as well as we might be seen as competition. As I am working on a solution I could use help from your people."

"You'll have it."

"Something else, Jason has been friendly with the Commander even working for him . . . I love my son and I can't protect him."

"Jason is very intelligent and fortunate to have a family who loves and cares about him, he has his reasons for working with the Commander, trust him." VE'AR wouldn't reveal the true reason for Jason's working aboard the Battalion. They ended the evening on a positive note with respect for one another.

CHAPTER III

GALAXY—PLOT

Commander Scott began planning how to take Bright Star from the human inhabitants and to destroy the fragile government headed by the military comprising human and Narin. He had sent a probe filled with toxin to the Narin home world before the Battalion reached Bright Star. He wanted to cause dissension between the Narins and humans as he bribed some of the residents who could play on the fears of the people concerning the purpose of the Narin presence. He found Jason after he had finished repairs for the day on the Galaxy.

"I owe you Jason, you have exceeded my expectations; meet me aboard the Battalion as soon as possible."

"Yes Sir."

Jason talked with VE'AR first. "He's going to use the truth monitor again."

"I'll be there Jason . . . another thing, he has sent a probe filled with toxin to our home world."

"When?" Jason was shocked.

"On their way to Bright Star."

"The Commander didn't reveal that. He's trying to destabilize our government pitting Narin against human . . . what about the probe?"

"We're working on a way to stop it, as it's proving to be very challenging, several fail-safes were added by the Commander to insure that it would reach the target, if destroyed it could send the toxin over several areas of space."

Jason was devastated over this. "I must meet the Commander now."

"I'll be there as before." Jason left.

Commander Scott told Jason to prepare for a takeover on Bright Star. "We're going to move on this soon."

Jason wanted to ask him about the probe but it would allow him to know the Narins had figured it out. He was hooked up to a truth monitor as the Commander's number two questioned him.

"Are you loyal to us even over your Colonel Sobel?"

"Are you willing to forsake your Narin wife and children?"

"We will have Bright Star for ourselves, people and Narins will die. Is this acceptable to you?"

Jason was so stunned by the calloused attitudes of the Commander and crew that he hesitated to answer.

VE'AR gave him instructions telepathically, "You must agree Jason."

Then, "I agree to all this, it's a new world," Jason told them.

"Good, your loyalty is noted, you will be well paid."

In the meantime Jason and VE'AR, Colonel Sobel and four others discussed all that Jason had been told and what the Narins had discovered.

"We Narins have a plan, seven have left in our fastest ship to stop the probe from releasing the toxin, a long shot as you humans say."

"What can you possibly do?" Colonel Sobel asked.

"We can try to reconfigure space to throw off the trajectory of the probe sending it into another realm of space and into a large sun which will completely destroy the threat." VE'AR wasn't sure of the outcome as he tried to be positive.

"And if that doesn't work?" Jason asked.

"We will be successful one way or another, we will know in perhaps a year or longer."

"God speed," Colonel Sobel said as he looked in the direction of the departed Narin ship. He then sent out the military to quell any uprising.

A human was murdered a week later, shot. This was in the plan of Commander Scott. Two humans were paid blaming the Narins. He criticized Colonel Sobel for not protecting the citizens. The Colonel and four of the governing military met with the Commander as did VE'AR and two of his involved in the Narin part of the government.

"You are trying to cause dissension Commander, what are your reasons for doing so?" the Colonel asked but knew why.

"I'm only observing what appears to be a weak governing body, allowing no justice for crimes committed. I admire the fact that you essentially are the government; we on Earth have swift justice and absolute laws that all should work or be terminated."

"Creating jobs is a priority here, education also a priority, no termination for those unemployed or those who can't function due to health issues or injury." VE'AR was becoming aware at how calloused this Commander was, polar opposite to Colonel Sobel.

"Spreading your philosophy here is promoting ill will, especially where it concerns us," VE'AR said, "we are peaceful."

The Commander only replied, "I don't believe you, nor should you Colonel." Then he left.

Colonel Sobel and VE'AR took all this in then, "We all have things to do and after hearing this . . . where is Jason?"

"He left for Myra's ship an hour ago. The Commander has been testing him."

"Has he done anything to him?"

"Not to my knowledge, but daily we check for this."

"All right. Let me know anything at anytime VE'AR, I have a murder to investigate."

Two weeks passed, the reality that the Battalion was a weapon in itself had weighed heavily on Jason's mind. He located the area of the toxin as he wandered aboard the ship. An officer on the ship questioned him then brought him to the Commander.

"You were wandering past the permitted areas . . . why?"

Jason hadn't expected to get caught, now trying to be calm, he answered, "I was curious."

"Find anything?"

"As what? I'm an engineer, what would I find?"

The Commander smiled, "Do your job, don't wander again."

"Yes Sir."

Jason wasn't subjected to the truth monitor. He finished for the day then went directly to VE'AR telling him everything. "How do we deal with the ship?" They were in the park and night was approaching.

"Take it into the sun if possible. I have been consulting with Colonel Sobel and our scientists. Since Bright Star and Sanctus orbit a white sun, it could be reached conceivably before the toxin is released due to the melting of the hull."

"Then I can go aboard and feed their systems into my head and take the Battalion into the sun."

"I advise against it, the human body cannot withstand that much data being fed into the brain so quickly without dire consequences, stroke, death . . . I will take the ship, the Narin is the stronger species. I admire your bravery." VE'AR was sincere about taking the ship himself.

"Is it possible for the one piloting this ship to return . . ." he didn't finish his question before a gunshot was heard.

VE'AR fell, his attendant and Jason examined the wound. They took him aboard a larger Narin ship. Myra and the Colonel were notified. VE'AR was unconscious as the Narin doctors worked on him. Jason held Myra. They were there for several hours. Colonel Sobel then left to launch an investigation. Jason left soon after and met with the Colonel. He told of VE'AR's idea to take the entire ship into the sun.

"Don't you even think about it Jason."

"I'm not . . ."

"Good, I don't want to throw you in the brig. Any news on the probe?"

"Not a word. I better check on VE'AR and Myra." Jason did go back to see VE'AR and comfort Myra. "May I talk with him privately?" Myra looked puzzled. "I know he can't respond, may not even hear what I have to tell him being unconscious." She left them alone for a few moments. "VE'AR, I value our friendship, I hope you recover. I won't see you again, this is a one-way trip for the greater good." Jason then stood up and left. He went to a supply area and then took neuro-interface connectors and hid them inside his jacket. He had called Commander Scott when several of the crew were on Bright Star for the weekly gathering on Saturdays. He told the Commander he had new information for him.

"Come aboard Jason, I'll be in my office."

Jason beamed aboard. "I know the way," he told a guard. He avoided an escort and detoured into the control room. There were only two crew members present. "He wants to see us," he told them. They were bored so they left. Jason lagged behind, "I'll be there in a minute." He then uses the neuro-connectors to link him with the ship's main computer and sets up a forcefield between himself and the rest of the ship; the Commander rushes out and discovers to his horror Jason at the controls.

"Jason, what is this . . . what are you doing?"

Jason then sounds the alarm to abandon ship. "Leave if you want to live," he announced shipwide, then cut off the control units routing all control of the ship to himself, now beginning to receive the data quickly from the main computer. He started the engines. Colonel Sobel watching the beam down of several from the ship left quickly with soldiers who took custody of the crew. Myra became aware it was Jason.

"Jason, talk to me," the Commander said even as he and his soldiers armed themselves. Jason began plotting a trajectory to take the ship and all aboard into the sun.

"You have sent a probe filled with toxin to the Narin home world and then attempting to destabilize our government on Bright Star as you also planned to use the toxin here, against us, your own kind."

"False, I didn't plan to harm your world, I did want to have you as someone who understood and would be loyal to me."

"Somehow I admired you, battle hardened, knowledgeable . . . being your friend would, has proved costly."

"What are you planning?"

"The data is flowing into my mind as we speak, you should leave now, I can't . . . this a one-way trip for me and anyone on this ship. It will be flown into the sun once and for all ending the toxin threat."

Commander Scott became enraged, "I'll kill you Jason for this."

The engines now lifted the ship into a higher orbit and travelled a million miles from Bright Star, he then turned the ship to the plotted course to the sun. He had begun to falter as the data became too much for his brain to absorb, his nose began to bleed and his left ear. He set the controls, speed and course.

"Should I pass out, we have ten minutes," he told them.

The Commander wasn't one to give up, still trying to break down the forcefield or find a way around it.

Suddenly down a wide corridor came what looked like a man encompassed by fire. This frightened them. He walked toward Jason moving the forcefield to trap the men further. His appearance of fire subsided in favor of the VE'AR Jason recognized. He removed the neuro-connectors separating him from the computer.

"You're dead," Jason said in his weakened state.

"Hardly, it takes more than a bullet to kill one of us." He temporarily stopped the stroke which was ravaging Jason's body. "We must go." He stands Jason on his feet holding him steady.

"My left leg has been affected."

They walk down the corridor, VE'AR looks at the Commander and his soldiers as he says, "Have a good trip gentlemen." They find a small shuttle. VE'AR takes the controls and releases the docking clamps, he can't pick up speed.

"Have you ever driven one of these?" Jason asked being humorous.

"Not this model . . . if we don't reach Warp 3 or faster, we will be incinerated along with them."

Just then the Battalion began its journey toward the sun.

"I'm an engineer, let me try." Jason was being factious when he stated the obvious and began working with the computer and connected a small relay barehanded and remembers something from the ship's database that he tried. Suddenly the shuttle shot forward going Warp 4. VE'AR was nervous but handled the shuttle well and the situation. Jason passed out as his mind couldn't accept the flood of data and the damage it had caused.

The Battalion was now travelling Warp 6. It began to melt as it entered the sun's corona. A cataclysmic explosion occurred, the shuttle was rocked side to side, VE'AR remained in control.

"Jason."

"I'm ok, but you're bleeding." VE'AR didn't reply.

Three hours had passed.

CHAPTER IV

GALAXY—AR'TYN

VE'AR and Jason made it back to Bright Star, a crowd was standing outside watching the cataclysmic explosion of the Earthforce Battalion several million miles away. The crew members of the Battalion began cursing Jason and VE'AR even trying to strike them as they expressed anger over the destruction of their ship and loss of their commander and those who died with him. The Galaxy security soldiers held them back as best they could. VE'AR and Jason moved as quickly as possible. Myra braved the crowd and got to them. Jason was taken aboard the Galaxy escorted by VE'AR and Myra to sickbay. The Colonel came quickly to check on both men. VE'AR was reluctant to leave Jason but finally had himself doctored. He gave his report to the Colonel giving Jason the credit.

"I merely rescued him, he did the rest."

"Good job to both of you . . . as you can see the three of us won't win any popularity contests, an uprising has begun by the forty crew members who survived." The Colonel then walked outside and made an announcement. "All of you from the Battalion will be housed in tents for the night, food and water will be supplied—there will be a military patrol standing guard. Tomorrow an announcement about the events of tonight, until then."

Morning came, everyone was uneasy about the Battalion crew. The Colonel had hoped Jason and VE'AR would join him in addressing the events last evening. He also talked to Jason's father about his role in making the toxin that had harmed so many.

The Colonel addressed everyone present, outside and inside the ship and buildings. "Fellow travellers, it was with great expectation that we journeyed from our home world two-hundred years ago . . . we were almost vaporized on our journey by a white sun when our trajectory changed while we were in stasis. A Narin came aboard, awakened a young man and together they saved the ship and all of us. We had met the first of a new species. Back on Earth a toxin created only with the purpose of defending against aggressive life forms, created by one of our scientists before we left was shot out into deep space essentially precluding any encounter with any species whether friendly or aggressive . . . this action was taken before we left Earth; it was not our intention to release this toxin, a top secret project of Dr. Jackson Kindle . . . misused, it harmed the Narin race, yet they didn't retaliate and have the capacity to do so. When the Earthforce Battalion arrived, hundreds of years had passed on Earth. This ship had been designed for exploration and war, it carried within it the toxin, tons of it, so potent it could kill virtually anything including us if we were deemed an enemy to the policies of Commander Scott. There were those who investigated the purpose of the Battalion who personally heard from the Commander's own lips what he planned to do and to take over Bright Star when we were eliminated. I authorized the investigation and the actions taken. Jason Kindle gave everyone on board the Battalion a chance to beam off the ship then he took it into space and plotted a trajectory into the sun killing all aboard as the ship and its poisonous cargo were destroyed. He was rescued by VE'AR the Narin leader who himself was wounded. Jason also suffered serious injury as both saved us and the Narins from catastrophe. Now I present VE'AR, Narin leader."

"One human, Jason Kindle proved that we could exist together; we are not aggressive but are more than capable of defending ourselves. We are now partners out here with the human race and are sharing our technology with our human counterparts especially as it relates to medical issues and scientific technology."

Jason's father now stood up, "I am Dr. Jackson Kindle, I created the toxin and I wish I hadn't, it was misused. I am making it my mission to do all I can to dissolve the clouds of it floating in space from two-hundred years ago and to undo what it did to the Narin race and what it could do to the human race if used against us."

Jason now stood up with some difficulty a day after his stroke which wasn't recommended. "Give me a moment," he said as his nose began to bleed. Those from the Galaxy held him in high esteem for saving the ship and all two-hundred lives as they travelled across the Milky Way to their new home. "I am an engineer, I have a wife and children. I liked Commander Scott but his views and ideas were flawed. He sent a probe filled with the toxin to the Narin home world, it hasn't been stopped yet. This is the same toxin as you are now aware of, sent from Earth two centuries ago. The Narins weren't our enemies but should have been due to the clouds of poison sent into their realm. As I worked aboard the Battalion, the Commander also revealed to me that he considered that humankind here on Bright Star was weak and intended to take this world from us one way or another. There was no other option than to take the Battalion and twelve others including myself into the sun to destroy the threat. I had given opportunity for everyone aboard to beam off the ship before departure. I was then rescued by a Narin who came aboard, VE'AR, who I consider a friend and is family."

The Colonel had the last word. "I authorized the actions taken. Any attack on us or our Narin friends will be dealt with immediately with the severest of consequences, banishment to a nearby moon or possibly death. Any dissatisfied who want to leave, we'll make it possible and leave you somewhere with food, water, building materials . . . on your own, or you can join with us and make something of this world. Those of you who want to stay register aboard the Galaxy today and be assigned quarters. That is all."

Jason was taken to sickbay where the stroke continued to ravage his body. Soon, as the doctors worked over him, his eyes went into a blank stare, his breathing shallowed.

"We can't save him," the doctors said.

"Please leave us for a moment." VE'AR leaned over Jason. "You're going to die very soon, allow me to help you . . . you love Myra and the children, we are friends you and I . . . will you accept my help?"

"I will," Jason said in his thoughts now barely able to form a thought.

"Open your mind to me." Every thought Jason had would now be revealed to the Narin leader as Jason didn't struggle now to keep his thoughts private. VE'AR worked over him, his form changed as he expended energy.

Myra had been crying, her form had become pale, saddened over Jason, her love for him was strong.

Hours passed since VE'AR began to bring him back. They both stayed with him. Marco, Allison and Jason's parents wouldn't leave as others came by to wish him well again. They knew VE'AR had tried his best to save him. Myra sat by her father through the night. Hours passed.

Jason opened his eyes. "I'm still in here VE'AR," he related this message by thought.

VE'AR stood up and walked over to Jason, "So are we, we won't leave you."

Jason then closed his eyes and slept.

"A good sign," the doctor said, "whatever did you do to bring him back?"

VE'AR gave no credit to himself for this miracle.

Later in the afternoon Jason was sitting up, Myra hugged him, his arms and legs weren't responding but he had thanked VE'AR for bringing him back. "Seems I need physical therapy," he said then laughed.

"Everything in your head is healing and it will all heal eventually . . . your body should follow," VE'AR told him.

Weeks passed. The new arrivals had decided to join those on Bright Star, both humans and Narins. They would be schooled, all had been taught only how to live aboard a warship preparing for war, not schooled generally above their duties aboard ship. All were detoxing from an addictive powerful drug required to be taken by all crew members to insure loyalty.

Jason had been fitted with a neuro pack attached to his spine allowing his arms and legs to work a few hours a day without overtaxing his system, it was the best the Galaxy doctors and scientists could do.

A variety of subjects would be taught by several instructors. Myra, the sciences, Jason and Henry, engineering, Jackson Kindle, botany and hydroponics; the Narins would teach navigation, terraforming and cloning, others taught medicine, cooking, music and about space probes.

As Jason taught his two classes, he still sensed the anger of some for destroying their ship, the Narins felt it as well as being partly responsible.

The neuro pack had not allowed Jason the freedom to be a husband to Myra. They talked about it. VE'AR became aware of it when he was around them, he felt their frustration. He spoke with Jason one evening.

"I know there is nothing else that can be done here for you Jason but I will suggest this, that you and Myra and the children come with me to visit Sanctus and our science ship might be able to help."

"I owe you VE'AR, you stopped the stroke and saved my mind. I would do anything to be a husband to Myra again and a complete father to our children."

"You have overcome great odds to save the Galaxy and all on board and remove the threat to the Narins. As a respected member of the family I ask you to give us this chance to give you back what you lost."

Jason thought for a moment, "How long would we be there?"

"It depends, at least a month."

"Explain to Myra and me what they might do."

He brought in Myra, they sat and listened.

Jason later talked with the Colonel, Henry, his parents and Allison.

"If you get married Allison . . ."

"I'll wait, Marco wants you there as much as I do . . . just get well and that will be the best present you could give us." She hugged him.

The Colonel remarked, "I would like to see this terraformed planet."

"You have an open invitation," VE'AR told him. "There are risks for Jason."

"As I see it, you're the best chance he has."

Later, VE'AR and Myra talked privately.

"When I was repairing his mind, I heard music."

"Humans respond to music even more than we do, it can be calming."

"There was one song that kept repeating itself, over and over."

"That would be 'Bittersweet Symphony', he . . . we really like that one."

"Have you played him some of ours?"

"He likes that too, spectral music through the banwith from the stars and comets fascinates him. Have the fertility specialists found a way of reversing the condition of our people?"

"Not yet. Jackson Kindle is working closely with them and finding an antidote may not be possible."

"Would our people be open to taking human partners, would you be opposed to it?"

"Humankind is ruled by emotion, sometimes driving them to irrational behavior and deadly consequences."

"Jason and I are the first, our children are as you said, 'the best of both worlds'. Ask them, we need our children if we are to survive."

VE'AR touched her face. "We'll help Jason first then discuss the other."

A week later VE'AR, Myra, Jason, the children, a doctor from the Galaxy and an attendant travelled to Sanctus. Once there they beamed aboard the science ship. Again out of respect everyone aboard changed to human form. Jason spent the night there to be rested and ready for surgery the next morning. He and Myra were amazed at the changes on Sanctus and the Narin population which had grown as others travelled there from NARIN'MAR to explore and learn about humans.

VE'AR and Myra encouraged Jason the next day as he was taken for surgery. Two devices would be implanted in his lungs resulting in permanently being able to exist in a Narin atmosphere aboard the science ship. The Narin air had healing properties and a potential for healing Jason's body.

Hours later Jason awakened.

"The devices are working properly," his doctor said standing beside the Narin doctor who assisted him. "You are now able to breathe in both atmospheres."

"Now what?" Jason asked.

"Probably tomorrow we start you on a regiment of exercise and breathing the Narin air in small quantities gradually increasing both."

Later, Jason was alone with Myra, he drew encouragement from being with her.

"I wonder what it would be like to be normal again, to hold you, to hold our children."

She kissed him, "You will."

"Where is VE'AR?"

"Probably asking questions about you."

"Thanks to him I haven't had another stroke and my mind seems clear, I owe him."

"I brought up the subject of extinction without children, inter-marriage between humans and Narins."

"What did he say?"

"Wait on that one until Jason is better then we'll discuss it."

"Anything, any news from Bright Star?"

"Nothing yet."

VE'AR was escorting the children around the science ship, they were distracted from worry as they saw amazing things. They had the ability to breathe in a Narin and human atmosphere. He was proud of them.

The next day Jason was taken to a type of hyperbaric chamber. A scientist, one of several working with him told him what to expect.

"I am MAR'TYN. The Narin atmosphere is in your terms 20 psi; you will now be placed in this chamber and receive a concentrated saturation of the Narin air."

An hour passed.

"How are you feeling?"

"Like my arms and legs are stronger."

"Can you move your arms?"

"Slightly."

"Now your legs."

"Not yet," Jason had guarded optimism about this.

"They should in time."

"Where is VE'AR?"

"He has been here with us monitoring your progress. He is now with the children."

"Are they behaving?" Jason seemed upbeat when he saw Myra across the room.

"Oh yes."

Back on Bright Star the Narins were learning a great deal about their human counterparts as they attended courses taught by humans. They helped to build new communities for the humans and it was reciprocated as the Narins began to settle in; they were envious of those who had children trying to imagine joining themselves to humans and having children as Myra and Jason had. They were becoming very respected due in part to Allison, Marco and others who pushed for welcoming the Narins as neighbors and friends. Some still resented their presence. They were cautioned to always have another accompany them wherever they went as a precaution.

A young Narin male decided not to take the advice and went to a popular night spot on the Galaxy. He sat at a small table alone drinking tea, watching, learning. He could hear their thoughts. Three women, former crew members of the Earthforce Battalion were at a table several feet away. One was particularly pretty and obnoxious as they noticed him. In human form his hair was brown, shoulder length, around six feet tall, good looking. The pretty woman was tough and crude, she walked over to his table.

"Sit . . . please," he said. She did. Her long hair was black and curly, her face was light tan, she was tall and in dark pants and shirt. "What is your name?" he asked her.

"Wanda and yours?"

"AR'TYN." He could feel her dislike of the Narins.

"Why are you here alone?"

"Observing people, listening to music, it's unlike any music I have ever heard."

"How long will your people be here?"

"I don't imagine we'll be here very long."

"I hear Jason Kindle isn't well, good riddance."

"He's a hero."

"He destroyed our ship and killed our commander along with twelve others. We'll all be better off when all of you leave."

"I am here in this place to find a wife." His statement startled her.

"You're looking for a wife here? Narins don't come here . . . are you looking for a human wife?" She then got up and left for her table before he could answer. Then he got up and left, not wanting to read her thoughts at this point. He walked up and down the non-restricted areas of the Galaxy. The Colonel saw him and joined him in his walk.

"Good to see you Colonel."

"And you AR'TYN."

"I am fascinated by that hotspot, the Blaze. The music is loud and unusual."

"You were in there?"

"Yes, just people watching and listening to Earth music."

"If you decide to go there again take someone else with you, it's not the best place to be especially if you're Narin."

"I was made aware of that."

"There are other places, higher quality you could enjoy."

"I'm looking for a wife, human."

"What?"

"You are aware that the majority of our race cannot reproduce with each other."

"Yes, VE'AR made me aware, our scientists are working on the problem and there are other places to look besides the Blaze. Let's go for coffee, you like coffee?"

"It's good."

The Colonel showed AR'TYN an alternate place to meet human women."

"Are you married?" he asked the Colonel.

"No, I never married, seems I'm married to the Galaxy."

"Your ship?"

"Yes."

"Ever . . . ?"

"Oh yes, but as a starship commander and military matters that always took precedence, I never had time for a wife."

"More of us will face reality, intermarry or become extinct."

"Generally the Narins are held in high esteem."

"I appreciate hearing that."

"Are you staying aboard a ship or here?"

"Aboard a science ship, one of two we have."

"Rest well, I have to tend to my wife," he laughed.

AR'TYN returned to his ship, his thoughts returned to the woman he met that evening and the music at the Blaze. He was a scientist and was generally happy even as he wanted a mate and have children as Myra and Jason had. Many Narins began thinking this way and not all were going to wait on VE'AR to give his blessing even as respected as he was as their leader. Cloning hadn't worked for the Narins physically even though they could clone other life forms.

The next day the Colonel assigned a guard to follow AR'TYN as soon as evening came. He walked alone among the masses, standing out, wearing the traditional white metallic suit and colorful fabric thron stretched over one shoulder and across the chest tied on one side, he was looking for a mate trying not to think of Wanda since she wouldn't be willing. He went to the coffee shop which was a better meeting place. Narins were also present and treated well and there were several human men and women there, most were unmarried. He began reading a book <u>Adventures of Tom Sawyer</u> as he drank his tea. An hour later he left and as he walked by the Blaze he heard her voice. He turned in her direction and walked in, sat several tables over pretending not to notice, this time indulging in a cup of hot chocolate another favorite. She noticed him and came to his table. He motioned for her to sit.

"Did you come to see me?" she asked.

"That depends . . . I am enjoying this book."

"<u>Tom Sawyer</u>? I read that book as a child."

"I find it fascinating."

"What do you mean it depends?"

"It depends on if you'll spend time with me."

"You shouldn't be here, Narins aren't safe here."

"Probably I shouldn't."

"What will it take for you not to pursue me?"

"I'm not pursuing you," he said as he drank his chocolate. "I would like to spend time with you, only talking to you, nothing more."

"It will cost you . . . only to talk?"

"Yes."

"All right." She attempted to discourage him by charging him. "When?"

"Let's begin tonight, how much?"

"Five credits for tonight."

He knew she was trying to discourage him. He reached into his pocket and took the currency and subtly pushed it across the table. She seemed surprised that he agreed. They then talked for over an hour about a variety of subjects. He told her he was a scientist and about his people and home world. She revealed that she was third in command of the Earthforce Battalion and was taking classes to learn another profession that could be used to maintain cruisers.

Later she went back to her friends, he left for his ship, it was late, her friends were concerned.

The guard assigned to watch AR'TYN reported to the Colonel. "Sir, he went back there again, seemed to want to talk with someone and picked the roughest, crudest woman he could find, the third officer on the Battalion, Lieutenant Wanda Sykes. He just left."

"All right, get some sleep, we'll talk tomorrow."

"Yes Sir."

Wanda wanted to be with someone, she never considered a Narin. As they talked for several evenings she learned more about the Narin people, he learned more about her and what it meant to be a human female and a lieutenant. They took walks on the Galaxy and outside in a recently constructed park. She was going to miss the next evening with AR'TYN to be with someone she had a relationship with on board the Battalion as it travelled to Bright Star. That relationship had soured in recent months. AR'TYN didn't become angry even though he had feelings for her that grew stronger each time they met. She had feelings for him but didn't give in to them. She knew from the way he treated her, with respect, that he wanted to be with her on a more permanent basis.

The next evening he went to the Blaze knowing she wouldn't be there. Her two friends were there but didn't approach him. He wanted her and to be where he first met her. He read his book for a while and left. He didn't return the next evening doubting that she would want him. She was there and looked for him.

He returned the night after with another book <u>War and Peace</u> pretending not to notice her. She came and sat across from him.

"Where were you last evening AR'TYN?"

He looked up, stopped reading, "I had to work late."

"And you're reading <u>War and Peace</u>."

"It is a lot of information about your world."

"We're always at war, that's all we know, war and defending ourselves."

"Were we a threat to you humans?"

"Why are you asking me this?"

"Your ship arrived carrying a powerful toxin, the poison that threatened us with extinction."

"I don't know about any toxin used against anyone, Narin or human."

AR'TYN knew she was covering for her crew. "My apologies, it has been a stressful day, I am not angry with you."

"Let's talk."

He started to pay her, she wouldn't take his money. They talked for over an hour, even laughing, his mood began to lighten. "Is your relationship with this man serious?" he asked delicately.

"I've known him a while, it's not serious."

"Be with me Wanda."

This surprised her. "As in . . ."

"Make love to me, allow me to love you as your husband."

"AR'TYN, you are special, a Narin I actually like but you couldn't keep up with me in matters of a sexual nature, joining, let alone be a husband to me."

He closed his book and looking at her said, "Are you challenging me, my abilities? I would outlast you."

"All right, let's test one another . . . where?"

"I live and work on the larger ship, no privacy."

"I live down the corridor, let's go."

They both left.

The Colonel was contacted by the guard following AR'TYN.

"Leave them alone, there is nothing we can do at this point."

Once they arrived at her small compartment they removed their clothes. She had quickly gotten in bed as he continued removing his traditional Narin clothing.

"What do you really look like?" He looked so human and very handsome.

"I have simply rearranged myself to look human, not so different." Once in bed, "This is different, give me a moment," he said, "I have read up on this."

Wanda was amused but didn't laugh. Then he joined with her. Neither one had experienced anything like this. Afterward, both seemed very satisfied with the experience. He was exhausted but managed a smile as he looked at her. As he attempted to leave the bed she grabbed his arm and pulled him back for more. They did. When it was over, he had expended so much energy that he couldn't stand for a few moments.

"You win," he said.

"I think we both did," she replied.

"Got any chocolate?"

They both had chocolate to drink and talked for a while. He left an hour later for the research ship. She didn't tell her friends nor did he tell his.

The next evening he sat in his usual spot at the Blaze. Wanda's two friends were becoming concerned and advised her to call security.

"He's not a bother and I'm definitely not afraid of him. I'll go over and tell him he doesn't belong here."

"Does he insult you?" one asked.

"No, not at all, just ignore him. Give me a minute," she told them. She then sat across from him as always.

"Today I'm reading <u>Adventures of Robin Hood</u> . . . do you have plans?"

"My schedule is clear, want to meet?"

"I'll be there. Are they telling you to stay away from me?"

"Something like that . . . put your money away."

He left after a while and met her at her place. They ended the evening walking outside in the park, there were now lightening bugs which were a recent addition to the insect population on Bright Star, they delighted everyone. The moon was like gold and one and one-half times the size of Earth's. There was a small gathering around the recently formed lake; there were plans for more lakes to be constructed and for enlarging an ocean several hundred miles away. The stars and constellations were becoming familiar to the astronomers and gazers. There were plans to build a planetarium.

"Where is your home world from here?" she asked.

"Around five-hundred-thousand light years going back across your galaxy toward Earth and beyond the galaxy near the constellation Belshai, the warrior. I've never been to Earth."

"I was actually born on Mars. Not all our problems in our solar system were solved when we left Earth."

"That is unfortunate. Was your ship intended to destroy our home world?" He continued to press her for an answer about the toxin's purpose.

She wouldn't answer, "Let's go back inside."

He escorted her home not pursuing this. They talked about other things but he needed an answer at some point, he would be patient with this one, he loved her.

The Colonel was very aware that AR'TYN was courting a Battalion officer whose loyalties were in question. They had been together two months. She had been taking mechanical engineering courses and working aboard the Galaxy. He was taking a course in human culture, he tried to refrain from reading her mind, it gave him an unfair advantage and he might not be able to accept what she was thinking about him. She had secretly enrolled in another course regarding the Narin culture, not even telling him.

A week later a soldier from the Battalion followed AR'TYN to the beam up point to his ship. The man confronted him with threats concerning his liaisons with Wanda, some heard the confrontation.

"She is mine, you're not human, leave her alone or face the consequences."

AR'TYN turned facing the man, "Does she love you?"

"No business of yours." The man was angry and left after making his threats.

AR'TYN went to the Blaze the next evening, he didn't see Wanda, her two friends were there and came over to him.

"She isn't here, she has been injured."

"Where is she?"

"Sickbay . . . find who did this to her."

AR'TYN left quickly. He found her there covered in bruises. The Colonel and two of his men arrived. She was barely conscious as he held her hand.

"Someone threatened me last evening saying she was his and if I continued to see her there would be consequences. Narins see very well in the dark. He was a soldier from the Battalion, I can identify him."

"I'll need you to identify him as soon as possible. A guard will remain here for her protection."

AR'TYN touched her face then left with the Colonel. He identified the man. Military police were sent to bring him in but couldn't find him. AR'TYN was very angry.

"Don't take matters in your own hands," the Colonel told him, "our people are looking for him."

"I understand, I'm going to stay with her tonight."

"Sounds good, I'll look in on you both tomorrow."

"Be well Colonel."

He went to sickbay, she was now conscious. He held her hand and sat by her.

"He was coming after you," she could barely talk.

"He found me last evening, only threats, you weren't so fortunate. I identified him from the Colonel's database."

"Be careful, he's unstable."

"Did you love him?"

"I thought I did before I met you."

"He's going to have to deal with me now."

"AR'TYN, if you harm him, you've turned back any progress our two species have made together and you'll face banishment, don't do this if you love me." She was tired and fell asleep, he stayed.

The Colonel and security had searched for the man unable to find him.

Three days had passed, Wanda was now home, her friends were very attentive as was AR'TYN. They weren't aware that AR'TYN and Wanda were intimate. Wanda asked them to allow him to be with her overnight to protect her. They didn't try for intimacy until she recovered.

The fifth day since she was attacked, there was a visit from the Colonel and two security detail.

"It seems the man, Thomas Bruffel, a sergeant with the Battalion, was found murdered last evening."

Both AR'TYN and Wanda were there together as the Colonel told them the news.

"Where were you AR'TYN last evening?" The Colonel already knew.

"I was here with Wanda."

"All evening?"

"Yes Colonel I was."

"Wanda?"

"I am certain AR'TYN didn't do this but I can't remember . . ."

This statement surprised the Colonel but not AR'TYN who knew she was traumatized and conflicted, her old life was about abuse, orders and battles and it was about to consume her again taking her away from him. He had to let the events play out.

There would be a trial, VE'AR had left Sanctus to attend; Jason and Myra remained on Sanctus as Jason recovered. He talked with the Colonel and AR'TYN.

"Why?" he asked AR'TYN.

"I have feelings for her, she is conflicted and knows the truth about several matters including the toxin. When she comes to herself and sorts things out she will collaborate my story, she is the only one who can. Your security detail left earlier that evening Colonel."

"And if she doesn't?" VE'AR asked.

"Then my faith in her was unfounded."

"You could face banishment or death."

AR'TYN said nothing more as a representative of the law began counseling him, a human. The reality of the situation was beginning to sink in.

The Colonel and VE'AR left AR'TYN and his counsel to discuss the case.

"How is Jason?" the Colonel asked.

"Improving considerably, now able to breathe Narin air which is part of the healing process. He and Myra plan to return soon, the children are growing . . . I am always aware of our impending extinction. I haven't yet given my blessing so-to-speak to join with humans."

"Jason and Myra are reasons to believe it can work," the Colonel said.

"I respect that Myra mated him and he loves her completely but the human heart is hard to understand, prone to be irrational and angry."

"But we're capable of love and compassion among other things. They're your people . . . our people might be persuaded to join with the Narins to save your race if you agreed."

"It seems AR'TYN decided on his own."

"We'll win VE'AR. I'm keeping him here for his safety."

"The brig?"

"No, an adjoining room to my office. We don't know who murdered Master Sergeant Thomas Bruffel, we're checking for witnesses and the security footage."

"I'll leave you now Colonel, there is much to do . . . I ask one favor." VE'AR got permission to talk with Wanda in the Colonel's presence.

"AR'TYN needs your help now Lieutenant Sykes. He will face banishment or death if he is found guilty. Only you can substantiate his story. What does your heart tell you to do?"

"I don't remember," she said. "I wish I could." She became emotional. VE'AR knew she had strong feelings for AR'TYN and she knew he was innocent.

Wanda doesn't visit AR'TYN. Her past was pulling at her, the beating she received at the hands of Thomas Bruffel brought back a part of her that she had discarded when she fell in love with AR'TYN. Now she was confused as her old nature began to take over again.

The trial date came quickly, a week later. There were no jurors, the Colonel was judge and would pronounce sentence. AR'TYN sat with his lawyer and the prosecutor sat across the room, also human. The courtroom aboard the Galaxy was filled. The events leading up to that evening were stated. Two friends of Wanda stated that AR'TYN came to the Blaze and pursued her.

His turn came to testify. "I met her, I fell in love and knew she had good qualities and could, I hoped, love me. We . . ." he seemed to shut down for the moment. "I was angry at what was done to her but I didn't retaliate against Mr. Bruffel even as he threatened to harm me."

Wanda was beginning to fracture inside as she began to testify. "AR'TYN was special, we joined, my choice, I knew I loved him." She looked at her Battalion shipmates as she said this. "He was angry with Master Sergeant Bruffel seeing how badly he had beaten me, he didn't leave my side including the night of the murder. Thomas Bruffel had been my lover for a year as we travelled here but he was cruel and I no longer wanted to be around him, he went ballistic threatening harm to me and to AR'TYN if I didn't break off the relationship. AR'TYN couldn't be with me and commit the murder . . . and now something I have also been asked . . . the Earthforce Battalion was going to attack the Narin home world with the toxin it carried and launched a probe months ago to do this very thing and to attack Bright Star to make this planet ours to be used as an outpost. The Commander revealed this to his Second and to me his third; only two others also had this revealed to them, this was so, I say this of my own free will."

Everyone attending the trial was quiet, then gasps over the testimony given by a top officer on the Battalion. Wanda's two friends were in disbelief not having known the information that she had just presented.

"Not guilty," was the verdict as announced by Colonel Sobel.

Wanda and AR'TYN left together to start a new life. He asked VE'AR for his blessing which he gave. They would officially be united in a ceremony. The Colonel then went with security to the brig and talked with a prisoner. "Lieutenant you'll be placed in a facility where you'll receive the best help we can give you, you won't be executed or banished."

"Was the young Narin cleared?"

"Yes, we'll keep this quiet, the only other one to know is VE'AR of the Narins."

"Yes Sir."

Neither AR'TYN nor Wanda were told about the capture earlier of the true murderer with hope that Wanda would testify in AR'TYN's behalf and also reveal the purpose of carrying the toxin aboard the Battalion.

Months passed, several other Narins sought humans to mate with, even going to the Blaze and the usual coffee shops. VE'AR was pressured to allow these unions. Several of the Battalion crew then united with a Narin partner. More houses were built, farms were started, businesses of all types were begun and more children were born.

The entomologist, Dr. Vu had a flourishing business as he worked with human and Narin scientists to improve upon creatures that would pollinate and others that would be beneficial in other ways. Unfortunately an experiment to make Earth mosquitoes into pollinators failed miserably and were released by accident; they were now a larger species and more aggressive to everyone's disappointment. Butterflies and praying mantises were his next project, two of the most beautiful and fascinating creatures on Earth.

VE'AR had left briefly for Sanctus and returned to Bright Star with Jason, Myra and their children. In four months Jason had improved considerably. They caught up on the progress made there and were astounded seeing many who were pregnant and several had delivered early in under four months if the mothers were Narin . . . Myra wasn't so lucky.

Allison and Marco married now that Jason and Myra were back; he was best man and Myra was maid of honor. The Colonel officiated even though there was a minister who had been aboard the Galaxy, Pastor Ames and now officiated at a church on Bright Star, but his business had begun to grow as more of the population married. He was now training an assistant pastor.

The son of a rabbi, Jonas Zondervan was officiating at Bright Star's only temple; he was basically taught by his father who remained on Earth unable to travel to the new world, and was self taught for the rest. He was basically familiar with the rituals. A large menorah was made for his temple by the Narins who were gifted in crafting metal sculptures. There were now other places of worship for the diverse cultures that were brought to Bright Star.

The Narins had rituals of worship in a single dome building recently constructed. Services were held twice a week or as each Narin decided for themselves.

Sanctus not only served as a Narin outpost and sanctuary for humans should Bright Star be attacked but as a source for science and medical research which benefitted Narin and human needs. VE'AR would stay on both Bright Star and periodically Sanctus. He hadn't been to his home world NARIN'MAR in nearly two years; he was still revered as undisputed leader of the Narin civilization. He and Jason retained a special bond for one another which led to more unions between Narins and humans.

Jason and Myra lived aboard her ship while their house was built, Jason helped in its construction. He continued his teaching not feeling ill will this time from the students comprising those from the Battalion. Many were pregnant and happy as they were schooled, the male students also had for the most part a change in attitude. Some of the classes were made up of human men who had taken Narin women as wives.

Myra continued teaching and added advanced chemistry. Schools prepared to educate the child student population due to recent births. Jackson and Bella Kindle were teaching botany courses. The Narins taught a number of subjects including better ways of cloning farm animals increasing the population and food production. The Narins loved cheese more than even humans so cattle and goats were prized.

The Colonel, scientists and military both Narin and human collaborated on a more powerful security grid for Bright Star similar to the one setup by the Narins on Sanctus. There was a strong feeling among the Narins that Earth was again sending ships into deep space with the same intent to kill off any competition Narin or human. Battalion I had sent a report to Earth before being destroyed. AR'TYN felt it as he was working in the fields after a day's work aboard the science ship orbiting the planet. The fields surrounded a newly constructed house for Wanda and himself.

"The ship will be arriving in a year or less, a warship," he told Wanda, "will you leave to join them when they arrive?"

"Look around AR'TYN, look at our children I'm carrying," she held her stomach, "I made my choice, I'm not going anywhere." They kissed.

CHAPTER V

GALAXY—THEY CAME

Another ship came from Earth. They were prepared for war, they carried both weapons and the toxin, a more potent version. They remained in a low stationary orbit above the planet's surface. The security grid around Bright Star was up and running, human-Narin technology, the ship would not penetrate the grid as a safety measure; the Commander and five of his crew beamed to the surface. He was welcomed but suspicions grew about the warship which was almost identical to Earthforce Battalion I. It travelled through a wormhole at faster speed cutting travel time by years as the Battalion I had. Colonel Sobel invited them aboard the Galaxy; his security, VE'AR, Jason and others of the Galaxy crew were there. The Commander was young, tall and military from his hair cut to his dark blue uniform.

"I'm Colonel Sobel, my Second Lieutenant Benoit, Chief Engineer Mr. Ferris, Assistant Chief Engineer Mr. Kindle, VE'AR leader of the Narins, his attendants and my crew, welcome. What brings you to Bright Star and carrying this toxin in your warship?"

"We have come on a mission of an unpleasant nature. I'm Commander Neal, the toxin is only carried on deep space missions and only used if needed to defend ourselves. My mission is to take Jason Kindle back to Earth for trial on charges of murder." He looked at Jason as he said this thinking Jason was only a young troublemaker, destructive and out of control. Jason couldn't believe what he was hearing and stood motionless, no expression whatsoever.

"We had proof of intended harm to the Narins and to us, witnesses, Jason's testimony and much more," Colonel Sobel told the Commander.

"Twelve men and Commander Scott perished as they were flown into the sun," Commander Neal replied.

"I gave them a chance to beam off the ship, several did and lived," Jason said.

"Nevertheless, there will be a trial, here on Bright Star or on Earth."

"Do you really want to risk a war?" Colonel Sobel asked. "I authorized his actions to save our community here and to protect the Narin home world from the effects of the toxin, however, Commander Scott sent a probe before arriving here filled with the poison to their home world . . . the Battalion crew should have been tried for their crimes." Colonel Neal seemed unfazed by this revelation.

VE'AR was very protective of Jason and their attempt to punish him for saving lives by destroying the threat would not go unchallenged.

There was a trial a week later held aboard the Battalion II warship. The Commander, as if to intimidate both human and Narins on Bright Star revealed that several battle class ships would be launched from Earth if they were attacked or denied bringing Jason back to Earth should he be found guilty. The trial began, Commander Neal was judge and found Jason guilty even with witnesses testifying on his behalf. He was immediately placed in confinement under guard on the Commander's ship.

Colonel Sobel spoke with VE'AR who were both at the trial. "They will terminate him for doing the right thing." VE'AR listened then left.

Jason was allowed to see his parents and sister. Myra and the children were there as he said his goodbyes. No one was allowed to travel with him. The trip would take one year.

"Is there nothing we can do?" Myra asked VE'AR.

"Their laws are clear, Jason was found guilty."

"It's not right."

"I didn't say it was, this isn't over, not yet."

Myra looked at VE'AR with an understanding of his role in the situation.

"You are planning something."

He touched her face and hugged her as he had seen Jason do. "Tell no one, not even ours. We will say we journeyed to the home world."

"Safe journey," she said concerned about both Jason and her father.

The Battalion had left Bright Star two days earlier. The Commander talked with Jason as one of the doctors put drops in his eyes. "These will cause temporary blindness since you can pilot one of these warships," he said, "should you escape confinement and the armed guard."

"Under law," the doctor reminded the Commander, "he should be permanently blinded for the trip to Earth."

"If you do that, I'll drop you off at the nearest moon."

"But . . ."

"I'm the Commander, no sight at first, no permanent damage, understood?"

"Yes Sir."

Jason was nervous about his eyes but controlled himself. "How will I die? The drops are working, I can't see you."

"I suppose firing squad, quick. Leave us," he said to the doctor. They were now alone except for the guard standing a few feet away. "Do you wish to make a statement?"

"About what?"

"About how all this started."

Jason hesitated for a moment then, "My father Jackson Kindle created the toxin before we left Earth some two-hundred years ago. The military misused it to clear areas of space removing any competition so-to-speak but it harmed the non-aggressive Narins. When our ship, the Galaxy went off its trajectory, a Narin saved us. As we began our new lives on Bright Star and getting to know the Narins, the first Earthforce Battalion came with the intended destruction of us on Bright Star to retain the planet for themselves and to destroy the Narins and their home planet using that toxin they carried. The only way to stop their assault was to pilot their ship into the sun but first allowing those who wanted to survive to beam off. Unfortunately the Commander and twelve others stayed in an attempt to take back the Battalion. I was rescued . . . these are the facts as I stated in the trial."

Commander Neal then commended Jason for his bravery which surprised him, "I do believe you."

"Then what is all this?"

"We can't allow you to discredit the military, back home the military rules and it will rule space, as much of it as possible and stamp out any competition. You will die so others won't become well meaning heroes teaching people to kill off the military when things don't suit them or they feel threatened."

"I'm glad you cleared that up," he said as he listened.

"A sense of humor, you'll need it Jason . . . get some sleep."

Jason was more confused than ever. He tried to rest, his thoughts were of Myra and the children and was there a way out of all of this. He was carefully monitored in his confinement, his vital signs could be seen on a wall unit outside his cell as well as on the Commander's computer and in sickbay.

Two weeks had gone by since Jason was taken aboard. The doctor and two staff members came to take him for an examination. He didn't have sight yet and became resistant to their taking him; he fought the doctor and the guard who called in another guard.

"No," Jason said defiantly, almost hysterical at this point.

The Commander was notified of the skirmish and saw Jason's life signs which were off the charts.

Ralph, his guard, now had Jason in a choke hold. "Commander!"

"I'm coming, don't do anything drastic."

"Jason let's back up," Ralph said, "I'm lowering you to the floor, sit against the wall."

Jason obeyed, out of breath, perspiring, he offered no resistance now.

"What's going on Jason?" Commander Neal asked when he arrived. Jason didn't answer, still sitting on the floor against the wall of his confinement breathing hard.

"We were taking him for an examination, he then went ballistic fighting us," the doctor said.

"I can't see, I don't know what you're about to do to me." He was still resistant.

"What is all this about?" Commander Neal asked the doctor.

"We have to examine him, its required procedure."

"Bring the drops, give him two hours, after the examination bring him to my office."

They sat Jason in a chair and applied the eye drops.

"Can you see now?" the Commander asked.

"Yes."

"Do this, it won't be grueling, we'll talk about it afterward, agreed?"

"Yes." He didn't resist this time as he went to sickbay. The Commander was there but Jason didn't know it.

"Evidence of stroke," the doctor said. "Your brain seems to be capable of working all areas at once." The examination continued, "Two implants in your lungs of alien origin, enabling you to breathe the Narin atmosphere, nitrogen, carbon dioxide and methane. Physically aged ten years." There were more thorough tests then the examination was complete. Jason was then taken to the Commander's office.

"Why did you resist an examination?"

After a long pause, "The last examination I had, they were going to wipe my mind of the knowledge I had been given but were going to push it further until I died. I endured repeated grueling interrogations, humiliating painful physicals to wear me down until I gave up the Narin who saved the Galaxy and all aboard from being vaporized. The Colonel's orders had been altered by an overzealous lieutenant who wanted me dead. Apparently I haven't gotten over it."

The Commander then said, "You won't need another physical, you'll be allowed two hours of sight everyday then we go from there . . . agreed?"

"Yes, agreed."

"Now behave yourself." Commander Neal was beginning to be protective of Jason as he gained respect for him. The guard took him back to his confinement. He had one hour of sight left to see, to read. His life signs reflected an almost calm as he listened to music over the ship's intercom.

Two months had passed since he left Bright Star. For two hours a day he was able to study and read favorite books, nothing on piloting a war class starship however. Jason had also begun losing weight, not eating much which became a concern to the Commander.

"Jason, if you don't eat, your muscle tone goes, your mind goes, you die."

"What does it matter? I can't see most of the time, I'm really already dead."

"Well that's a downer . . . it does matter. You have to eat or take it through an I.V., then shots to stimulate your appetite."

"Eight hours of sight in the morning hours and I'll eat . . . anything."

"Four hours."

"Eight."

"Six, no more."

"Eight and . . ."

"And what?"

"I'll think of something."

The Commander laughed. "Eight hours in the morning." He allowed this privilege not normally given to wanted felons. "And you'll eat anything." He started Jason on an exercise regiment which included games as racquetball, basketball, self-defense, anything to keep fit which was all important as they travelled through space; a muscle building supplement was also added to his meals daily. Two women crew members Sergeant Blondell and Private Forbes would participate with them time-to-time in the games.

Jason and the Commander talked often about Earth and the conquest of space. "In several hundred years since the Galaxy left Earth not that much would be called advanced except ships that travel much faster and the use of wormholes on deep space flights as needed.

"Flying cars?" Jason asked.

"In a manner of speaking . . . you are young Jason, eighteen now?"

"Eighteen."

"You were aged ten years, tell me why."

"So my mind and body could accept a vast amount of data to pilot the Galaxy. I had the help of a Narin woman who placed herself in harm's way to do so."

"And you married her, two kids later, do you still love her?"

"Yes, very much."

"What can you tell us about them?"

"They're peaceful, technologically advanced, not aggressive, curious."

"And they accepted you?"

"Yes."

"What did they get from you? What did they want? Everyone always wants something."

"I didn't give them anything . . . I married the daughter of the Narin leader."

"The leader as in leader of the whole race?"

"Yes, VE'AR, you met him."

"Impressive . . . and the fact that you had to grow up so quickly for the responsibilities."

"How old are you?"

"I'm thirty-five, does it show?"

"That seems young."

As time passed, Jason and Commander Neal developed a friendship and a respect for one another, Jason never forgetting that the Commander would have him executed once they reached Earth. He was given more privileges and allowed to visit certain areas of the ship. The Chief Engineer of the Battalion, Manuel Ovilla, asked him about boosting the engines' performance. Jason studied the engines by computer and holograph, too risky to take him to the actual engine area should he attempt sabotage. He suggested changes which did help knowing that there wouldn't be any incentive to do so, the sight time would never be increased.

"It will unfortunately get me to Earth a month sooner," he told the Commander.

Two more months passed, the Commander read up on Military Earth Law in an attempt to find some way to allow Jason to live; he sometimes drank to forget the responsibilities of commanding a warship. Trials and executions weighed heavily on him.

One evening he went to visit Jason who was struggling to sleep and was blind again.

"Jason, are you awake? The monitor wasn't registering sleep."

"Commander?"

"You up to talking?"

"I think so, where are you?"

"Sitting in a chair facing you . . . there is no way to stop this, our laws are clear. I've been studying them, no loophole."

"I'm resigned to it, not happy about it . . . are you married?"

"Only to this ship."

"Our Colonel Sobel said the same thing, he's a good leader, very military."

"You respect him?"

"Yes, very much . . . do you agree with everything the military says without question, blind obedience?"

"To a degree, in our best interest." Commander Neal thought for a moment then, "No."

"Then change the rules."

"It would take years, maybe a generation, you wouldn't be alive to see the changes."

"It still matters."

The Commander thought on these things then, "Goodnight Jason." He left.

The next day he had Jason brought to the observation deck.

"Look out there, we are in an area of space filled with stars and developing ones. Open the overhead shield," he ordered, "you can begin taking readings," he said to a scientist, an Ethiopian who was dressed differently from the crew. "Explain, if you will, some of this to Jason, he's interested in astronomy."

"I am called Dr. Planck, chief scientist here, my specialty is radio astronomy. This ship is extraordinary in that one-third of the top outer portion is literally covered with radio telescope dishes and two optical ones receiving electromagnetic readings from stars, comets, anything out there and as you might already know they produce light waves and sound waves; these are measured after being collected by a correlator for proper analysis . . . listen now, a pulsating radio star, approximately sixty-million miles away, it is classified as a pulsar; computers direct the rotation of the dishes. This particular star flashes optically at the same frequency as the radio pulses. Electrons in interstellar space affect the velocities of the different radio waves; the longer the wavelength, the slower the velocity. These electromagnetic radiations are observed that are one millimeter or longer in wavelength."

In about half-an-hour Dr. Plank spoke to Jason about quasars. "These faint stars are among the brightest known objects in the universe, some have a luminosity of twenty trillion suns or a thousand Milky Way Galaxies. They are not really stars because of their enormous luminosity; these objects became known as quasi-stellar radio sources, "quasi-stellar" means "starlike", or quasars. The distance to the closest quasar from Earth is 240 Mpc. Most date back to much earlier periods of galaxy formation and are found in deep space; these redshifted objects are not all strong radio sources but there is one on the viewing screen, an optical image of one."

In the area of the control room where they were, the crew at times enjoyed listening to soft music in the background as they navigated and passed various areas in deep space. As more signals from stars were recorded, Jason asked questions totally fascinated.

"Coming up on a black hole," the Commander said.

"Large," Dr. Planck said, "a billion times the size of the Earth sun."

Jason stood up suddenly, he still had one hand cuffed to a chair still at the observation window sitting several feet from the Commander and crew piloting the ship. The guard who was armed and standing by Jason ordered him to sit.

"Sergeant," the Commander said, "you can stand down, I'm armed and if Mr. Kindle makes a wrong move, I'll shoot him myself."

Jason laughed but Sergeant Mills wasn't amused, nevertheless he sat.

For several minutes the black hole tugged at the Battalion. Jason observed it and a star it was feeding off of.

Later, he was returned to confinement after they left that area of space. In a few hours the Commander stopped by.

"Dr. Planck is on a whole different level."

"I never expected to see all of this and have it explained by a scientist, I didn't understand everything."

"No one totally does. We're having a basketball game tomorrow . . . come join us, a foursome . . . what's in your head Jason?"

"I really enjoyed this today . . . and then I started to wonder what does all this matter? I'll be dead in six months."

"A diversion. My crew and I might not survive this mission or the next, but that is flawed thinking to do nothing; you, all of us need exercise and interaction, reading alone isn't everything. You probably couldn't handle this advanced basketball, it gets very rough . . . fouls, fights break out, blood, bruises . . . let me know." He left.

The next day Jason decides to join the game, he changes clothes. All are wearing the usual tight black shorts, black T-shirts and gym shoes. Two men, two women.

"Private Forbes, Sergeant Blondell, Jason has decided to join us." He explained the rules to Jason. "Basically there are none."

The game got quickly intense and very rough.

"Are you making this personal?" the Commander asked him.

"Certainly not," Jason said with a grin.

An hour later they all sat together drinking anything available, everyone was bruised, Jason had nosebleed as did the Commander. They began sniffing a substance Jason recognized as cocaine, he declined.

"Takes away the pain," Sergeant Blondell remarked.

"So does ice," he said as he placed a bag of ice on his jaw and gave one to the Sergeant.

Later, the Commander whispered to him, "Do you want a woman tonight?"

"They are beautiful, I only want one woman, my wife."

"Just thought I'd ask, Sergeant Blondell is an excellent crew member, loyal and will be with me tonight."

Two weeks later the Battalion stops above a small planetoid that had a valuable supply of a mineral used to make fuel on Earth and also weapons. Jason is allowed to watch as a smaller ship is sent to the surface with three of the crew. The location of the mineral is found and drilling begins. An asteroid is coming dangerously close in their direction, the Battalion fires on it but several large pieces come in the direction of the large ship, the Commander orders shields up and a tractor beam to take the pieces and pull them away from those on the surface.

"Reverse one-third impulse," he orders and drags everything out into space then, "tractor beam off."

Thirty minutes pass.

"Sir," one of the crew says, "another asteroid is headed straight for the planetoid."

"How large?"

"The size of Texas."

"When?"

"Twenty minutes."

The Commander warns the small ship on the surface, "Get out now, one's coming."

Five minutes pass, "We have no engines."

"What the Hell!"

Jason heard this, "I know about that cruiser, allow me to help."

They pull up a holographic image, Jason then studies it and asks them about the control panel. He has them to re-route power in an unorthodox way. It works, the small craft lifts off quickly and makes it to the ship which leaves the area as the planetoid is cut in half and shoots out into space.

"Good work Jason," the Commander said.

The Battalion Chief Engineer also thanks him. "The ship, crew and contents are safe."

A few days later another basketball game, the usual bruises and blood. The competition between Commander Neal and Jason escalated, the game became very intense, the women players finally bowed out. Finally it was over.

"Jason, we ran overtime, you have five minutes of sight," the Commander said.

"Shit," Jason said as he quickly left with the guard.

Sergeant Blondell remarked, "You did that on purpose," and gave the Commander a dirty look.

"Me? I did, he has made this so personal almost like . . ."

"He's punishing you for taking him from his family to be executed in two months."

"I'll see you ladies in a while." He leaves to catch up with Jason and the guard. Ralph has escorted Jason who simply sits in the chair in his confinement. He is bloodied, smells of sweat and feels an overall sense of being helpless and having no hope spurred in part by sixteen hours of blindness everyday.

"Jason, talk for a moment?" the Commander asked.

"Why not?"

"Why are you doing this?"

"Doing what?"

"You know what, you're making this personal."

"I appreciate all you've done to help me through this, it isn't going to end well. I am angry but anger accomplishes nothing."

"If you still want a sonic shower, I can hand you a bar of soap and a towel, that was my retaliation keeping you until it was too late."

"I think I'll take that shower now."

As time went on they talked about the Earth-Mars Wars.

"I was raised military, placed in a starship as a Commander at a very young age, twenty-five. I always envisioned being happy but that has been put on hold, no wife, no children."

"Well not yet, there's still time."

"I keep telling myself that."

"You mentioned earlier that your mentor was an Admiral."

"Yes, Admiral Breedlove. When my parents were killed in a war here on Earth, the Admiral took me in and continued my training in the military which led me to the Commander's chair on a warship. I became like a son to him . . . he had two sons who became doctors, married, had children. He is still flying a warship, honored for many acts of heroism, a ship was named for him. I hope to live up to his expectations, I admire him."

There were still the games, basketball was now not played as aggressively, star systems to observe and anomalies throughout space. Jason saw many things on his way to Earth from that observation window.

Another month passed, they arrived in orbit above Earth then landed on a huge landing pad by other large warships and cruisers. The Commander took Jason to a detention center and found out his execution date.

"One week from today . . . I didn't want it to come to this, the penalty is death for destroying military property or killing military personnel. It doesn't matter why or to have witnesses testify on your behalf. I allowed testimony to satisfy everyone and you that all voices would be heard. Your death will be quick, no do-overs with a firing squad. You will be standing against a wall, your hands will be bound on two posts on either side of you, a heart monitor will be attached to your chest."

As he listened to the Commander, Jason tried to remain calm for the moment masking his fear.

"Would you have committed these crimes in retrospect?"

"I never wanted to harm anyone but with the information we had, yes I would do it again and die with them."

The Commander then stood up to leave, "hungry?"

"I don't know how I could eat." Jason now sat in this Earth confinement.

"Till tomorrow then."

That night the Commander made some calls as he again read up on current changes in the military law in a desperate attempt to save him, it seemed there wasn't a way.

Morning came. The Commander took Jason on a tour of Washington D.C. where he was now stationed and where the execution would take place. For the hundreds of years that had passed on Earth since the Galaxy left over two-hundred years ago, there weren't any big changes for the better; some changes reflected wars that had taken place over years, never rebuilt. Jason asked him about this. Interplanetary wars had done the most damage. There were a few landmarks and monuments still in existence that Jason remembered.

Days went by. The Commander played one last game of basketball against Jason then later on to a grooming shop.

"We need to prepare you. After we leave here there are uniforms to select from, how you're dressed will be important. I will announce the charges against you and the punishment."

Jason missed Myra and the children, VE'AR and his parents and Allison more now than ever. The Commander had become a friend and would be the only one on Earth who understood why he did what he did.

The day of the execution there were several in attendance, those whose relatives had been killed aboard the Earthforce Battalion, some military and the others, mostly curious who knew about him. As he was being prepared for his execution he began to hyperventilate.

"Keep it together Jason," Commander Neal whispered, "you have a following, some are here, they're looking to you for strength."

Jason then struggled to remain calm with no emotion. As he stood against a wall he saw the soldiers in uniform ready to take his life. His hands were bound to posts on either side of him, the monitor was placed over his heart, a restraint was used to hold him against the wall. The Commander then announced the crimes and punishment. Jason closed his eyes. The guns fired but he wasn't struck. He opened his eyes to see the bullets stopped in mid air; as everyone watched he realized something had stopped his execution. The Commander stood up and told the firing squad to "stand down." Then VE'AR appeared standing by Jason, he freed him, Jason was in disbelief.

"I am VE'AR leader of the Narin race, this execution will not be carried out. Our first encounter with the human race didn't go well as a toxin was spread through space to stamp out any competition; its intended use was to kill lower forms of life detrimental to humans as they pushed out into deep space. The toxin has harmed our people beyond measure. Over time we met our human counterparts and formed an alliance of sorts. For a year five of us have been aboard the second Battalion ship to visit us learning everything we could about humanity as warships would continue to invade space from planet Earth with destruction as their mission. One human aboard, Jason Kindle was taken from us to be executed even as he tried to save his new world, Bright Star from the threat of annihilation and the Narins from an attack on their home world with the deadly toxin carried by the first warship to reach Bright Star. We had considered destruction of planet Earth, all of you seem to be doing a good job of that yourselves. Our decision not to destroy your world was based on information we gathered as we travelled here; how Jason was treated was a factor. You are a destructive species but worth saving. You will find that space has been reconfigured so you will never send your warships to our doorstep again." VE'AR then changes form looking like fire, the other four appear as human.

The Commander approaches Jason and the Narins are watching carefully. "I'm glad for the outcome."

"I know," Jason said, "they know," looking at the Narins . . . "I had no idea they were aboard."

"Are all of us prohibited from finding Bright Star?"

"If you're not in a war class ship, you're welcome to visit. Space will be altered, we'll guide you in." Jason then looked at VE'AR who didn't disagree with this. Jason, VE'AR and the other Narins beamed aboard their ship which had not been detected as it was piloted by other Narins and followed the Battalion to Earth.

The Commander now realized that the Narins were powerful, able to destroy Earth but chose not to. Everyone there for the execution was in amazement over what they just witnessed especially those who were there to support Jason.

Aboard the Narin ship VE'AR talked with Jason again citing his reasons for not revealing his presence aboard the Battalion. "We were monitoring your situation and prepared to rescue you should it become necessary. It seemed the only way to determine what to do about Earth and the threat and that included how you were dealt with aboard ship . . . the Commander was determined to spare your life if possible and for that reason he will be permitted to visit as you determine. You showed great courage even as you were about to be terminated."

"All of you took a risk. I respect your decisions in these matters VE'AR, especially not to destroy my home world."

They talked often over the ten months it took the fast Narin ship to reach Bright Star. The brave Narins who pursued the probe to NARIN'MAR were feared dead.

When they arrived Myra couldn't believe he was home, safe, she couldn't keep her hands off of him, he was as passionate. Colonel Sobel congratulated VE'AR and the other Narins on the rescue and talked to Jason even hugging him.

The Narins did what they said and altered space so no earth ship could ever find Bright Star, Sanctus or the Narin home world.

Commander Neal had considered leaving Earth after Jason was freed months ago. Others felt as he did wanting a new start. He had been told emphatically not to approach in a warship but he and the others would be taking Battalion II with the improvements to the engines provided earlier by Jason; they could technically outrun the other ships. He talked with his crew who were loyal to him, they discussed how and when to leave.

The next week he had them move provisions onto the enormous warship as well as any other personal items. He talked with a mission specialist to go on a delivery mission to the moon Io to bring fuel and supplies. He presented a fake request form. The mission was approved for two days from that day of request. He would bring his Second who had accompanied him on all missions, Lieutenant Colonel Brandon Wells and all members of his crew. Another private came aboard to benefit from the flight by logging more hours, this was a concern to everyone aboard. Everyone was preparing.

Then it was time, Commander Neal picked up his papers confirming the mission as approved, then he returned to the ship.

"Where is Sergeant Blondell?"

"There is a problem Sir," Master Sergeant Ralph told him.

Just then the private who was assigned to the Commander's ship walked by, "I'm Private Sussman Sir, can I be of assistance?"

"Yes, help them move these files to the ready room."

The Private then assisted the others.

"What about Blondell?"

"A car has followed her to every place she has been today including the store where she is now."

"Surveillance. I'll be back." He left quickly, calling her. "Meet me out front, ignore the car."

She met him out front. He walked with her in the direction of her apartment. "I'm scared."

"I know, try to stay calm like we're on a mission . . . I'm going to do something now that I don't normally do in public."

"You're not going to unzip your pants out here are you?"

"No, nothing like that . . . just go with me on this, that car is still following." He began to touch her shoulders then touches her sensually and they kiss then walk up the front stairs of her apartment.

One of the two in the car then says, "They aren't going anywhere for a while."

Soon after, the Commander and Blondell quickly leave out a back door. Once aboard ship they confirmed their departure with the mission specialist, the huge doors covering the ship bays where the ships were required to land were opened. They rose in the air around two-hundred feet then began forward thrust, slow at first. Suddenly they were called back.

"This mission is declined," came the transmission, "return to the ship bay immediately."

Commander Neal ordered that no reply be given. "Increase forward thrust," he said. The bay doors began to close, they made it out, barely. "Increase to warp two." Two smaller cruisers were ordered to follow and force them to return immediately. They fired on the Battalion, then unable to penetrate the shields the two ships positioned themselves in the path of the Battalion firing as they did so. The crew of the Battalion had no other recourse than to defend themselves. Commander Neal gave the order, "Return fire." It had deadly consequences. Now he and the crew were all guilty of murder as Jason was and destruction of military property. He now began to regret his decision to leave Earth, but they couldn't turn back. It would take around eleven months to reach where Bright Star had been and wasn't now. They increased speed to warp 6.

VE'AR told Jason about Commander Neal commandeering the warship and leaving Earth. "It is armed carrying no toxin, he jettisoned it and destroyed it with the aft thrusters even as Earth vessels are still pursuing."

"Why a warship? I told him how to reach us."

"When he reaches us I believe we should lead him in, I don't sense aggression, I do sense his desperation in taking the Battalion."

"How long?"

"Around eleven months, perhaps sooner."

"How can you know all of this when these things are happening light years away?"

"As a Narin we have certain abilities, some have a much stronger sense of things but I have help aboard his ship, two of our own unseen, to help him, I can understand their thoughts."

"I envy that ability. I'll look forward to their arrival and the preparation to be made."

"Jason, they might not make it."

"At least the best hope is having Commander Neal at the helm and your people there."

"They could be casualties as well, a suicide mission as humans would say."

This was of great concern to VE'AR and Jason.

"I'm teaching a class which ends in two hours, meet me after?"

"The Grill?"

"See you there VE'AR."

Buildings had literally changed the landscape of the planet. Other towns were started, businesses of all types had emerged, more schools, more marriages, an increasing number between Narins and humans with VE'AR's blessing and more children. Jason and Myra's children were growing up quickly which was characteristic of Narin children; both had brown eyes like Myra and light brown hair like Jason.

VE'AR's influence was evident in their lives, he was very respected. When Jason was rescued months earlier he was able to overcome the repressed feelings of being taken from Bright Star, from Myra and the kids as he talked with VE'AR on the return journey. Myra also had those feelings when Jason was taken and sought the council of Bella Kindle and of VE'AR upon his return.

A government building was now under construction. The seat of the governing body was still aboard the Galaxy, still headed by the military. Narins and humans would share equally in the decisions through a council.

Farms were a part of home ownership. Crops were abundant and were sold to several market places in the towns. Animals were raised on some farms to be sold or kept as food sources. Several new species were introduced both on Bright Star and Sanctus, a result of cloning by the Narins; they shared their technology with human scientists.

A bartering system was used or a system of using credits in the form of a card or currency to buy anything.

Two attorneys had opened offices aboard the Galaxy helping families with legal matters and settling disputes. Generally houses were built and given to families, but they in turn were to help construct houses for other families in need. The mortgages were attached more to businesses or to those who wanted to add to their houses or farms.

Two months had gone by, Commander Neal and his crew were followed by another warship, Earthforce Battalion III and two small cruisers. The Battalion Commander, Admiral James Breedlove made several attempts to communicate with him. The improvements that Jason made to the engines kept Commander Neal and his crew out of weapons range for now.

"Commander Neal, this is Battalion Commander Breedlove, come in."

Finally Commander Neal replied, "What are you doing out here Sir?"

"Trying to stop you."

"We made our choice to leave Earth."

"I mentored you, treated you like a son, why have you done this?"

"To join others who got tired of the military way of doing things . . . people die if they disagree."

"Surrender and I'll do everything within my power to help you, help all of you."

"You've done a lot for me. It seems strange to be on opposite sides now, we're wanted felons and would surely die for our crimes."

"Then I'll have to stop you one way or another."

"It's good to hear your voice again Sir although not under these circumstances, Commander out." The transmission was ended, Commander Neal didn't know how he would deal with his friend and mentor when he caught up with them.

Another two months went by, seven to go to reach those on Bright Star. Communications Officer Vann alerted the Commander, "Sir, another unauthorized transmission, that makes five since we left Earth. It seems to be coming from different areas of the ship, no signature."

"Probably a spy communicating with Breedlove's ship."

"Who would?"

"That's a good question, the obvious one might not be the one."

No one trusted Private Sussman, he had wanted access to a weapon and had an unusual curiosity about the engines, wanting to study them.

More transmissions came from Battalion III. "We're gaining on you, you'll never be happy out there, you're . . ."

Commander Neal terminated the transmission and went to his office, he had a drink, sitting quietly for a few moments then fell asleep. He agonized about what was ahead for him and his crew. Sergeants Ralph and Blondell met with him later.

"I feel badly about all of this, that I caused the calamity we're in."

"Commander," Ralph said, "we were all for this, everyone wanted their chance to leave Earth forever . . . we'll all make it together or we'll all die together having made the effort."

"I agree with him," Sergeant Blondell said, "each one of us made our decision."

Commander Neal was moved by this and encouraged. He called a meeting. "Is everyone in agreement to find Bright Star whatever the cost?" Everyone agreed. "Suggestions anybody?" he asked.

"Keep going, we can't turn back," his Second replied.

"We don't want to turn back," said another.

"We can start over, it will be different."

"That's what we're hoping that it will be different," the Commander said.

"Well, let's get back to work, we have several months to stay ahead of our pursuant."

Everyone was encouraged to stay fit, to read, to stay positive. Games were played, education was encouraged; Dr. Planck who had joined them on this journey would study the universe and document his findings. Commander Neal would regularly meet with his crew, they had ideas and suggestions, he listened, even Private Sussman seemed in favor of leaving Earth and made suggestions.

Ten months into the journey one of the engines had malfunctioned. Jason's repairs which had been documented were studied.

"Sabotage," came the reply from Chief Engineer Ovilla, "we have a saboteur aboard."

"How long?" the Commander asked.

"If I can repair it, five days maybe . . ."

"We don't have two days, do your best, Breedlove is closing in."

"Yes Sir."

Several of the crew began to look for anything suspicious. Each one offered to have the truth monitor prove their innocence, the Commander didn't want this, he trusted them.

Two days passed, Engineer Ovilla and his men fixed the main engine. It wasn't as efficient as before but it could still outrun the other Battalion which had moved closer in those two days of repairs.

Another month passed, as they got closer to where Bright Star had been, so did the smaller cruisers which accompanied Battalion III, they fired on the Commander's ship, the shields were taking damage, Battalion III was closing in. Suddenly there was shouting in the navigation room, Commander Neal turned as a gun was fired in his direction, the bullet was deflected and hit Sergeant Blondell, another shot killed his Second. He stood up and saw a stranger struggling with Sergeant Ralph who killed him. They attended to Sergeant Blondell and pronounced his Second, Lieutenant Wells dead.

"Who is this?" The Commander demanded as he looked at the unknown assailant lying dead on the floor.

"He apparently came aboard in one of the crates and as everything failed to stop us, decided to stop you . . . that bullet was a kill shot, yet it was deflected, reminds me of another incident," Sergeant Ralph told him.

The Commander knew there was someone unseen helping them aboard ship, Blondell was taken to sickbay, her wound was serious.

Just then he gave the order to fire on one of the cruisers, then the Battalion III came straight for them then stopped, Commander Neal maneuvered his ship to face the enemy.

"Our weapons are off-line," the weapons engineer said.

"If we're going down, we'll ram their ship," the Commander told the crew.

"Jason, if you know we're here . . ." he didn't finish the statement as the ship was jolted from enemy fire. "All ahead one third, attempt to ram them."

Breedlove's ship was moving into position to disable their ship. Suddenly Commander Neal's ship was taken, the warship and all aboard into a different realm of space above Bright Star. The other ship simply saw them disappear and had lost their signature signal and had no way to pursue. They would keep up the search without ever finding them. Commander Breedlove didn't want to kill the young Commander and his crew.

Commander Neal, his crew and the two Narins that had been aboard beamed down to the surface. Jason, VE'AR, Colonel Sobel and his security forces surrounded them.

"Colonel Sobel, we are surrendering this ship and ourselves. Sergeant Blondell is in sickbay and is receiving medical attention for a bullet wound . . . my Second was killed by a saboteur." Commander Neal didn't know how they would be received especially by Jason who then came forward and shook his hand.

"It took you long enough to land on our doorstep," Jason said.

"This was the only way we could outrun them, in the ship you modified over a year ago."

The Colonel came forward and shook hands, "We need to debrief you and your crew, welcome."

VE'AR didn't shake hands but nodded indicating approval. "You will be secure here, our ways are different."

"We understand, we have no ties now with Earth and are considered criminals there worthy of the death penalty." He looked at Jason when he said this. He then thanked the two Narins who had been aboard and saved his life.

Jason knew what Commander Neal had risked in coming there. They would talk in the days to come. Sergeant Blondell was improving. The death of his Second had a profound effect on Commander Neal as being the one who caused his death. He would be buried with honors on Bright Star.

Myra and the children stood by as several, some with skepticism, greeted the new arrivals. She was still upset over Jason's incarceration and nearly losing him to an execution.

The ship would prove to be a valuable tool for the inhabitants. Commander Neal saw the Narin ships above Bright Star. The Galaxy was the only ship to remain permanently on the surface and wasn't considered a warship even though it had a large arsenal of laser cannons and other weapons to defend herself. Ship bays and landing pads were in the process of being expanded to accommodate more human and Narin ships while others would remain above the planet in orbit.

The new arrivals, twenty-three were given temporary quarters aboard the Galaxy. Several days passed as everyone was allowed to visit different areas and become familiar with Bright Star. Jason and Chief Engineer Henry were the first to be given complete access to the Battalion ship to further study the engines and Jason's improvements led by the Battalion Chief Engineer Ovilla.

Commander Neal told Jason and VE'AR how remarkable, "The timing was of being taken in before Commander Breedlove destroyed our ship or us ramming his ship when our weapons failed was unbelievable. Neither one of us wanted to kill the other; a saboteur really did a number on us."

Colonel Sobel conversed with Commander Neal about the events. "Everyone will settle in and find their calling. Since you are military and a judge familiar with military law, flying large warships, your knowledge puts you in a special category."

Commander Breedlove wasn't going away anytime soon as he continued to search other areas of space in an attempt to find Commander Neal and his crew.

CHAPTER VI

GALAXY—BREEDLOVE, THE SEARCH

Jason and Commander Neal, who wanted to be called Colonel Neal or Steven, now flew missions to find habitable planets or moons as outposts and search for a crystal fuel or a facsimile on each planet they were assigned to report on, giving chemical composition. The crystals would produce a chemical that would power star ships and the power grids on Bright Star, Sanctus and Earth. Landings were frequent as samples were gathered for further analysis.

On one such trip they landed on a planet's surface, they saw ancient structures, a city but deserted now. The area where they landed their cruiser gave way suddenly not allowing a takeoff. Both were injured, Colonel Neal's arm and three ribs were broken, Jason's leg was fractured. He transmitted a distress signal from the smaller craft. Both men were able to crawl out. There were trees, Jason built a fire, the temperature was falling rapidly.

"Hope they'll find us in time," Jason remarked.

"They will," Steven said trying to sound reassuring. "How's the leg?"

"Still there and you?"

"Not too bad." Steven was in a great deal of pain but had been conditioned by the military to ignore it to a degree, Jason was aware of this.

They had retrieved some insulating cloth as protection against the cold as well as rations, there were no medications. Steven admired Jason's bravery and how he matured emotionally to handle most situations which were very challenging.

"I had considered going military," Jason told him, he respected and looked up to Steven.

"Why? You're already helping in military matters as a civilian, with your background you're providing for military and civilian needs—don't create problems for yourself and Myra."

"Are you and Sergeant Blondell going to make it permanent?"

"Perhaps . . ." Just then Steven passed out, pain and exhaustion along with the cold had taken its toll.

Colonel Sobel had repeatedly tried to reach them, interference from some unknown source was blocking their distress signal, he sent a cruiser to find them.

Two days later a ship appeared overhead, it wasn't a welcome sight.

"It's Breedlove," Colonel Neal said, "we're in deep . . ."

He beamed down with five of his soldiers and a medic. "Well, who have we here? Two wanted felons, Commander Steven Neal and the infamous Jason Kindle Engineer."

"How did you find us?" Colonel Neal asked.

"Your distress signal led us right to you, we've been out here for months."

"And now?"

"Take Mr. Kindle to sickbay." He assured Steven that no harm would come to Jason.

"Whatever you do, don't let them give him an extensive physical."

Commander Breedlove listened. "Now what to do with two felons one of which I mentored like a son who is injured."

"Execute us here, not the humiliation of taking us back to Earth."

"Let me think about this while you're in sickbay."

"Clever, putting that spy aboard my ship, he tried to assassinate me wounding my sergeant and killing my Second."

"I know of no spy that was put aboard your ship. We did receive communication from someone on your ship who was apparently, we thought a disgruntled passenger or crew member." This revelation about a spy was disturbing to Commander Breedlove especially when he was contacted to bring Commander Neal and his crew back to Earth. He then contacted Colonel Sobel.

"I want something Colonel and I'll return both the Commander and Jason, both are injured, they are being tended to after the ground gave way beneath their ship which we will also return to you."

Colonel Sobel had a meeting with the top officials on Bright Star. "He wants to come here, he's carrying the toxin, made a proposal to return both Jason and Colonel Neal in exchange for their help and ours in mining exploration for the much needed crystals."

"We can alter space again," VE'AR said, "but they have Jason and the Colonel to bargain with and the toxin."

"Why mining?" Colonel Sobel's Second, Lieutenant Benoit asked, "Earth has a number of mines extending even outside the solar system."

It was decided that Commander Breedlove would be allowed to visit Bright Star on a beam down while his ship stayed in a stationary orbit outside the grid guarded by Narins and humans in patrol cruisers.

"I understand your concerns about the toxin," he said upon arrival. "Am I addressing Colonel Sobel? I'm Commander Breedlove."

"Ordinarily, I'd say welcome and yes I am Colonel Sobel."

"We are returning Jason Kindle and Commander Neal, their injuries have been addressed . . . the smaller cruiser will also be returned. We need this particular crystal for fuel, Earth is depleting hers, the skills of your people could prove useful to us. We have been scouring the universe for these crystals and you have found a source, the planet of an ancient civilization where we found your people. We want to work side-by-side with you to mine those crystals."

"These aren't the exact crystals Commander, close enough though, probably enough to fill our needs on Bright Star and several years for Earth." He didn't mention Sanctus as a precaution.

The meeting lasted two hours as the Commander and his entourage met with Colonel Sobel and his officers including Jason and Colonel Neal, the Narin hierarchy headed by VE'AR and his officials and scientists. Assignments were made, deals were forged out which would rely heavily on those who would be mining and drilling deep into the planet's surface.

Colonel Neal learned more about Colonel Sobel and his presence during the Earth-Mars Wars which had earned him enormous respect. He tried to live up to the assignments given him by the Colonel especially being paired up with Jason, but doubts came easily especially after seeing Commander Breedlove and realizing he had disappointed him deserting the Earth Military Force.

"I'm starting to believe I can't fit in here, all I've ever known is war," he told Jason.

"But haven't you wanted something better than what you left behind . . . maybe for yourself and Sergeant Blondell?" Jason asked.

"A dream."

"That can be a reality to be a part of this, the ultimate challenge."

The teams began working together. One of the replicator systems aboard the Galaxy was replaced with one of the more powerful units from the Battalion II. Drilling equipment was replicated as well as engine and cruiser parts aboard the Battalion II, III and now the Galaxy. The Narins participated in the replication of parts and mining activities with the others from the Battalion ships and the Galaxy. Jason, as an engineer and pilot joined with Chief Engineer Henry and the engineers from the other ships to maintain the efficiency of these ships involved in the mining efforts. Colonel Neal and Jason also teamed up to find other sources of the crystal on the planet.

Something seemed to be causing the planet to reactivate itself as the miners drilled and the crystals were taken aboard the larger ships. The drilling commenced hundreds of feet away from the ancient ruins out of respect for a civilization long extinct. The deepest point of drilling on the large planet was one-hundred miles.

Many of the women who weren't part of the military participated in the mining efforts with those who were involved. Myra flew one of the smaller cruisers against Jason's advice.

"Too dangerous," he said.

She had earlier voiced her concerns over his participation. Jason's parents and Allison took care of the children. VE'AR was also aboard one of the Narin ships to assist. Marco, Jason's brother-in-law and good friend as well as Lieutenant Vann, communications officer under Colonel Neal, worked on the participating ship's communications as needed.

Three months passed, there were now thousands of tons of the crystal that had been mined. In that time, sounds began emanating from the planet which also orbited the white sun of Bright Star and Sanctus with a thirty hour rotation period, the size of Earth having a breathable atmosphere for both human and Narin visitors; this was as much a mystery as the ancient ruins. The planet was named KA'OW by the Narins which meant 'The Ancients'. The sounds, which were continuous, were more of a low frequency humming sound, not harming anyone as yet. The ruins continued to rebuild themselves as the mining continued. The Narins didn't detect any intelligent thought from the planet. Scientists had been flown there to investigate and document the events.

Colonel Neal and Commander Breedlove had patched some differences since meeting again after he and Jason were rescued on KA'OW.

CHAPTER VII

GALAXY—THE EXECUTIONS

It was time for the Battalion III to take the now million tons of the crystal and return to Earth. Someone that looked familiar from Admiral Breedlove's ship pretending to be his Third in Command appeared at a meeting of the leadership on Bright Star; Jason and Colonel Neal were there. That someone stood up at the meeting wearing a different uniform, that of a judge, different from a starship commander's who also had judicial powers as Colonel Neal and Colonel Sobel.

"My name is Jonathan Iglesis, my title is Judge and I will pronounce judgment now. Commander Steven Neal and Jason Kindle, engineer, you both are guilty of murder and willful destruction of military property including a warship and two cruisers; the penalty is death for both."

Jason and Colonel Neal were in a state of disbelief and shock. There were protests from those attending the meeting.

Colonel Sobel had his men in the courtroom to keep order. "The first problem Judge Iglesis is that you haven't given one a trial and you have no authority here as I am the Commander under military law and the judge who determines guilt."

"I do have the authority. Jason Kindle's execution was stopped prematurely, we have adequate proof of charges against Commander Neal by Earth law. This gives me the authority even over yourself." He handed two execution orders to Colonel Sobel. "They will now be taken into custody and executed aboard the Battalion III tomorrow."

The Colonel, Admiral Breedlove, VE'AR and Judge Iglesis then talked privately with Jason and Colonel Neal. No one was allowed contact with them.

The next day they were prepared, wore appropriate uniforms. The large room was filled, Myra sat by VE'AR, Jason's parents, Allison and Marco. Jason was prepared first, the charges were read then the guns fired, he was pronounced dead, Myra wept, VE'AR held her, Jason's family was in turmoil, the grieving began, then Colonel Neal was prepared, the charges were read then the guns fired, he was pronounced dead, his crew grieved for him especially Sergeants Blondell and Ralph. Admiral Breedlove showed little emotion.

"These executions have ended, the penalties are paid," the Judge said.

The bodies of Jason and Colonel Neal were moved to the morgue aboard the Battalion III. No life signs were registering. DNA samples were taken to prove the identities of the bodies and of death. Certificates were signed by the Judge, Admiral Breedlove, Colonel Sobel, and VE'AR. These were the witnesses and the doctor aboard who took the DNA samples and pronounced both dead.

Afterward, Colonel Sobel and VE'AR were there to send the visitors back to Earth even shaking hands.

When Myra and VE'AR went to the morgue on the Galaxy where the bodies had been moved, she shrieked when she saw both men sitting in chairs being pumped with fluids.

"What is this? You're alive," she ran to Jason holding him, crying. She then saw Colonel Neal, "Both of you executed, still alive?"

"Yesterday, Admiral Breedlove told us his plan of an execution to satisfy the penalties for Steven and myself, five were in on it, we weren't allowed to tell anyone," Jason told her.

"The penalty for both of us was death and it has been paid," Steven said, "even if we travel to Earth which is unlikely . . . it might raise questions." Sergeant Blondell was now standing by Steven with her arm around his shoulder.

"VE'AR did you know?" Myra asked.

"Yes," Colonel Sobel replied. "Only five of us knew, no one else outside the circle; it depended on what the guns of the executioners were loaded with and to make everyone believe it was real."

"The Admiral might return," Steven said.

"Hoping he does?" Colonel Sobel asked.

"We'll see," he replied with a smile. "He said his goodbyes this morning."

Myra understood the deception realizing Jason wasn't allowed to see her. VE'AR had kept her from reading his thoughts or Jason's the day of the execution; she forgave this in favor of freeing her husband once and for all. As for everyone who witnessed the executions the truth was that somehow they lived and didn't question how or why.

CHAPTER VIII

GALAXY—THE PLANET REACTIVATED

The mining was about to cease as enough of the crystals were mined to power the ships on Bright Star for years as well as a power source for the planet. The changes continued on KA'OW, still no signs of a life force, yet the ancient ruins continued to repair themselves. Several scientists Narin and human were brought to the planet to study it. Three ships were in orbit keeping watch over the scientists. One ship did a deep probe scan, suddenly there was a different sound emanating from the planet, a human scientist was suddenly engulfed by something unseen, he couldn't breathe, fell and died. Others saw nothing but a large crystal that laid beside him.

"These crystals were taken to Earth," a scientist named AR'TYN said who had met and married a Battalion officer.

"They left one month ago," Colonel Sobel told him.

"These crystals are alive and if they reach Earth . . ."

"You're the only one who believes these are alive, what do you base your analysis on?" the Colonel asked him.

"A gut feeling as you humans say, we could have been destroying the inhabitants here without even knowing it."

"One has died, how do we communicate?"

"They made the first move, the death of one of yours, I suppose we do nothing more here in the way of mining their world." As AR'TYN walked away, he saw something facing him, he stopped suddenly.

"What is it?"

"I don't know Colonel . . . it was a form standing in front of me, dark, like it was covered by a cloud then reaching out with an arm covered in crystals."

"Did you sense a living presence?"

"Some type of living matter, not life as we know it." He picked up the crystal next to the dead scientist and left in the Narin ship for Bright Star three days away.

Later, during a meeting, "We have to reach Commander Breedlove's ship," Colonel Sobel said, "we sent a transmission yesterday."

"It might be possible to reach them but would we be in time?" Colonel Neal asked.

"Henry?"

"Sir, Jason and I could revamp the engines on two cruisers but catching up with the Battalion with a month head start, I don't know."

"Then get on it, solicit all the help you need. Colonel Neal, this mission is under your command."

This surprised him. "Yes Sir," he replied.

That evening AR'TYN saw the form again in his bedroom. Wanda was still sleeping as it began communicating with him in his thoughts, he was trying to not act frightened as he saw it more clearly now. It stood there several minutes looking like it was covered in crystals. It came toward him, he was standing by the bed. As the Crystal form reached out and touched him his thoughts became one with the creature—he conveyed his concern that his wife not be harmed. His form began to change from human to Narin as he lost control.

The next morning Wanda found him sitting on the bed next to her, his eyes were open, he looked calm, looked human. She quickly called the Colonel who called a medical staff, they arrived soon after. VE'AR was there.

Wanda was frantic when he wasn't breathing. "I found him like this, I heard no sounds and found this crystal beside him when I awakened earlier."

VE'AR tried to communicate with him telepathically, "He seems to be in a trance, he is alive, not breathing but being sustained somehow."

"Can you reach him?" the Colonel asked.

"Not yet."

The doctor examined him.

Then, "Let me try something," Wanda said. She whispered in his ear these words, "I want you, now."

For a few moments nothing happened then, "Yes," he said then looking at Wanda. She hugged him, he seemed disoriented.

"What did you say?" the Colonel asked.

VE'AR knew, but didn't say, nor would Wanda.

They questioned him, he saw that she was safe then as she sat by him he revealed that the creatures were these crystals.

"One communicated with me and made me realize that we have taken some of them and their children . . . the Crystal Entity knows we did this out of ignorance and we must make it right. Stop Commander Breedlove before he reaches Earth or Earth will be taken over by the Children . . . I will be accompanying you on the ship you send as will the Entity."

"AR'TYN, don't go," Wanda pleaded.

"I don't want to leave here or leave you, but lives are at stake, we must hurry."

Preparations were quickly made. Colonel Neal and Jason would each pilot a large cruiser. Marco and Lieutenant Vann came aboard as communications experts, VE'AR and AR'TYN, three other Narin scientists and five human crew and scientists joined the others. Sergeants Ralph and Blondell were also part of the crew. The Crystal Entity was then brought aboard Colonel Neal's ship. Those other Crystals taken to Bright Star would be quickly returned to KA'OW by the miners and crews aboard smaller ships to avoid a disaster.

Commander Breedlove hadn't received the transmission from those ships in pursuit, the Crystals had blocked the signal, but the ships were gaining on the Battalion after three months. Odd things began happening aboard the ship, both VE'AR and AR'TYN felt it even light years away.

There was a meeting held on one of the cruisers still traveling warp 7 to find Battalion.

"If you can AR'TYN, communicate with the Crystal to stop any action against us or Commander Breedlove and his crew," Colonel Neal said.

"VE'AR could you plant a thought to confuse the crew as to where they are, routing them back to us?" Jason suggested.

"Perhaps."

Just then the Crystal Entity began to grow and stood upright.

"Whatever you do don't fire on it," Colonel Neal told them. Sergeant Ralph reholstered his weapon and moved away from the Entity which now stood facing AR'TYN. It touched him as it communicated, then it suddenly turned, looked around then back at AR'TYN. They continued to communicate telepathically for a few moments then the Entity returned to its small crystal form. AR'TYN was drained.

"It wanted to know how long before we found the children aboard the other ship, I said I didn't know, we were doing our best but there was some disruption aboard the other ship that we suspect was coming from the Children. It didn't communicate about the disruption."

Breedlove's ship was now at an all stop, there were energy discharges all over the ship, the engines had shut down, there was activity in the storage area where the Crystals were stored. The two cruisers in pursuit continued to transmit a warning. Commander Breedlove recorded a message in the ships log. ["Battalion III at a dead stop—activity in storage facility where fuel Crystals are stored, attempting to send a distress signal to Bright Star, not expected to reach Earth for five months."].

VE'AR and AR'TYN both attempted to communicate with the Battalion. VE'AR was successful as he telepathically reached Breedlove. ["The Crystals are living entities that are the Children, do no harm to them, we are coming, quickly approaching your location, do not travel to Earth with the Crystals, should you do so, Earth is doomed. Remain where you are, engines off-line . . . I am VE'AR."]. He heeded the message. The storage facility was now surrounded by a force field while they waited. A probe had been sent to Earth relaying the distress call and warning Earth to destroy the Battalion before they entered the Earth's atmosphere with the Crystals on board which would mean they had taken over the ship, no one alive to communicate. Breedlove advised his crew of a transmission to wait for the rescue, he didn't mention how the message had been sent, by telepathy.

"We didn't receive a transmission Sir," his communications officer told him.

"In any case we stay here, we wait."

"Yes Sir."

The air supply was now in jeopardy even as the two cruisers were approaching. Breedlove then made another entry into his personal log. ["To Commander Neal: I admire your courage though I would have preferred that you stay aboard your warship and continue your career. I am proud of you, if I don't see you again, be happy, you have new challenges ahead, goodbye and good luck—Breedlove."]

A week later they caught up to the Battalion, no one responded to their transmission then ten beamed aboard, humans and Narins, AR'TYN was one of them carrying the Crystal. There were energy fluctuations and they discovered that the controls to the ship were covered in crystals. They found the storage area, there was movement as some of the Crystals began to mature. The crew was found, Commander Breedlove and his entire crew had barely survived.

"Is Steven, Commander Neal with you?"

"I am," he said as he had come on board. "Did you think we weren't coming?"

Breedlove laughed, "We're in a bit of a mess, just got your transmission yesterday. VE'AR had sent me a message telepathically a week ago, we complied. The force field around the storage facility had weakened but allowed us to escape to another storage area, in other words 'havoc' has dictated this mission."

AR'TYN put the Crystal in their midst, it then grew and communicated with him; "The instructions are very specific, the Entity will call the others, all of them back to the storage, control of the ship will be given back to Commander Breedlove and his crew. I am to stay with the Entity in storage until we return them to KA'OW, the same name you have given the planet. We leave now. No one wanted AR'TYN to stay with the Entity and the Crystal Children.

"Will you be harmed?" VE'AR asked.

"I don't know."

"Could one of us stay with you?" Jason then asked.

AR'TYN asked the Entity, "Yes."

"Then I'm coming with you."

"No Jason, I'll go," Colonel Neal said. "VE'AR, will you pilot my cruiser?"

"I should be with AR'TYN but I will pilot the ship."

Commander Breedlove understood the danger they were facing, that they were all facing. He talked with Steven, "We might just make it Steven, if we do, there is much to discuss."

"We'll make it Sir." They shook hands.

Steven left with AR'TYN who carried the Crystal, they entered the storage facility; just then the Crystal grew and stood between the two men and the other Crystals. It told them to sleep until they were awakened. Steven was then probed by the Entity, AR'TYN read his thoughts and that of the creature. Within minutes it released him, he sat on the floor drained of energy.

He spoke to AR'TYN, "I felt no intent to harm or kill us, it wanted to learn about us."

"It knows about both our species, our weaknesses as well as our strengths. We have no defense against them."

"I thought the Narins would . . . changing into fire, bending space."

AR'TYN laughed, "Perhaps in time."

"How did you and Lieutenant Sykes hook up, since we have time to talk? It's probably too private to talk about."

"No, I don't mind. I met her at the Blaze. I liked the strange music and people watching. As a scientist I needed to explore, to find a wife outside my species."

"The toxin?"

"Yes, many of us cannot pro-create with each other, our race is doomed to extinction if we don't consider other options. The Lieutenant was there, walked over to my table and said, 'I wouldn't be safe at the Blaze'. As time went on we fell in love as you humans say . . . we have a small farm and two kids. What about you?"

"I have someone, my Sergeant, Shirley Blondell, she insisted on coming, I plan to marry her, make things right with my mentor, a father to me, Commander Breedlove. I gave up a promising career as a warship Commander and a judge to his disappointment."

"Those two things might still serve you well; I hear you are able to pilot several different ships and cruisers . . . he must still be proud of you."

"Seems to come naturally to me, piloting ships."

"Do you still dislike us, our species?"

"I never disliked the Narins, I didn't trust you because I didn't know anything about you except what I was told. Jason helped change that and now I hope we can work together for the greater good."

"I am a scientist, considered young at one-hundred of your years. Some of us live considerably longer; we are trying to extend the lives of our human partners, that is one project I am devoting time to . . . this is one of those greater good things."

Steven smiled, "Hope you succeed for all our sakes."

Back on Bright Star, the smaller cruisers and mining ships were quickly returning the Crystals to KA'OW. Both Lieutenant Sykes and Myra were determined as ever to assist in this effort to protect their planet, still piloting cruisers as the transfer of the Crystals continued. They missed their husbands, fearful of the outcome when they found Breedlove.

Several Narins had travelled light years to stop a probe filled with toxin from reaching their home world NARIN'MAR. Commander Scott of Battalion I had sent the probe nearly two years earlier to virtually extinguish any hope the Narins had of reproducing with one another. His lieutenant had earlier confirmed this as fact and the documentation in his ship's log and Jason's testimony. VE'AR had contacted NARIN'MAR. It was confined that the probe had been neutralized in some manner and was no longer a threat, however that was a year earlier, no one could reach the brave Narins on that mission and search and rescue hadn't found them. They had crash landed on a small planet but interference kept their distress signal from being picked up and interfered with their telepathic abilities or others attempting to contact them in that manner.

Two years earlier when the Narin ship pursued the probe which had a two month head start to reach its target, the Narins were distraught over how, "Our home world will be adversely affected from this; if the toxin is even released in space without a direct hit it could be more lethal, we can't simply destroy the probe with the fail-safes in place . . . we must be creative in its destruction."

"Agreed," another said.

"We can't run this ship any faster," a Narin engineer told them.

"Then we must try another approach, to reconfigure space as we did to protect Bright Star from those who would destroy it, but we must get closer to the probe."

Ten months passed, as they got closer to the probe they began to reconfigure space to throw off the probe's trajectory and confuse it into taking a different route. Four of the Narins had sat joining mind to mind to confound the probe. Hours later the probe was headed in their direction, it was gaining on them. They had considered a super nova to destroy the probe and its contents, then a small sun was considered. The ship then passed in front of a black hole a billion miles across and was active, the engines strained against the intense gravitational pull as the probe was given orders by the Narins who convinced it to now move toward the black hole and with a tractor beam sent it into the event horizon, they were able to pull away in time but not before damage was sustained by their ship. A garbled message was received by NARIN'MAR ["The threat is over . . ."], then the crippled ship crashed several light years away on a habitable small planet where they were now stranded for over a year.

On the Battalion, the crew and scientists were dealing with their problems. AR'TYN temporarily lost his ability to look human as the entity probed him again. Steven saw this. The Narins were beautifully shaped beings, somewhat like humans, their faces paled into a soft blue white as they were about to lose control or were saddened. Anger usually caused a reddish glow and then sometimes appeared as fire; they tried to mask these mood indicators and look human.

"AR'TYN?" Steven was concerned.

"It was more draining this time," he said.

"Are they feeding off our energy?"

"This one is, while trying not to harm us, they seem to need an energy source." Steven then used his communicator talking to VE'AR and Commander Breedlove simultaneously.

"The Entity has put the others into what appears to be a sleep state. AR'TYN has suggested that the creature is feeding off our energy and when the others awaken, they'll be eager to be fed. Can you figure out a way to feed them with an alternate energy source?"

"We'll work on it Steven," Commander Breedlove told him.

"I don't know how much more AR'TYN can take as it continues to feed off him more than off me."

"We will come up with a solution," VE'AR said.

In the coming days AR'TYN and Steven were fed an energizing diet, then exercising, watching the research on a televised unit, every reading was monitored. AR'TYN as a scientist and Steven who was familiar with energy problems aboard long duration flights were now involved in the research. It was suggested that they should be put in stasis in that storage area only after a source of energy was available for the creatures. As each exercised, ate and then rested, their electromagnetic energy was measured. One radio astronomer on board was observing the electromagnetic radiation from an exploding star which had corresponded to that of KA'OW, the Crystals' home planet. A sample was brought aboard the ship, tested then placed in the storage area where the Crystals were and would attract them as well as three larger ones and the main Crystal to the electromagnetic waves produced to feed on. Then as the Battalion with two escort cruisers headed for Bright Star, AR'TYN and Steven were placed in stasis chambers; AR'TYN had earlier conveyed the reasoning behind this and assured the Crystal that an energy source was now available that wouldn't become lethal to Narin or human. Then they slept, their electromagnetic readings were now very low. Everyone breathed a sigh of relief. The young Crystals were nourished as they awakened every fifty human hours; three older ones and the main Crystal had a longer duration then slept. The storage unit was still surrounded by a force field and carefully monitored. A month passed.

Breedlove had met everyone involved in his rescue, learning about two different species, the Narins and the Crystals. Jason talked with him about Steven and how they became friends now working together on Bright Star.

"He gave up a promising career . . . he didn't seem happy, it was more of a duty to perform . . . if he's happy now, then I am glad. He should marry." Breedlove realized the pressures of the job had caused Steven to drink.

"He's embracing new challenges and I believe he will marry," Jason said, "you gave us both a second chance."

Just then Judge Iglesis walked in, "Someone mention a second chance?"

"Good to see you again Judge."

"Didn't I see to your executions?" He laughed, but Jason couldn't.

"Maybe we don't need to go there," Breedlove said to his friend.

VE'AR entered the room with an attendant.

"I'll check on Steven and AR'TYN," Jason told them, as he passed by VE'AR he nodded in respect.

They had an exchange of ideas one of which was finding a substitute for the Crystals, since they couldn't be used for fuel. The Battalion had been scanning for a substitute, there were some possibilities which were noted.

The main Crystal awakened and began to communicate with AR'TYN. It did even as he was in stasis, it didn't attempt to feed off him or Steven. Then it simply remained standing for several days. The scientists aboard decided to awaken AR'TYN. When he came to himself and saw the Crystal motionless but standing, he realized that there had been an attempt to communicate. "The Crystal has told us where we can find the Narin survivors, bring me a star chart. All survived the initial crash, we don't know if any are living now; also, there are three sources of crystal fuel." A chart was given to AR'TYN inside the storage and two scientists assisted to find both the Narins and fuel sources. Jason was also involved since Myra had downloaded the Galaxy's database star navigation charts into his mind years earlier.

A meeting was held, AR'TYN used a communicator to participate as he would not leave the storage facility as promised to the Crystal which hadn't moved.

"Admiral Breedlove?"

"I suggest having one of the cruisers rescue the Narin survivors and the other escort cruiser to investigate at least one source of the crystal fuel. Take precautions and anyone necessary to complete the missions. We on the Battalion have the urgency of returning the crystals to KA'OW as soon as possible. Good luck everyone."

The plans were finalized. AR'TYN was placed in stasis again, the Crystal then returned to a sleep mode.

Three months passed, then a transmission.

"Commander Breedlove, we have found the survivors, alive and well . . . on our way to you, Cruiser I out."

There were shouts of joy from both the Narins and humans aboard. They would make a two month journey before reaching Battalion. There was concern for the other cruiser, piloted by Jason.

Two months passed then a transmission from Cruiser II.

"Commander Breedlove, we have found three confirmed sources of the crystal fuel, what the Entity told AR'TYN was fact. The deposits are so plentiful that the fuel needs will be met for years on Earth, Bright Star and Sanctus. Scientists aboard took samples, we are on our way to join you in about a month . . . did the Narins survive?"

"Yes, they did," VE'AR answered.

"Great news."

"Now get yourselves back here," the Commander said humorously.

"Will do, Jason Kindle out."

They reached Battalion in about forty-five Earth days. The samples were tested again. Steven and AR'TYN were still in stasis. Everyone who participated in the rescue mission and in the scientific mission for fuel was congratulated. Jason knew several of the Narin scientists and doctors from a previous encounter when a stroke left him a cripple.

Bright Star was now free of any crystals, all were taken back to KA'OW. The residents had now heard from the Battalion and the Narins who stopped the probe not expected to arrive home for four more months. VE'AR also reached out telepathically praising those involved.

Lieutenant Sykes and Myra became friends and both had shared anxieties about their husbands and the dangers they faced but their efforts helped keep Bright Star from being overrun by the Crystal Entities.

CHAPTER IX

GALAXY—MEMORY REVISITED

Months later, three Narins who had been banished to a moon for violent crimes escaped and travelled to a small planetoid to free a fourth, their leader. They travelled to NARIN'MAR in disguise to find VE'AR and continued their search for him and Myra. They learned of humans through records sent back by VE'AR and where he and Myra were. They didn't regard humans as a threat. Before they reached Bright Star, VE'AR was aware of their escape and impending arrival. He didn't care for this Narin male, AR'BIN; he was troubled that he was coming. He and VE'AR were always on opposing sides and AR'BIN had a single minded purpose to destroy VE'AR in some manner and would take Myra for himself. VE'AR would never have approved their union. He made Colonel Sobel and Jason aware.

Upon their arrival, VE'AR, the Colonel and a security detail were there to meet them. VE'AR then met with AR'BIN.

"You are married?" he asked Myra who also agreed to meet with him.

"Yes, Jason will be home soon."

"Human?"

"Yes, we have two children."

VE'AR attempted to read his thoughts but AR'BIN had masked them, he was powerful but VE'AR was able to understand that his intentions weren't honorable. Myra didn't like him and realized that both VE'AR and Jason were in danger, the Colonel was warned.

"Why your visit?" VE'AR asked.

"You banished me to that planetoid years ago for an uprising that would have brought NARIN'MAR into a new age, as you see I escaped."

"Not one of peace, you sought the ways of war; death and destruction followed you always."

"I want to reclaim my birthright Leader, I want Myra at my side."

"And me and those loyal?"

"To banish you and if necessary those loyal to you. Myra has taken a human husband, he must separate himself from her or be terminated."

VE'AR became angry and began to change form but quickly composed himself. Myra heard everything. AR'BIN retained a human form for the time being. Jason arrived and met the stranger. VE'AR had telepathically told Jason more about this visitor.

"Good to meet you Sir," he said trying to mask his apprehension.

"Do you know who I am?" he asked Jason speaking in English.

"Yes I do," he said as he hugged the children, "you're AR'BIN of the Narins."

"How was school?" Myra asked him pretending to ignore AR'BIN and kissing him on the cheek.

"The classroom was packed, I took Harold's class, out sick, it went well and you?"

"The science class finals were today, we'll see how well it went."

"Perhaps I should leave now and meet with you VE'AR and Jason tomorrow."

"Sounds good," Jason said, not willing to welcome the guest to stay. AR'BIN left.

"He's one angry Narin," VE'AR said, "I might not be able to stop him."

"Your powers are strong," Myra said.

"Once we allow ourselves to go beyond a certain limit, certainly killing, certainly hate and revenge, sometimes we cannot retain that self-control that we had and end up as AR'BIN is now."

They had dinner together as they contemplated this.

"Why did you banish him VE'AR?" Jason asked.

"He was attempting to divide our people and cause an uprising, an insurgency. He is responsible for the death of your mother, Myra."

Myra was in shock. "You never told me . . . you said it was her time."

Jason was surprised at this revelation.

"He is my brother's son, he must be stopped and not harm you or Jason and the children."

"And my mother?"

"We'll discuss it at a later time."

AR'BIN was bent on revenge and wasn't interested in Bright Star or the human—Narin population. He and the three Narin conspirators who had escaped their prison planet a year earlier and rescued him began to study Bright Star gaining information about VE'AR's influence and Jason's role in the situation.

"Why not destroy this world, both Narin and human?" One asked AR'BIN.

"It would only ignite those loyal to Leader and all out war, we can do without it for now."

They met the next evening aboard AR'BIN's ship, Myra wasn't there for her protection.

"I want what is mine," AR'BIN told VE'AR, "my place as leader."

"You are no leader, you conquer, you take, no matter who is harmed."

"I can request a duel to the death and you must answer or you forfeit your right. As for you Jason, you must give Myra to me."

"I will not, she isn't property to be given or taken."

"Or be terminated if you do not."

"Where do you plan to establish your new world after you destroy NARIN'MAR?"

"I am not going to destroy our home world, I demand only loyalty."

"At any cost?" VE'AR was frustrated and angry.

Then Jason said, "I won't give her up without fighting for her."

AR'BIN looked at him as he said, "A fight you couldn't possibly win, nevertheless I will allow you this . . . Leader, what is your answer to me, a duel or . . . ?"

"I will relinquish my position as leader."

Jason's expression was one of disbelief but he said nothing.

AR'BIN had expected more from VE'AR. "You are up to something."

"I am tired, take your rightful place as leader."

"What about him?" pointing to Jason.

"We'll talk."

"No changing my mind VE'AR, I will meet you AR'BIN in a place of your choosing."

"Then it is settled. I will contact you, one Earth week and tell you where." VE'AR and Jason left.

Jason couldn't handle this, "VE'AR?"

"We have to prepare you Jason."

"Try preparing me with the truth."

"Let's go inside so our thoughts won't be known to AR'BIN. I'm not relinquishing anything and we will plan together how you'll defeat him. We must talk to your father, we need his assistance." Jason was very puzzled.

After their meeting with Jackson Kindle, Jason and VE'AR went to Myra's ship where she and the children were instead of their house.

"Myra, Myra, where are you?"

The children were in bed, but no Myra. Jason became frantic. Just then VE'AR received a message from AR'BIN.

"I have her, she will not be violated or harmed. I will contact Jason."

"Jason, he has her, he just now contacted me, he will not harm her."

Jason just sat, no emotion. VE'AR sat by him. "Everytime it seems that there might be a peaceful existence, the world comes crashing down around us."

"Jason, we will win, my powers are greater than his, he doesn't begin to know what I can do to him, but it must appear that you are facing him alone. Physically you can't defeat him, he can read your thoughts. Allow me to enter your mind and block your thoughts."

"I'm listening," an exhausted Jason said.

They talked for over an hour with VE'AR's closest confidantes and Colonel Sobel and two of his officers. A plan was made. Jason talked with his family and Steven, not telling what the exact mission was but his father knew as he was working with VE'AR and Jason.

Myra had been taken to a small moon several light years away, AR'BIN had given her something to calm her as she had resisted and filled her mind with doubts about Jason and his faithfulness to only her. He had also planted doubts in Jason's mind before leaving Bright Star concerning her as being unfaithful to him.

"Why have you taken me?" she asked.

"Others of our kind are awaiting us, you will be my mate."

"Never to see my husband, my father or my children?"

"How could you allow a human to mate you?"

"He is more of husband to me than you could ever be . . . and I mated him."

This startled AR'BIN. "He is coming here to fight for you and I will kill him . . . I will bury him here. In time you will forget him."

This talk sickened her. "And Leader?"

"He appears broken, initially showing anger and resistance, he then seemed passive, he won't be a problem. I will banish him to stay on Bright Star never to see you again or NARIN'MAR, he will be with his grandchildren. I will be merciful."

"What did you do to my mother?"

"He told you I caused her death . . . I did. My mother had died, my father wanted another son to become his heir, not me. VE'AR allowed your mother to join briefly with my father to carry his child, she was willing. This male child would have kept me from seizing power from my father and VE'AR. I gave her the choice to terminate the child before it was born or die, she wouldn't, I murdered her. My father tried to avenge her, then I murdered him. VE'AR then banished me, no longer co-ruler with his brother, my father, he became the undisputed leader of NARIN'MAR. Your mother should have listened to me and lived."

"It doesn't faze you, what you have done."

"Be very glad that VE'AR is going to live. I cannot just banish Jason, I must terminate him."

Myra's heart ached, her appearance became pale.

Aboard an orbiting Narin ship on Bright Star, VE'AR, Jason, Jackson Kindle and three scientists prepared for the conflict with AR'BIN. VE'AR's essence was transferred into Jason, then he was put into stasis until Jason's return. Jackson then gave Jason a shot of the toxin; he rested a few hours then prepared to leave. The trip would take a week in a smaller cruiser. He was advised by his father to take a shot of a newly developed anti-dote that he would be carrying aboard ship as soon as possible after his encounter with AR'BIN. The toxin was lethal to humans in heavy doses and Narins in that it caused sterility.

"If you die, VE'AR dies, his essence will be destroyed," Jackson told him. He hugged Jason who felt the toxin spreading throughout his body.

"I'll return Dad, we'll all return . . . wish me luck."

"I do son."

Jason left. From the beginning of his journey he had thoughts of past encounters and this one didn't promise a happy ending either. He had doubted his ability to complete the mission successfully. As he slept part of the time to renew his strength, VE'AR taught him and prepared him, Jason wasn't aware of this and he wanted to communicate but didn't sense VE'AR's presence.

In a week he found the moon and saw the Narin cruiser on the surface, he landed several yards away, AR'BIN was waiting for him still in human form, his three collaborators stood by their ship, Myra was inside. He and AR'BIN approached each other.

"I'm not carrying a weapon," Jason said.

"I can defeat you easily, you're a weak species."

"You're using contractions . . . nevermind; if you want to impress Myra, put away your powers and make it a fair fight and when I die Myra will know I fought for her, can you at least do that and allow me to die with some dignity?"

"I will, she will see that you died bravely, she is there in the ship."

AR'BIN began planting doubts in Jason's mind to force him to remember his worst experiences and to lose his focus.

"She doesn't love you Jason," AR'BIN now began taunting him verbally. He couldn't read Jason's mind clearly not knowing his body was laced with the toxin due to VE'AR's presence blocking Jason's thoughts. He now realized that VE'AR was helping him as he fought. AR'BIN and Jason exchanged blows, each was bleeding. Jason used a form of self-defense he learned from Steven, AR'BIN had his own self-defense technique which was very effective against any opponent.

"Are you going to call your friends to help you win against one human?"

"No need, you're wearing down." AR'BIN becomes frustrated when Jason is still fighting him.

Jason now begins taunting AR'BIN. "How could she end up with someone that murdered her mother and with no conscience?"

AR'BIN begins to turn red with the appearance of fire.

"She is watching, better not do the fire thing."

He then changes back to a human appearance and throws Jason to the ground and is now literally on top of him, choking him. He can't free himself so with all his strength he scratches deep gashes into AR'BIN's face and left hand. Suddenly AR'BIN feels something is different.

"What did you do?" He is no longer choking Jason who moves away from him and is now speaking Narin, he didn't know how he knew the language.

Then VE'AR begins to talk through Jason, this frightened AR'BIN. "What you are feeling is the toxin created by humans to conquer space, it will weaken you." Jason stood up then he took on VE'AR's features, that of a body covered in fire, VE'AR's face now staring at the enemy, he struck AR'BIN with incredible power and the other three Narins. AR'BIN defiant to the end rushed toward Jason to destroy him striking him physically with a surge of power. Jason fell, VE'AR's essence left him and attacked AR'BIN with all he had. AR'BIN now lay dying, VE'AR was going to do more and also kill the others.

"VE'AR don't, you're not like him . . . you'll be killing both of us."

VE'AR listened as Jason toned his anger so he wouldn't go beyond the limit and become like AR'BIN. VE'AR then spoke to AR'BIN. Jason didn't know what he told him. AR'BIN would be buried there and given respect. The other three Narins would be left on the moon with supplies, a rescue would be signaled, they were very afraid of VE'AR who now returned into Jason's body.

Jason had now given himself the anti-dote for the toxin which worked quickly and now he could bring Myra to his cruiser, she was in shock. He then towed the Narin ship belonging to AR'BIN back to Bright Star, a week's journey.

VE'AR praised Jason for his courage and handling of the mission and as they shared Jason's body, he felt VE'AR's words of encouragement.

"Myra hasn't slept this much, ever."

"That is the way she will heal herself."

"I've never witnessed anything like this VE'AR."

"My powers are great but I am not a warmonger, we are a peaceful race but occasionally there are the exceptions."

Jason understood and had agreed with VE'AR not to reveal all that happened on the small moon, it might cause fear and mistrust of the Narins.

By the second day Myra woke up, Jason was asleep, she kissed him, he opened his eyes, she knew he was all right, he knew she would recover.

"I remember you fought bravely."

Jason kissed her. "Your father and I fought together, his essence is in me now."

"How is this possible?"

"Just take my word for it . . . AR'BIN was surprised; he gave you a sedative so you wouldn't resist."

"Yet I was conscious as I watched the events happening. I was so despondent, the thought of life without you, not seeing VE'AR or our children ever and to be with AR'BIN caused me to shut down . . . make love to me."

"I really want to do that but not while VE'AR is in my head."

She laughed, "All right, I can wait. We are towing the ship?"

"Yes, there might be crucial information stored in the main computer. The other three Narins with AR'BIN will be rescued shortly and taken back to NARIN'MAR for trial."

A week later they reached Bright Star. Jason was taken to a Narin facility where VE'AR's body was in stasis. His essence was removed from Jason who spent the night there as he was checked periodically. VE'AR was also kept that evening. Myra was thoroughly examined, it seemed she was not harmed physically by anything that was done to her; the stress however, from seeing Jason about to be murdered had an adverse effect on her mentally.

Jackson Kindle talked privately with Colonel Sobel, VE'AR, Jason and Myra and those involved in the mission; everyone was made aware of the events and the outcome.

"The anti-dote cannot undo what was done to your people VE'AR. We're still working on it with your scientists, we will find an answer."

"I know that you and your scientists are. There are always challenges, some we must handle with help," he looked at Jason when he said this.

A few days later Allison and Marco had invited a large group of friends and family to their house, one of the newer houses to be constructed on Bright Star. It was a celebration of cultures and friendships. Marco was telling about his new business in communications that he opened with Lieutenant Vann. Allison, however, was now struggling with the reality of not being able to become pregnant. Doctors were working to remedy this. Everyone seemed to have a good time even with many who were dealing with problems of everyday life.

Myra stayed quiet for most of the evening. Bella Kindle noticed. She sat by Myra.

"You are special to all of us Myra, my son loves you more than life."

"He fought for me, putting himself at risk, about to be murdered."

"I know . . . Myra, are you feeling all right?"

"This incident was very traumatic for all of us, but being taken from Jason and my father and the children has affected me in ways that I can't describe. I believe in time things will be normal for us again."

Bella hugged her, "I want you to talk to me whenever, I admire you and am your friend as well as your mother-in-law."

"I know why Jason turned out as he did having you and Dr. Jackson as his parents."

"And you know how much we admire VE'AR."

Myra smiled.

A few hours later, the evening ended. Allison and Marco were bidding their guests goodbye.

"Tell JAS'AR and MY'AR to come visit," Allison said to Myra and Jason.

"Who?" Myra asked.

"The kids," Jason said.

Everyone just pretended they didn't hear this.

"Oh yes, the children will," Myra replied.

"Goodnight."

VE'AR heard everything, even Bella's conversation with Myra.

In the following months Myra became so distracted that teaching her classes was impossible. She spent most of her time sleeping, ignoring the children and not filling her time with anything. She and Jason weren't intimate. He talked with her as often as possible about the situation and how doctors might help. Allison was for that time a surrogate mother to the kids as they stayed with her and Marco.

"VE'AR, what has happened to Myra? Why?" They met after Jason's class.

"AR'BIN. He had planted seeds of destruction in her mind should she escape him; these thoughts are eating into the very fabric of who she is and erasing her memories of those she loves."

"He tried that with me, but you were in my mind and the thoughts had no effect."

"That is why."

"What can we do?"

"I'm taking her to NARIN'MAR with your permission and asking that you accompany us."

"I . . . yes, how soon before we leave?"

"Tomorrow. It will take several months to reach our home world. There will be two stasis chambers prepared. One of your doctors has downloaded information about human physiology and specifically yours."

"Why is this about me?"

"Grief can cause problems along the way, we can't foresee them but we have to be prepared."

Jason said his goodbyes to his parents, Marco, Allison and the children. Colonel Sobel and Steven were very concerned.

"All the luck Jason." They shook hands.

"I don't know when we'll return, VE'AR is adamant that we bring Myra to his home world."

They departed Bright Star in a medium size Narin cruiser. Jason was given a physical then dressed for stasis. At first he was reluctant then agreed. He understood Narin and could speak it, he didn't reveal this but VE'AR knew. The doctors aboard thought it would be in Jason's best interest to sleep and not be stressed over Myra's condition over the long trip as she was also put in stasis.

Months passed, Jason was awakened.

"We are in orbit over NARIN'MAR," one told him, our rotation period is thirty-six Earth hours."

Myra was removed from stasis and brought to a medical facility. Doctors worked over her. She and Jason had two small beds in a room of the facility. VE'AR and one doctor began to explain what was about to happen.

"Myra will die . . . not in the same sense as the death of a human, not a natural death from old age or a death from an unnatural cause as my mate experienced. We are not like you, in this death Myra will be purged of the damage inflicted by AR'BIN, she then will grow again from the few cells remaining back into herself, not a clone, not anything or anyone else but Myra."

Jason listened carefully, "Will she remember me, the kids, love?"

"Yes, she will . . . she cannot rebuild until she dies."

"How long?"

"It could take a year, perhaps longer."

Just then Myra opened her eyes, Jason took her hands as he knelt beside her bed, he kissed her. She closed her eyes and died. Tears welled up in his eyes, he then collapsed by her side. Two doctors began to work to save him.

Five days later he came to, lying on a bed next to hers. He was being fed fluids but managed to sit up and look at her. VE'AR had been sitting, keeping watch on both Myra and Jason.

"How is she?"

"Beginning her life over again." There was a pale glow emanating from her and the outline of a physical form beginning to take shape.

Jason was calm as he watched for several minutes. Then he looked at VE'AR, "I need a haircut and to make myself useful while I'm here."

VE'AR smiled, "I want to show you NARIN'MAR and introduce you to several acquaintants and I have a suggestion to take up your time . . . and they won't address me by any special title even as their ruler, I am only called VE'AR or Leader."

Jason was convinced that Myra was in good hands and left with VE'AR and his entourage to see NARIN'MAR by land and from space. It was three times the size of earth. The planet appeared pale red with several large silver rings circling vertically as the planet rotated horizontally orbiting around a white sun. There were three moons. There were light pink, blue clouds, mountains, valleys, the oceans were pale pink and blue. Land masses were clay red. Buildings were generally huge, tall and dome-like with elaborate geometric designs covering them. Their atmosphere was composed of nitrogen, methane, and carbon dioxide at 20 PSI. There were also arid areas on the planet where nothing grew, but generally farms dotted the landscape, forests were generally located in the mountainous areas.

For several days Jason visited factories and market places; he saw a huge docking bay filled with Narin ships and cruisers, then on to see schools and universities, ancient sights and much more. He was fascinated. Out of respect, those who knew who he was changed into human form as they saw him with VE'AR. He was exhausted as they reached the hospital where Myra was.

"You could teach subjects on engineering, you know navigation and piloting, you speak Narin . . . consider teaching about the human race," VE'AR suggested.

"I'll consider it." Jason liked the idea. "What ages?"

"Two classes every four Narin days, adults then children; a Narin day is around thirty-six Earth hours."

"When?"

"As soon as you're ready, this particular school is easily accessed on foot."

Jason decided to live at the hospital facility with Myra, the room was small but very adequate. He would talk to her not knowing if she could hear him. Her form was changing daily. VE'AR would later assist her in remembering what she knew before the incident.

Jason began classes. He wasn't in a uniform but slacks and a dress shirt. He was inwardly grateful for this diversion and a chance to meet the Narin population. He was at first asked questions about Myra and how she was. The classroom became crowded as he spoke.

"News travels fast," he said, "she is improving thanks to VE'AR and the Narin doctors. We have two children who are Narin and human, we are the first to join. We live on a planet called Bright Star thousands of light years from here across a large galaxy we call the Milky Way. Earth is where I'm from and the human race began. It lies across the same galaxy in the opposite direction . . . it was my father who created a toxin for our government to protect us in space as we travelled to our new home; it was misused and caused problems for ourselves and our Narin friends, we are attempting to reverse its effects."

"How did you join with Myra?" a student asked.

Jason laughed nervously, "That's a secret between us. I will attempt to tell you about our world, Earth and our new world Bright Star. I will throw in some English words time to time." He showed them star charts of constellations as seen from Earth and the solar system and pictures of wars which had devastated so many and polluted the atmosphere. "Mankind is basically good, at times warlike. Those of us lucky enough to have left Earth two-hundred years ago were leaving to make a new start. Our life spans are considerably shorter than our Narin counterparts, but in stasis we don't age. Myra found our ship drifting in the path of a large sun, off on our trajectory, she came aboard, awakened me from stasis and together we got our ship back on course. We fell in love and married." Jason then showed them more pictures of Earth and Bright Star, trees, animals, farms and the beloved Galaxy ship.

By the end of class he was surrounded and welcomed. The second class for children had begun. The Narin adults were looking in from outside to hear more. Two hours later he ended the session. He walked to the small room in the hospital that he shared with Myra. VE'AR congratulated him on his first day. Jason began to smile again as he told about both classes and being welcomed along with some unexpected questions. He then gave Myra his full attention asking VE'AR how she was doing. He pointed out changes in Myra's genesis state.

"Every day there are changes. And I'll tell you now, Narins are not embarrassed easily, even children will ask you anything especially since you're a hero to them and the only human they have ever seen . . . are you up to joining me for dinner?" He knew Jason was tired.

"Will she have someone here?"

"Yes, always."

"Then I'm going."

The streets were made of smooth pearl white stones. As they rode in a small hover craft, the most popular mode of travel besides walking, they visited several areas filled with stores, restaurants and office buildings. One restaurant was very popular. It served a variety of things and had a replicator that made anything. Jason described pizza in detail even to the molecular level which it replicated. VE'AR was amused.

Jason tried the pizza, "Not bad." He was encouraged to try Narin variety foods. "Different, good," were his remarks.

"As a son of botanists I imagine you have tried many different fruits and vegetables," a Narin told him.

"Yes, but these seem more potent, a rich taste."

There were those Narins who followed them, curious to see their Leader again and the only human they had ever seen. When they had finished dinner Jason shook hands and asked VE'AR for more sightseeing. They saw a large Narin temple, this was the largest one, filled with ancient scrolls and symbols of worship. Then on to the building housing the seat of government thousands of years old. Then they departed for the hospital facility where Jason and Myra lived. He praised VE'AR for the tour of this beautiful world.

A Narin woman was now assigned to cut his hair and help with any other needs as organizing his research papers as he taught school, she would even see to his meals as needed, he tried to pay her but she refused, she considered it to be a gift of friendship to help him.

Six months had passed.

It began to rain as Jason watched Myra that morning. He leaned over and kissed her. "I'll return in about four hours," he told the attendant. He enjoyed teaching.

That day after class he ate a sandwich as he sat quietly on a bench in a park reflecting on the recent events. Suddenly he looked up and saw a light created by the sun's rays reflecting off the rings surrounding NARIN'MAR, it was incredibly beautiful. He sat for several minutes then heard someone.

"Mr. Kindle?"

Jason looked to see a Narin male. "Yes, I'm Jason, sit please."

"I am an instructor at the Mar University here . . . our town here is PAL'EO. I am curious, do you appreciate learning about ancient civilizations?"

"Tell me your name."

"My name is SA'MAR."

"Good to meet you and yes I do appreciate learning about the ancients."

"Then accept this, it is one of the oldest of our books." SA'MAR then gave Jason a disc. "It contains many things, music is one of them, star charts are also visible in holographic form, it can be played on a special unit, VE'AR can request one for you."

"Why are you doing this?"

"Because you appreciate us, you have come a long way." SA'MAR hesitated for a moment then, "Visit me tomorrow at our university when you have time, there is something important I must tell you."

Jason saw apprehension and concern in his face, he also out of respect took on a human facade when he was with Jason. He left,

Jason then left for home. A nurse was there with Myra. He studied the changes since morning as he sat and talked with her.

VE'AR came by, "Is this a good time?"

"Yes, come in . . . more changes," he said upbeat.

"She is going to be Myra again, be patient."

"That's all I can be. I met someone today, a professor from the Mar University contacted me as I sat in the park, SA'MAR was his name. He gave me an ancient book, literally gave it to me. I'm to meet with him tomorrow. Who is he, VE'AR?"

"SA'MAR is one of the foremost astrophysicists in our world, he wouldn't meet with anyone normally outside of his field of study. There is something important, urgent to tell you."

"What is it?"

"Talk to him first then we will discuss the matter."

"I guess I can wait."

"Did your classes go well today?"

"Yes, and I enjoyed the park afterward, it was very peaceful. When the light from the sun hit the rings, it was fantastic, beautiful."

"Could you ever be comfortable here?"

"Permanently? Not permanently, but I could spend time here off and on. I miss Earth, but even more Bright Star."

The next day after classes were over, Jason walked to the university and met with Dr. SA'MAR.

"Thank you again for your generous gift."

"This news isn't good for your world. I am an astrophysicist. Your world is attempting to harness a power source and will bring on its own destruction."

"When?"

"It's a feeling and there are signs as they begin harnessing higher forms of energy, probably two years. The Earth's sun is showing energy fluctuations as a new way of draining off that energy is being evaluated."

This news was devastating to Jason. "Who would I present this news to?"

"Only another astrophysicist connected with this project. I would have to go with you to present the facts as I have calculated should you travel to Earth, we might both die in the effort."

"The fact that you would risk your life to save my planet speaks volumes about you and the Narin population."

"Tomorrow then."

Jason returns home, VE'AR is there.

"Now that you know, what will you do?"

Jason sat, looked at Myra, touched her face then walked into another room with VE'AR.

"What would you do VE'AR? I'm asking for your counsel. The only home world I knew growing up now about to be destroyed."

"You have a life elsewhere now, a wife, children, humanity that you travelled with to Bright Star . . . I would advise you not to go there even with a willing scientist like SA'MAR. As for what I would do, anything to save my home world."

"I can't just stand by if there is a chance."

"I could make you forget."

"Yes, you could . . . I respect you and your counsel as I would my father's which is saying a lot, but even as I grew up he allowed me the freedom to make hard choices, some were devastating to me."

"The Earth's sun is showing signs of energy fluations which could over tax the collectors; five, perhaps more of the planets in your solar system will be destroyed, incinerated. I don't want this for you or your people but there is nothing we can do, our interference could be seen as an act of aggression and start a war. If you go with SA'MAR they might not listen, might not be in time . . . but you have already decided. I cannot be there for you Jason, I must be here for Myra."

"I'll know where to find you and my wife when I return."

"You'll need a small ship and stasis chamber, SA'MAR must have an implant to breathe the Earth atmosphere. You'll need to leave as soon as possible."

VE'AR hugged Jason who then left for a meeting with SA'MAR.

Three days passed, Jason left a note for Myra, then with the trajectory set in for Earth and having studied the Narin ship thoroughly he and SA'MAR departed. Jason knew and agreed that no Narin but SA'MAR should be involved in this mission.

They would find the Institute of Astrophysics in Washington, D.C. and locate chief scientist Dr. Hanna Sol once they arrived.

CHAPTER X

GALAXY—WHAT ON EARTH

Eleven months had passed. Narins traditionally didn't trust wormholes, their ships' engines destabilized them so the trip took longer. They were now in orbit above Earth undetected, hidden by a cloaking device which involved bending light. Jason and SA'MAR beamed to the surface now looking for the scientist Dr. Hanna Sol. SA'MAR now had taken a human facade. They rented a room at a hotel. They did research and then proceeded in the direction of the Institute. They had to walk through a large park, pristine and beautiful belying the fact that there were reminders in debris fields of past wars. As they walked, SA'MAR opened a piece of pas'ce, like a stick of gum and threw the wrapper on the pavement. They kept walking and saw a sign, 'No Littering,' it read. Then a voice.

"Stop, both of you!"

They turned to see a man in uniform carrying a gun and a night stick who was very angry.

"Sir?" Jason asked.

"Your friend has littered our park."

"I apologize," SA'MAR said, "my first trip to Earth."

"Not good enough, pick that up first trip to Earth."

He did, then they turned to walk away.

"Not so fast, it is forbidden to chew gum or eat here in this park."

"Next you'll throw us in jail," Jason said exhibiting sarcasm.

"I just might or give you a stern but needed warning and maybe a beating."

"Don't do that, this is beyond ridiculous."

"I'll show you ridiculous, I'm taking you both to jail."

"No, you can't," SA'MAR said.

"Yes, he can."

They ended up in jail. Jason's fingerprints gave more information than he could have ever imagined. He was brought before a magistrate.

"There is nothing on this other one with this book of calculations but Jason Kindle has an extensive history with us including execution." The magistrate then questioned Jason. "You were executed aboard Commander Breedlove's ship ordered by Judge Iglesis, yet here you are."

"Yes Sir, I was executed and died but somehow I exist . . . here is my scar. Unless I'm a clone and I don't think I am, I am Jason Kindle."

"Who is he?" pointing at SA'MAR.

"Someone who must talk to Dr. Hanna Sol," SA'MAR replied.

"What is your city of origin?"

"Echo Province on Mars?" Jason said.

"Let him speak for himself."

"I really don't know."

"Mental issues," Jason remarked.

"Put them both in a holding cell," the magistrate said, "until we finish our investigation."

Hours passed.

"Could you reach Dr. Sol with telepathy?" Jason asked SA'MAR.

"Perhaps."

"SA'MAR, you will get your chance."

"I hope so."

That evening SA'MAR began to focus on the astrophysicist Dr. Sol with a warning that his calculations were incorrect and Earth was facing its worst fate. Within a few hours Dr. Sol arrived at the magistrate's office.

"You are holding two men, I want to see them."

The magistrate's assistant agreed knowing who and how famous Dr. Sol was.

"I am Dr. Sol, am I addressing Dr. SA'MAR and Jason Kindle?"

"Yes," they both replied.

"We have come a long way, can we meet with you privately at the Institute?" SA'MAR added, "And just call me SA'MAR."

"Yes, the magistrate will release you tomorrow into my custody . . . could I see your notes, the calculations?"

"They are written in another language but take them," SA'MAR told him.

"I have a decoding multi-language super computer."

"It won't work on this."

"Until tomorrow," Dr. Sol said puzzled.

Both men were uncomfortable, SA'MAR struggled to relax and keep his human form. Jason fell asleep, he began to dream about years past on Earth.

"How was school?" his mother asked him.

"Good, the botany class is very interesting. The air is getting harder to breathe, can we stop this greenhouse effect?"

"Your father and I want to discuss something with you and Allison over dinner . . . your question will be answered then."

There wasn't much activity outside anymore. Jason loved basketball which he normally played twice a week indoors at school. He and Marco, a close friend, were teammates and also on a bicycling team which practiced indoors in a large stadium due to toxic air. Both boys and Allison, Jason's older sibling, were into swimming. She was also a budding gymnast, all were very competitive.

Jason went to check on the plants in the botany lab which was attached to their modest house. His father, a botanist, was in his office there talking to a man in a military uniform. They didn't notice Jason who was behind a wall unseen, listening.

"We don't need this so potent Major and what are the plans for using it?"

"It will be used to eliminate any threats to the Galaxy or its passengers essentially clearing a path for exploration and colonization of deep space."

"Will it be carried aboard the ship?"

"Perhaps."

"This could harm us if it mutates or is made more potent."

"You created this from a space microbe we found years ago, you have done well Dr. Kindle, the best in your field, let us decide now." The man left.

Jason came in a few minutes later. "Dad?" He saw several chemicals, bottles labeled, beakers half filled. "What are you working on?"

"Improving what we are growing."

Jason knew better as he checked the plants and read labels.

"Time for dinner," Allison said as she stood at the door.

"Let's go Jason," his father said.

As they ate, Bella Kindle and Jackson gave them the news.

"We are leaving Earth in five months for a new home thousands of light years from here. The Commander of the ship, the Galaxy, will be someone we know, Colonel Sobel."

No one said a word.

Then, "Happy Birthday Jason, you're fifteen today," Bella said.

"I was hoping you were about to say 'April Fools'," he remarked.

"It's no joke," Allison said, she was sixteen. "Who will come with us?"

"There will probably be a lottery of sorts for the remaining seats. Those whose professions would be most valuable in building a new society would come first, certainly doctors, scientists, engineers, teachers, the Colonel and crew, his military and whoever else . . . there will be others aboard who will also contribute in meaningful ways."

"Our global warming is proving too dangerous to remain here," Bella said.

"Are we going?" Allison asked, "is it by lottery, do we have . . ."

"We're going," Jackson Kindle said. "It's already been decided."

"Curtis?" Jason asked.

"Yes and others, cattle, chickens for food, cloned embryos of several farm animals which will be frozen for the trip, replicators for certain foods, for clothes and machinery . . . and for you Jason, replicated pizza." At that Jackson laughed.

"We need Marco and his family," Allison said. "He can help with communications."

"You love him?" Jason asked, "he's only sixteen."

"None of your business," came a swift reply.

"Don't mention this, that we are going, not even to Marco."

"He's my friend too," Jason said.

"Don't . . ." Jackson told him.

That evening Jason did talk with Marco and told him. He was in distress upon hearing the news.

"A lottery? Get us on that ship Jason."

"I have no control over this, nor do my parents, I want you aboard, Allison needs you. Most of the spots are taken I was told."

"There is a reason I must go, Allison and I love each other . . . we slept together and she might be pregnant."

Jason just stood there looking at Marco in disbelief. "Of all the people I would have trusted, you were the one I believed would treat my sister with respect . . . you slept with her? Took advantage?"

Jason and Marco got into a fight, both sustained bruises. From then on a rift was created between them. He didn't tell Allison about what they had discussed but when Jason returned home there were questions and Marco, the next day, was also questioned by his parents. Marco was pushed away from Allison at every turn by Jason. She questioned why. Later, Jason had told her to pretend that she and Marco had married secretly and that as her husband he should go, never mentioning that Marco thought she might be pregnant, true or not. It worked, Marco and his family would be leaving as well. Jason still pushed him away in an attempt to protect Allison. Jackson and Bella realized that he had discussed the trip with both Marco and Allison and a marriage as a pretend scenario not realizing what Marco had told him. They were glad that Marco and his family would be going.

School and other activities continued on Earth then the last month everyone made final preparations to leave. Allison showed no sign of a pregnancy, she wanted Jason and Marco to heal the rift, she didn't understand why the bad blood.

Every family had a small compartment aboard the Galaxy. The medical facilities were up and running. Jackson Kindle set up the botany lab, school and classes were assigned, recreational facilities opened, small stores were due to open; all of these activities were a dress rehearsal of what was to come once they reached their new home. The stasis chambers were the most intimidating as they were assigned for each person on board, two hundred in all.

The military had pushed to send the toxic substance on board the Galaxy but the Commander, Colonel Sobel refused. They had earlier, unknown to all the passengers shot a probe filled with the substance into deep space to clear the way of any possible obstructions or life which would impede humankind reaching out into space.

Fifty years into the journey the ship's main computer went off trajectory. Myra came aboard to save them, Jason assisted her after being removed from stasis, they fell in love. He wanted her back and to spend his life with her. The dream ended.

"Jason, Jason."

He woke up, "SA'MAR?"

"Dr. Sol is here for us, let's go."

They went with Dr. Sol to the Institute; he had asked that Jason and SA'MAR be remanded to his custody until they went before the magistrate again. SA'MAR explained his calculations.

"What language is this?" Dr. Sol asked.

There was a pause then SA'MAR spoke, "Narin, I am a Narin." As if to drive the point home he changed form then back again. "My people and I want to save Earth from this coming disaster. Jason is in this whatever it takes and came with me. We knew the result of this attempt to pull more energy from your sun."

"I've heard of your species and Jason Kindle." They shook hands.

For several hours Dr. Sol and SA'MAR discussed their calculations, opposing views, Jason listened carefully, he wanted to study the engineering aspect of the project.

"What we have been doing for over a solar year is pulling energy off our sun using a man-made equivalent of a black hole. The energy pulled in is then routed to solar energy collectors on five planets," Dr. Sol explained.

SA'MAR countered, "The energy will be drained at an increased rate by the black hole, when the collectors can no longer efficiently collect due to the overflow of energy then the energy will strip each planet of all life. As you know, your sun will have burned up its hydrogen fuel sooner in its central core, the fusion will continue as the sun expands from a yellow star to a red giant, engulfing Mercury, Venus, Earth, Mars, and probably Jupiter as it continues to burn the last of its hydrogen fusing it into helium. Everything will happen billions of years sooner as everything is accelerated, so there are the two worst case scenarios.

"Then what?" Jason asked him, "I have read books on this but if everything changes then . . ."

"The same ending . . . when all the nuclear fuel is exhausted and thermonuclear reactions will cease over thousands of years, again not billions, the sun will have become a small dense star, a white dwarf, a dying star. The most immanent of most concern now are the collectors becoming overloaded." The calculations of SA'MAR were proved correct.

"We are desperate here, wars and more wars have been fought over fuel. One of our own ships was due to return with a crystal super fuel."

"That ship never made it," Jason said. "The fuel was in the form of crystals which were living Entities and Commander Breedlove had to return the Crystals to the planet they originated from. We on Bright Star, our new home and Commander Breedlove's crew are joined in evaluating and mining three planets with crystal fuel, enough to create enough energy on Earth and the other planets . . . he will come with the fuel."

There were days of discussions, recalculating, frustration, then the sounds of agreement. Jason in the meantime had been allowed to study certain aspects of the man-made black hole with someone who designed it, Astrophysist and Engineer Dr. James Weed who didn't realize that SA'MAR was a Narin.

"Good to meet you Sir," Jason said.

"And you, everyone seems to have heard of you."

"Not all bad, I hope."

"No, not all bad, you have a following."

"So I've been told."

"We had hopes of continuing to use this design, but after conversing with Mr. SA'MAR and Dr. Sol, it appears we're in disagreement."

"I am fascinated with the design, my training doesn't include astrophysics, but I understand the concept."

"And what do you think?"

"Its concept is brilliant, but according to Dr. Sol and SA'MAR the calculations were flawed."

"We can't exist without fuel, how soon will Commander Breedlove return here? Is he bringing a fuel source?"

"I don't know how soon, but he is bringing a source of fuel."

"Hopefully . . . you and Mr. SA'MAR should leave here and we'll deal with our fuel problems. The mechanized black hole will be our salvation and if we find another fuel that is efficient then we can discuss what we should do."

Dr. Sol then said, "If the Mechanism malfunctions or is too efficient in taking the sun's energy you see for yourself what those calculations are telling us."

"Are you going to the Council crying wolf?" Dr. Weed asked him.

"I feel I must."

"They can't hear you if you're banned."

A police force then entered, Dr. Weed took all the calculations but couldn't find SA'MAR's.

"Where are they?"

"You saw them I haven't moved them from this room."

Then Dr. Weed looked at Jason, "Take them, place them in a holding cell until further notice."

SA'MAR had bent light to hide his endless notes about Earth and the sun, describing in detail a looming disaster. All three were now in jail.

"Use your telepathy SA'MAR, as best you can to reach anyone who would want to rescue Jason Kindle and two friends from jail. Dr. Sol how big is the Mechanism now?"

"Approximately the size of Mars; a black hole so much smaller than the sun shouldn't be able to pull off its energy but since it is man-made it is more powerful and is actually capable of increasing its size which it has continued to do . . . there is no way to shut it down, those in control are in a very fortified area, probably inside a mountain. Dr. Weed absolutely believes he is right. In what he has created, he sees hope. It's almost like his creation has a mind of its own."

"Could he have placed his thought patterns in it? Could it be controlled in this way?" Jason asked.

Dr. Sol thought very carefully before he answered . . . "I saw the schematics of his creation but one page was missing, pertinent information on how its mechanical brain was constructed and would function. Nowadays we can use thought patterns in machinery as they work tirelessly saving hours, doing things more efficiently, but the machines were never intended to totally take over. No machine on this scale was ever given human thought patterns."

SA'MAR then said, "Perhaps I could plant a thought in the minds of Dr. Weed and the Mechanism . . . and I will try to contact those followers of yours Jason as well."

Two days later they were still incarcerated. Dr. Weed and security had again searched Dr. Sol's lab at the Institute thoroughly, not finding SA'MAR's notes. All three were brought before the magistrate who sentenced them to lengthy prison terms if they didn't leave Earth. They agreed to leave which was only stalling for more time. They were then released and met by several who were familiar with Jason's exploits and his having been saved from execution on Earth by a Narin presence three years earlier. They wanted to hear from him and the two scientists. These followers were part of a resistance that didn't accept what was happening on planet Earth and the way those that disagreed with the authorities in power were dealt with. Instead of inciting riots which would have had serious consequences for everyone, he and the scientists began citing the reasons for stopping Dr. Weed's project to those who would listen. Dr. Sol, SA'MAR and Jason were hidden by these people from Dr. Weed and the authorities as they wouldn't leave Earth. SA'MAR's notes were found by an ally and brought to him. He occasionally changed form when he became tired. He kept reaching out to Dr. Weed and the Mechanism to change their thought patterns.

Jason and SA'MAR asked to see other areas of Earth to see what had changed in the years since the Galaxy took flight and more recently the change since Jason had been brought there over three years ago aboard the Battalion. Many improvements had been made including parks and new office buildings. There were still piles of rubble from wars that were in designated areas of the city. Most of the monuments had remained intact. The atmosphere was cleaner with Dr. Weed's fuel solution which still presented a danger; from the air, they saw the solar energy collectors around the city.

Their extended stay had become increasingly risky but this diversion helped. "Three years ago I was on trial for murder and willful destruction, I had no intent to harm anyone, only to protect, I don't advocate violence even in these circumstances," Jason said.

"And now here you are again and the circumstances are as bleak as they've ever been, you are as committed to save this world as any of us," Dr. Sol told him.

The military police were looking for Jason and the two scientists. Three of the Resistance were captured and tortured, one was allowed to leave to relay a message to the others. Dissension would be met with the severest of penalties. Everyone who saw the one released was moved seeing that he had endured torture.

"What now?" Some were asking.

"No violence will still be the best approach, computers can do our talking." Jason repeated this as many times before.

Part of this enlightened Resistance was continuing to tap into the computers and security systems of the authorities and of the Mechanism and its creator. Several attempts had been made to rescue the two in prison who had been tortured.

"They're going to be executed," one told Jason, "they want you and the two scientists."

"This is devastating news," Dr. Sol said.

"If only Commander Breedlove was here with the alternate fuel and Judge Iglesis who might deal favorably with all of us," Jason was hopeful. "SA'MAR, listen for my thoughts and perhaps a warning."

Jason decided to turn himself over to the authorities for the two prisoners. Everyone had mixed feelings about this young man they respected.

Two days in jail, he was fed and basically left to himself. Dr. Weed then paid him a visit.

"Where are Dr. Sol and Mr. SA'MAR?"

"I don't even know, hidden somewhere after I turned myself in."

"I believe you. Are you advocating violence here? An attempt was made on my life . . . again."

"No Sir, I am not . . . only educating the public about this machine and its flaws according to Dr. Sol and SA'MAR, Commander Breedlove . . ."

"I know, I've already heard enough about a new alternate super fuel."

"Won't you consider it?"

"When his ship approaches Earth and the judge aboard, we will have to decide how to destroy him and the fuel or allow the ship to land and confiscate all of it as a bio-weapon requiring further study . . . I like that scenario better; of course I can't allow you to die since the judge confirmed your execution aboard the Battalion III. You are certainly no clone, Mr. Kindle. Did any Narin come with you? They can do surprising things as they did when you were about to be executed here on Earth."

"No Narin came with me, not even my father-in-law."

"I can hook you up to a truth monitor."

"Be my guest."

"We'll skip that one . . . you are going to wish you were dead by the time I'm through with you, there won't be a way to communicate any of this."

"To the point . . . I request one thing."

"What?"

"To see your creation in action from the facility where you created it."

"You've got to be kidding?"

"I'm an engineer, humor me, apparently I won't remember."

Dr. Weed thought for a moment, "I'm a god here, I have saved this planet and neither you nor your friends can stop me . . . I will show you the Mechanism as you asked, dwell on its magnificence as you are being brain wiped."

He showed Jason where the facility was. Jason carefully told SA'MAR through telepathy everything that was happening and where and to send a warning to Commander Breedlove's ship; he didn't know that AR'TYN was aboard which would be in their favor as messages were relayed.

"Do you and the Mechanism share thought patterns?" Jason asked Dr. Weed.

Dr. Weed turned to him, "And DNA. The Mechanism was the size of the moon, but in space it has grown to the size it needs to be to route energy off the sun more efficiently . . . artificial and intelligent."

"If something goes wrong then what?"

"It won't, but I can reason with it to shut it down or do it manually from here. And if something happens to me, the machine makes the decisions."

Two hours passed then Jason was taken back to jail by two military police. The orders were to have him tortured daily. He was afraid, but bravely submitted to interrogators, some of which knew about him and respected him. They were apprehensive and didn't agree with this and made the torture less severe over certain areas and not wiping his mind as ordered by Dr. Weed who saw him as a threat.

SA'MAR knew what was happening to him. With the information he had received from Jason, there was a raid on the facility to disrupt things. Weeks passed.

A security park attendant was at the police facility walking down a long corridor when he saw Jason incarcerated in one of the holding cells. They recognized each other from the park months ago. Jason was bruised from beatings and other forms of punishment were evident.

"This is pretty severe punishment for a gum wrapper," he told the man trying to be humorous.

"What did they do to you?"

"I believe it's called torture, Dr. Weed is cracking down on any dissent concerning the Mechanism."

"I don't trust the thing, there will be an accident, I just know it."

"This is why my friend and I travelled here to talk with Dr. Sol and Dr. Weed, it didn't go well for us or Dr. Sol."

"Where are your friends?"

"I'm not sure, but in hiding."

"I can help you leave here but where do I take you?"

"If you get involved, you might be sitting where I am . . . tell me your name."

"Murphy."

"I'm Jason. They'll be coming again soon . . . go, perhaps you can help me."

Days passed, the torture continued, scars were now visible, Jason was wearing down. He gave false information concerning the Resistance headquarters, but he didn't know where they were.

After Commander Breedlove over a year earlier carefully deposited the crystals back on KA'OW, freed Steven and AR'TYN from stasis without either having sustained bodily harm, he met with the miners who were working at one of the newly discovered sites. The Battalion III was loaded with a million and one-half tons of crystals that would be converted into fuel lasting for years for Earth and four other planets. Two large cruisers were also loaded and sent back to Bright Star. The mining would continue. VE'AR had contacted AR'TYN to tell Commander Breedlove and others about Earth's fate if not stopped from a flawed attempt to pull energy from the sun too quickly. Jason and SA'MAR, a Narin astrophysicist, and Dr. Hanna Sol were jailed when they attempted to shut down the method used to take the energy. Battalion III had been in route to Earth for eight months and AR'TYN had insisted on going and relayed the messages.

Myra had earlier been reborn on NARIN'MAR, VE'AR helped repair certain memories both good and bad to restore her mind completely.

"Where is Jason?"

"He was with us on NARIN'MAR for several months, then SA'MAR, one of our scientists told him of an event coming on Earth like no other in which, if not stopped would lead to the destruction of Earth and four other worlds. He left with SA'MAR. He stayed in that room with you for months, taught two classes a day about humankind at the school; he likes NARIN'MAR. Jason has no aspirations for glory, only to save those he loves and his home world. I was going to keep him from going, make him forget . . . he grieved deeply for you Myra, he can't yet return to you."

"Have you been in contact with him?"

"No, but with AR'TYN and SA'MAR. He and SA'MAR are apparently unable to leave . . . Jason remains jailed and under duress. We are still a few months from reaching Earth where we will rendezvous with Admiral Breedlove's ship . . . we will find them."

"I can't lose him or you Leader."

VE'AR didn't reply, he hugged her.

On Earth there had been flare ups from the energy collectors which were over taxed; each prime collector, big as a fifty story building was stationed in three major cities in each state as the one in Washington D.C. Each one routed the energy to smaller collectors from which each city would benefit drawing power. The Mechanism was very powerful and never shut down. There had been other assassination attempts on Dr. Weed's life—this activity wasn't sanctioned by Jason or the other two scientists.

Jason was sitting in his cell trying to sleep when he got a message from SA'MAR.

"Tonight, tell your friend we're coming tonight, Dr. Weed is going to kill you."

Murphy was able to move Jason to the outside as SA'MAR and two others assisted. SA'MAR bent light so that it wasn't evident that Jason had escaped.

"Murphy, come with us."

"I can't, I have a family . . . go quickly."

"Thanks for the help, wish us luck."

Their meeting place had changed. A doctor was there tending to his wounds.

Months passed.

"There is a ship coming, actually two ships," SA'MAR said, "Commander Breedlove's and VE'AR's."

"How long?" Dr. Sol asked.

"A month, perhaps longer . . . I don't know about the fuel situation, but they are bringing a possible substitute."

"The air has definitely become less toxic using the sun's energy but calculations have put the energy taken at twenty percent higher since this project went on line two years ago," Dr. Sol told them. He had an alternate lab a few miles away from the Institute where he, SA'MAR and Jason lived in an adjacent dwelling with some members of the Resistance.

"I was able to reach Dr. Weed, but he won't consider that he could be wrong even as I presented the problems of his calculations again to him telepathically as he slept. The Mechanism I cannot reach, but it is a part of Dr. Weed, I can feel him in the mind of the machine," SA'MAR told them.

A month later Commander Breedlove's ship was now in orbit, he knew about the current events and the threats against him and Judge Iglesis concerning the new fuel. Dr. Sol was contacted. Simultaneously a Narin force arrived to assist. VE'AR contacted the Battalion. They met. Jason and several of the Resistance were beamed aboard. Everyone knew what they had faced, many wore the scars of torture and imprisonment. VE'AR hugged Jason as Commander Breedlove and Judge Iglesis praised all for their sacrifice, they were especially moved when they greeted Jason. The plans now were made for taking down Dr. Weed and his creation.

Without warning the facility lost power, Dr. Weed was shut down with memory loss with help from the Narins, the Mechanism was confused into believing the sun was no longer a viable source of energy. It was dragged into deep space quickly by the Narin ship as Commander Breedlove ordered a force to apprehend and detain any who offered resistance to the deposit of the new fuel and to stop attacks on the Resistance. The fuel was taken to several facilities that had been closed down by Dr. Weed. The Mechanism would never return to the solar system but in deep space it was directed to a large sun where it would be studied by Earth and Narin scientists anxious to know how it was constructed.

The energy collectors were now being destroyed Earth wide and on the other planets. There was confusion over the changes that were taking place. Judge Iglesis, who was very high ranking joined with others worldwide and the military to make changes. Earth had a president but it was a weak position compared to the power of the military especially Admiral Breedlove who would join the Judge in creating part of a new political system. Those in the Resistance became part of this system as an Earth Council. Violence would not be tolerated by any group unless approved by the now three sided government.

A week later goodbyes were said, handshakes were given, VE'AR was thanked by both the Judge and Admiral Breedlove for his assistance and the Narin force and a special thanks to Jason and SA'MAR for their participation in trying to stop Dr. Weed and discouraging violent acts against him while protecting lives. VE'AR, Jason, and SA'MAR then travelled to NARIN'MAR. AR'TYN left with an Earth mining ship travelling to Bright Star.

Jason was examined aboard the Narin ship. He had several wounds and scars that were visible. An attendant had been rubbing the scars with a salve.

VE'AR asked the attendant to leave for a while to talk with him.

"We have the technology to deal with the scars . . . the scars that you carry inside yourself concern me, they are eating away at you."

"It seemed like a hopeless fight, but SA'MAR and Dr. Sol were doing everything possible to prevent any violence against Dr. Weed and save lives by other means of non-violent attacks to stop the Mechanism."

"You put your life on the line Jason to stop the destruction of your world and placing yourself in the hands of the enemy to be tortured on a daily basis. You stopped the violence as best you could."

"Earth is worth saving. We waited; after I was rescued months earlier you came and we averted a disaster. The Commander and Judge Iglesis now had the help they needed to win this. You were right to not appear aggressive bringing a Narin force to Earth before Admiral Breedlove agreed, you were right to stay with Myra as she was reborn.

I feel I deserted her when she needed me most. I love her more than life, my children, I respect you. Your guidance and counsel have meant a lot to me."

"I have enormous respect for you Jason . . . I am not always correct, you felt you had to give them that push in the right direction. You didn't abandon Myra, don't put that on yourself. She is waiting for you and knows you were by her side for several months and the reason you left . . . allow me to help you through this, I know you better than anyone."

"I trust you VE'AR."

"Even if I make you forget?"

"Don't go too far, I need my memories both good and bad."

"I won't."

Myra was aboard the ship and listening, she had seen Jason while he was asleep and was aware of his condition physically and mentally. VE'AR worked over Jason to help him through this latest crisis even as he regretted not going with him.

One evening she came to him. He was sitting in a chair in his compartment asleep. He wasn't socializing as his wounds were repaired. SA'MAR had asked about him as he related events on Earth. She touched his face and kissed him. He woke up and saw her.

"Myra? Am I dreaming? VE'AR never mentioned that you were aboard."

"I have been aboard waiting for the right time, I'm no image."

Jason stands up, "I . . ." he couldn't finish the sentence he was so overcome emotionally.

"You are healing," she said as she touched his face again and his arms. "Your hair is longer." She smiled.

He touched her all over. "I watched you die and then being reborn. It's really you." He kissed her passionately.

"I heard you taught classes, Narin adults and children."

"I enjoyed it . . . do you remember how very much I love you?"

She took his hands in hers and walked him to the bed. "Let me show you how much I still love you." She was careful with him as they made love due to his having been tortured. Both became very emotional, there were tears.

After two years they were back together and joined again. During the trip to NARIN'MAR both would help each other heal.

Later she asked VE'AR, "What did you make him forget?"

"Nothing. I made a suggestion that Earth would continue and could handle the current situations as all voices would now be heard and represented and that he was needed more now by those who loved him, his wife and children. There are two Narins now stationed on Earth to assist as necessary."

"Jason will be glad to know that . . . when we leave NARIN'MAR for Bright Star, consider coming with us, you are very loved and respected."

VE'AR hugs her, "I will consider it. Now for the ceremony, tell Jason."

Jason and Myra would again have a joining ceremony held aboard ship. His hair was cut shorter, he dressed in traditional Narin clothes for the ceremony as did she. He sat on the floor on a large rug as did VE'AR and three others who surrounded and questioned him; Myra was later signaled to sit beside him then the words, "It is done," were said by VE'AR. They kissed then stood up. There was a celebration of all kinds of foods including pizza. Everyone had a good time, it was more of a celebration of life as two lives were united again.

The ship they travelled in was very large and a prototype warship. Jason was allowed to learn certain aspects of the ship from the Narin Commander AN'ZAR. The scientists aboard took readings of the Mechanism as they passed by it, it left a strange signature. He loved the interaction with the Narin crew. They had been anxious to tell him about certain experiments and discoveries made aboard their ship asking him about his experiences on Earth and as a young man travelling into deep space to find a new world.

One music device, a banwith, was played by spectral light hitting certain parts of the device, it was pleasant. Myra had brought Jason's I-pod which was hooked up to speakers around the ship.

"Different," came the remarks, several enjoyed it.

Months later they arrived on NARIN'MAR. The population welcomed SA'MAR, Jason, Myra, VE'AR and the brave Narin's who removed the Mechanism. Jason and Myra began teaching; his two classes a day were completely filled, Myra taught beginning physics and her classes were full as well. VE'AR was preparing to leave with them in five months as he prepared those in change in his absence until he returned.

Jason told about Earth's struggle, the military and judges, the Resistance also called the Freedom Fighters, the Narin help, and the threat to the Earth from an overflow of energy from the sun being siphoned by a black hole. The changes in the government were also mentioned, especially how the Resistance was now part of the governing body.

Several Narin officials met with Myra and Jason urging them to stay even to giving them housing and their own pizza replicator, this amused VE'AR.

"They don't want you to leave," he told Jason.

"We'll return, I miss my family, our children. I've never experienced a peace like I've felt here." he replied. "Before we leave, I would like to see the ice boat races you told me about that happen twice a year here on NARIN'MAR . . . isn't one race occurring this month?"

"Yes . . . and you will watch it and participate." This delighted VE'AR.

"I've never done this so how would I participate?"

"You'll see."

"Days later Jason, Myra and attendants accompanied VE'AR to a frozen valley in a low lying area several miles inland on the large province I'SA. There were practice runs on the ice, Jason was totally taken by the sport. He met several of the competitors. This area was kept frozen by several machines regulating the climate one told him.

"This is JA'LAR our best competitor . . . my son-in-law Jason Kindle." They greeted each other, JA'LAR quickly changed to a human facade.

"I would be honored to have you as a partner in the competition," he said.

"I also am honored to meet you . . . I just want to experience this, certainly not as a competitor . . . what about a practice competition?"

"Let's do it then, tomorrow?"

That evening Jason read up on the ice boats and competition both by Narins and earlier competitions on Earth. He could hardly contain his excitement. They spent the night in a small nearby equivalent of a bed and breakfast.

The next morning Jason was outfitted for the sport. JA'LAR explained certain characteristics of his boat they would be taking. Jason reasoned that it resembled a two ton B class Skeeter, with side by side seats and a mast twenty-five feet tall and a boom fifteen-feet long with seventy-five square feet of sail area; the fuselage was wooden at a length of twenty-five feet fitted with skate blades called runners. JA'LAR had both jib and main sails unlike an old Earth Skeeter B Class.

As the practice competition continued Jason realized what skills were required for the sport and the physical strength as he used all of it to steer the boat with the halyards attempting to not tip over as they gained more speed. Tacking back and forth became all important to use the wind without allowing the sails to generate excessive horsepower. Both men were laughing as several lessons were learned in the few hours of the session. Jason was exhausted, but continued to learn. He would be there the next day for the competition and cheering for JA'LAR; he won.

Jason and Myra returned from the trip having good memories. They took long walks on the tranquil Narin streets, the small lakes provided time to reflect on the day's events after teaching their classes. They sat dipping their feet in the tepid water. Others came and sat conversing with them toward evening. The three moons provided soft lighting in the dark sky that glistened off the huge rings surrounding the planet.

They travelled several months in a smaller ship escorted by two cruisers when they left NARIN'MAR for Bright Star.

When they arrived there were several there to greet them. Colonel Sobel and Colonel Neal were among those to welcome them. Marco and Allison brought JAS'AR and MY'AR; they were so grown up. Jason and Myra held them very lovingly then Allison gave Myra and Jason a side view.

"You're pregnant?" an excited Jason said, he looked at Marco, the two shook hands, he hugged Allison.

"Myra, you had us worried," Allison said.

"As you can see I got through it." She wouldn't tell them about being reborn. "I can't, we can't thank you and Marco enough for taking care of the children."

Allison smiled and hugged her, "I want to hear everything."

143

"And congratulations Allison."

Bella and Jackson hosted a large welcome home for Jason, Myra, and VE'AR. Narins and humans shared in this.

Jason had given an update of the events since leaving Bright Star three years earlier. VE'AR confirmed the events and his actions with Commander Breedlove and Judge Iglesis to shut down the Mechanism and Dr. Weed.

CHAPTER XI

GALAXY—THE CHILDREN—JACOB

Starting their lives over again was an adjustment. Myra was now two years old but her body aged to what she been, still young for a Narin.

Of the ten habitable moons and planets Steven and Jason found for possible deposits of fuel crystals and as outposts, two had a form of microscopic life and a third, a moon yielded more than they could have imagined. At first they found small creatures with scales, lizard-like in appearance burrowing into solid rock by burning holes in the rocks with an acid like substance secreted from their mouths. They were documented but not moved from their habitats.

The terrain was similar to deserts on Earth and Mars, rock and sand, dry blowing wind, very hot. There were areas of a desert-like grass, sporadic at best. No apparent life outside what they encountered earlier. They kept walking, it would be dark in a few hours. This moon was orbiting a small planet with no atmosphere and they both orbited a medium size orange sun, on a distant arm of the Milky Way Galaxy; they approached a large hill and would climb to the summit before turning back.

In an hour both were exhausted, the atmosphere was arid, the wind unrelenting; they reached the summit. Both stood in stunned silence, they stood there for several minutes.

"What have we found?" Jason could barely comprehend it.

"Looks like a settlement and remnants of a space expedition gone awry."

The wind seemed almost calm as they climbed down the hill to investigate. They walked half a mile to a community, now extinct, with several structures used as housing, fifteen in all and all large to accommodate several. There was evidence of births from the furniture and toys and small clothing. Food had rotted from time gone by. There were books, journals, computers, everything needed to survive. A medical facility was nearby, some of the equipment wasn't familiar. Steven took a vial of medicine to be studied on Bright Star.

As they moved from there they discovered a large biosphere that had sustained many plants and animals and the Travellers in some manner besides providing a food source after arriving on the moon. There was also a water pump in the biosphere which sustained the need for water as it pumped it from the interior of the moon; no lakes were detected. There was an ominous sound of a wind chime somewhere in the area.

Then as they moved on they saw a large ship which had carried the Travellers there. As Jason and Steven studied it, the engines were unlike anything they had ever seen; the metal that the ship was constructed from was unfamiliar and the ship resembled nothing ever sent from Earth. As they stood there they saw a debris field orbiting this moon—pieces of metal of various shapes and sizes and certain objects probably carried aboard a ship. Had the Travellers arrived in two ships? Where did the debris field originate? They were able to enter the ship, it was large enough to carry ten passengers and had both stasis chambers and seating. There was no indication of children having travelled there. The ship's log was discovered inside.

"I can hardly take this in," Jason said as he watched the video log entries.

"They documented everything that happened to them according to this other log, a written one . . . the audible language and script could be human with perhaps an alien influence. It doesn't appear that another ship arrived before all these died."

Jason agreed. "How could humans make it this far without help?"

They stayed the night aboard the ship. The next day, ten hours later they again studied the surroundings, a sample of the ship's hull was taken for testing as well as taking the ship's video log and the scripted one to be studied.

Another half-mile from the ship bodies were discovered. Thirty graves and two bodies of those who buried the last before they themselves died, human looking; there was a symbol above each grave which was even more puzzling, a circle with a sunburst inside it and names that couldn't be deciphered. The clothes resembled human made goods. Skin samples and swatches of the clothes were taken. Jason and Steven wanted to bury the two bodies but resisted as scientists would study everything when an expedition would be sent from Bright Star and Sanctus.

As they were leaving, they took a sample of the debris orbiting that moon as well as several items for testing and study; both were in disbelief over having evidence of a human existence thousands of years ago in this area of space. When and how they died would be answered.

It would take them two weeks to reach Bright Star and deliver the news about the Travellers. Every scientist human and Narin wanted to see the logs documenting the ancient journey. Steven and Jason were asked many questions as several studied their own video documentation. DNA tests and carbon dating were run on the samples taken from the Travellers; there was an array of other tests to date the piece of the spaceship flown by those explorers and the sample from the orbiting debris field. It would take weeks to evaluate what was found, then an expedition of scientists was planned to that moon.

In the meantime other scientists had changed certain things to help the bio structure of Bright Star by ensuring the pollination of plants, especially food sources.

Dr. Vu, the entomologist had tirelessly worked to correct the mistake of creating bigger, more aggressive mosquitoes that were bred to pollinate, but didn't. Finally he took another insect, the bee and combined it with those new mosquitoes and the pollination tripled. Dr. Vu loved a challenge and created some interesting insect combinations which helped in crop production and the soil they grew in. Lady bugs that had a fluorescent glow were a favorite of his, they ate harmful pests and delighted everyone.

Dr. Kindle was given credit for several advances in botanical matters. Flowers and crops covered the hills and were abundant. He and Dr. Vu worked well together changing the bio structure of the planet.

Marine biologists added fish and other marine life to the ocean and the several lakes careful not to add aggressive species to the lakes. Humans would now fish for hours; Narins didn't understand the fascination with fishing but enjoyed deep water diving, studying marine life and periods of relaxation as they sat around the lakes.

With very little pollution due to a crystal power source, the residents of Bright Star and Sanctus enjoyed clean air and less turbulent weather conditions that had occurred on Earth which was now improving. The periodic times for rain and the seasons were in sync.

The last mission had a profound effect on Steven even more than on Jason, he wanted a family. He and Shirley talked.

"Sergeant Blondell and I are getting married," Steven told Jason and Colonel Sobel at an evening out as they discussed the findings of their last mission to that moon, which remained un-named and only a number, M13.

"Finally," Jason said.

"When?" the Colonel asked.

"When can you marry us?"

"This evening, next week, you tell me."

"A private ceremony, no fuss, tomorrow evening at the Galaxy chapel."

Jason stood up to leave and tell everyone.

"No Jason," Steven said, "this is very private."

Jason sat down again.

"All right, tomorrow evening, six o'clock Bright Star time," Colonel Sobel confirmed everything.

"Jason, be my best man?"

"Certainly, what about a bridesmaid or maid of honor?"

"Private Forbes, Shirley's friend."

"Who is Shirley? You've never told me her first name. I thought her name was Sergeant . . . Shirley?" Jason was joking, he knew her name.

Steven rolled his eyes.

"See you both tomorrow, don't forget to tell the bride," the Colonel said being humorous.

Steven assured the Colonel he wouldn't forget trying not to appear nervous. Jason offered to help him and Myra offered to help Shirley and her friend to prepare. Marco made the announcement over the radio station which reached everyone so everyone knew. The Narins not wanting to be outdone, had a radio station set up in part with Lieutenant Vann and Marco's help where the announcement was made in Narin even though they frequently used telepathy.

The chapel was arranged and decorated with various plants and flowers from the botany lab and several gardens on the planet. Food for the celebration was prepared by chefs and others dedicated to the culinary.

Myra knew Sergeant Blondell and had worked with her; she had accepted Colonel Neal as a special friend and no longer held any animosity against him for taking Jason away from her.

The next evening there was an overflow of people attending the ceremony. All officers and crew loyal to Steven also attended. He was nervous as he stood there in his dark blue military dress uniform and she in a white knee length dress and small veil. He wore his medals showing his military background from four wars and a special one for heroism while saving lives during his service. He wore the symbol of a judge below these other medals, a cross inside a circle with a star in the background. Shirley decided not to wear her three medals reflecting her seven years of service aboard Battalion II. Colonel Sobel conducted the ceremony flawlessly but restrained from laughing as Colonel Neal became tongue tied at times. Jason did laugh.

"I now pronounce you man and wife and introduce you as Colonel and Mrs. Neal."

Everyone clapped as they kissed. Commander Breedlove wasn't able to attend due to forming a part of the new government on Earth. A transmission was sent showing the ceremony. He sent his congratulations as soon as he knew. AR'TYN and Wanda were there, they gave a warm greeting. VE'AR and his entourage were there with their own greeting and a gift of ancient Narin origin thousands of years old depicting space travel through charts. He and Colonel Neal shook hands.

The celebration went on for hours as everyone ate and drank human and Narin beverages including varieties of wine, the effects of the Narin varieties were long lasting.

The next day everyone returned to an almost normal routine. Myra had added classes for pregnant Narin and human women as she continued to teach science and physics. Jason continued teaching engineering and courses in levels of navigation. He assisted Chief Engineer Henry as needed repairing and modifying engines as his chief assistant.

MY'AR and JAS'AR were in secondary school majoring in the sciences. One of their fellow students was a young Narin boy, Jacob, only six but equivalent to a ten-year old human boy in stature and understanding. MY'AR and JAS'AR were ten. The boy had physical problems. His Narin mother was RU'AR and his human father was

Evander Kowalski who worked with Henry and Jason. Manuel Ovilla, the Chief Engineer from Colonel Neal's ship Battalion II, had worked with Evander on different occasions and almost came to blows with him over disagreements on fixing various problems. Evander was a mechanic or Mech 6 as his rank was designated aboard Battalion I, Commander Scott's ship. He was midway to his sought after Mech 10 which would place him as a top level mechanic. He was an angry person, he had married a Narin woman feeling that he loved her and no human woman was interested. Their son had medical problems; physically the boy's system had shut down at times and he was crippled in one leg though still able to walk. The Narin doctors explained that this was a disease caused by weaknesses in his father's immune system and that there was little they could do to reverse it short of a trip to Sanctus and staying aboard the research ship as doctors worked to cure him, no guarantees. Evander became enraged as the blame rested with him. Human doctors were consulted and gave the same answers, one even chided him for drinking too much and that could have complicated matters. He took his son and left with RU'AR. She was the only one who understood how devastated he was over his son's prognosis. He wanted his son to be athletic and compete with the other kids. He was always depressed and gruff. She was able to calm him and soothe the hurt knowing he wouldn't interact as he should with his son.

She and Myra had a talk one afternoon after Jacob's class.

"What can I do Myra? JAS'AR and MY'AR are good friends to Jacob, they try to do things so he'll enjoy some activities besides studying."

"Perhaps Jason can work with him in a special athletics program for those who are having physical problems . . . I'll ask him. We know Jacob is exceptionally bright. What about Evander?"

"Angry, frustrated, verbally abusive, drinks . . . he doesn't hurt us physically."

Myra was saddened by this. She talked with Jason and with VE'AR. RU'AR gave Jason permission to work with Jacob to evaluate him for exercise and perhaps later integrate him into a sport. He didn't mention this to Evander, nor did RU'AR.

Several weeks passed. Talks with VE'AR seemed to point to the need for a specialist on Sanctus.

"The father was told about this," VE'AR said.

"Then told him that he caused the boy's problems and that there were no guarantees for a cure . . . I have been working with him on a special athletics program to see what he can do."

"Very positive, his father however, is abusive and might come after you because you helped the boy."

"Possibly, even JAS'AR and MY'AR are helping him, I should caution them."

The next afternoon the boy didn't show up for the athletic program. JAS'AR told Jason, "I was taking him to the athletic class when his father pushed me away, yelled and took Jacob home."

"He pushed you?"

"And yelled, cursing."

Jason was so angry he could barely keep it together. He sent JAS'AR home and walked to Evander's house. He knocked.

"Who is there?" a woman answered, she knew who it was.

"RU'AR, it's Jason Kindle, there is a matter I must discuss with Evander."

She opened the door.

"Is he home?"

"Evander, someone to see you."

He came to the door holding a beer, she knew what was wrong and moved out of the way.

"You shoved my boy and cursed him."

"So I did."

"This has to be settled, an apology to my son for starters."

Evander put down his beer, "Or settle it like men."

They started to settle it then Jacob appeared standing by his dad.

"You took matters into your own hands asking RU'AR, not me."

"Tomorrow in the school gym, private."

"I'll be there."

Jason was still fuming. Myra knew. He called Steven.

"I need a brush up on self-defense."

"For which one of the ten year olds in the athletic department? Or is it all of them?"

"That's very humorous," Jason said. "Evander Kowalski pushed and cursed JAS'AR in an attempt to punish me for not consulting him about placing his son Jacob in this special athletics program. He won't apologize to JAS'AR and certainly wants to settle this another way by beating the crap out of me."

"I remember him, he was part of the Battalion I crew."

Steven would help. They met that evening in a gym aboard the Galaxy.

"He has an advantage of being bulky, I am taller and could react faster."

They begin to spar. Steven reviews several moves in military self-defense. Jason did a daily exercise regiment but the self-defense moves and discipline were lacking.

"I should get back into this."

"Yes, you should . . . always be ready Jason for anything."

"How is Shirley?"

"Mrs. Neal is just fine, we'll get together soon, she is a better officer than a cook, things feel right between us."

"Good."

Both men sustained bruises over the hour and a half they practiced but Steven was confident that Jason would do some damage to the other guy even if he couldn't defeat him.

The next afternoon came. No one was watching as Jason and Evander talked then the fight started in the school gym.

"I told you why," Jason said, "to help his leg."

"He's my son and you will lose."

"You've already lost Evander. Your son needs you and you're not there for him."

Several, including Steven, quietly wandered in to watch the fight. By the time the two men noticed they didn't care that a crowd had filled the gym as they fought.

"Keep your nose out of my business."

"Technically Evander, you work for me."

"Going to fire me?"

"No, we need you there . . . just open your eyes to people who want to help."

He punched Jason again, Jason punched back and kicked Evander hard who had no recent martial arts training. They continued to pummel each other for several minutes hearing yells and comments from the crowd. Each was very winded and bloodied twenty minutes into the fight.

"Go Jason," Steven yelled for moral support.

Myra, JAS'AR and MY'AR were there with VE'AR and several Narins. RU'AR and Jacob weren't there.

"Let's end this," Jason said. "Open your mind to the possibilities for your son, would you do that?" Jason turned to leave.

Evander, furious, runs behind him with the intent of harming him as he holds a sharp piece of metal which had remained hidden.

VE'AR stood up, "Look out," he yelled startling the other Narins.

Jason turned and quickly crouched down as the man fell over him crashing onto the hard floor on his face, the piece of metal had pierced Evander's arm.

The fight was officially over. There was clapping. Jason stood over Evander extending a hand up but he wouldn't, then Jason turned and left.

"You did good," Steven said, "and that piece of metal could have done some serious damage."

Jason didn't answer regretting that it had come to a fight.

Jacob wasn't allowed to attend the athletic program but did attend school. Jason apologized to him for the fight but the boy understood why he did it.

VE'AR talked with Jason, "You were defending your children."

"But now Jacob will remain crippled and today's incident taught violence as a solution to disputes; no one was supposed to see this . . . and thanks for the warning."

In the days since the incident, JAS'AR and MY'AR were told to stay away from Jacob except while they attended classes together. Jason didn't work personally again with Evander. Engineer Ovilla said someone should have throttled the man earlier. Evander was closing himself off from everyone, even his family.

A week later several of the crew members, pilots, engineers and families were invited to a party given by Steven and Shirley. Evander and RU'AR didn't show, everyone was relieved. AR'TYN and Wanda were among the guests. VE'AR was there with several Narin pilots and engineers. Others helped Shirley with food preparation. Colonel Sobel brought a date, a teacher who had been aboard the Galaxy and had taught Jason, Allison and Marco a few years ago.

"This pretty lady is Angela McCormick." Everyone welcomed her. Jason gave his own greeting.

"You have quite a history Jason," she remarked.

"Seems so," he said.

"You, Marco and Allison were three of my favorite students, now all married. You mated him?" she asked Myra.

Jason blushed for a moment then walked away with Myra before she answered. "I can't believe she asked that, I used to have a crush on her."

"She seems very caring and she's pretty," Myra remarked.

"He needs someone, he has told several people that he's married to the Galaxy," Jason said. "As I recall Steven said that about the Battalion."

"And now he has someone."

In the meantime, Evander took his wife and son on a sightseeing trip to KA'OW in the guise of testing a newly refurbished cruiser that he had repaired. He was given permission, the security grid surrounding the ship bays was opened. RU'AR knew something was wrong, KA'OW was restricted from any who might travel there. She and Jacob had been told to bring warm clothes, food and water while Evander brought camping equipment, a locator device and a weapon.

VE'AR spoke to Jason. "There is a serious problem concerning the man Evander Kowalski, RU'AR and Jacob." They quickly met with Colonel Sobel. "He intends to terminate RU'AR, the child and himself." This was startling news to the Colonel.

"Apparently by landing on KA'OW, the Crystal Children might feed off their energy, another unknown in all this," the Colonel remarked.

Steven, Jason, Colonel Sobel, two soldiers, VE'AR, two attendants and a human doctor were now in pursuit. The trip would take three days.

Evander landed on a small mountain range overlooking the ancient ruins. It was very cold. Evander, RU'AR and Jacob beamed down from the small cruiser to the ancient ruins which were still active and changing even as the Entity Children had returned three years ago. They had changed into warm clothes and Evander insisted they sleep the night in one of the ruins.

"My husband, let us go back, we're so cold," RU'AR pleaded.

"We're here, let's look at the ruins, camp here for the night then go home."

She looked at him with an understanding that he intended for all of them to die. She began to plan how to save their son.

That night she took the boy and beamed up to the small ship. Evander pursued them the next morning, he had locked down the controls so no escape could be made. She and the boy had travelled in the night to an area of the mountain where they were safe for the moment. For several hours they hid themselves. RU'AR had reached VE'AR who was aboard a cruiser and approaching quickly. He relayed the information to the others.

They didn't land but kept the ship above the smaller mountain range in a stationary low orbit in the atmosphere. They knew about where she and Jacob were. Colonel Sobel and VE'AR found them but there was a problem, a landslide had cut off the path to reach them, Evander found them.

"Don't need your help," he told VE'AR and the Colonel who were still unable to reach the other side of the cliff.

"You do need our help, RU'AR and Jacob are counting on you to protect them."

"We'll stay together," he said, then looking at VE'AR, "what are you going to do, put something in my thoughts?"

The Colonel had Jason and Steven beamed to the other side of the cliff.

"Almost there," they replied.

Evander takes Jacob and walks to the edge, RU'AR can no longer protect the child, Evander is holding a knife. "He can't have a decent life."

"Seems he could if you stop this and start helping matters," the Colonel said.

Just then VE'AR begins to work on his mind, Evander tells him to stop. "I'll kill the boy."

Jason is coming from behind, Steven is hidden as VE'AR bends the light concealing him as he approaches. Steven grabs Evander as Jason grabs Jacob. There is a brief struggle as Evander is disarmed but RU'AR gets too close and slips on a rock and begins to fall backward. Evander breaks free and grabs her arm to save her, then he says something, then both fall over the cliff as he is gripping her arm. Both died. Jason holds the child close who is in shock. The bodies are placed aboard the smaller cruiser taken by Evander and is flown back following the cruiser with Colonel Sobel and the others.

Not much was said during the three days travelling to Bright Star.

"What now VE'AR?" Jason asked, "no parents."

"Love, medical help, a family who knows intimately about Narin children," he looked at Jason.

"I'm not qualified, he saw me fighting his father."

"Could you handle it? I believe you and Myra could. You have two children who represent both cultures, you both teach."

Jason thought long and hard, "We could foster him until he's adopted. I'll talk with Myra and the kids."

After returning from a two month stay on Sanctus, VE'AR and Jason had seen significant improvement in Jacob's condition. VE'AR decided to stay on Bright Star for the time being. Jacob was now officially adopted by Jason and Myra. He had the 'AR family name. JACOB'AR would continue to be called Jacob and was going to have a good life full of dreams and hope. He responded well to his new family and wanting to become like his father became very athletic and pursued engineering as well as his other majors. His brother and sister loved him and guided him.

In the months that followed, three expeditions had been sent to the moon of the Travellers, M13, each three months apart. No one could say, even the Narins, what language this was but it definitely was spoken and written by those aboard over twenty-thousand years ago; they were human. All a mystery to be debated.

What Jason and Steven hadn't told anyone was that since their encounter on M13, they both had dreams about that moon almost like a visual record of the journey beyond any documentation and in the background the sound of a wind chime.

CHAPTER XII

GALAXY—THE CHOICE

Three years passed. There were considerable changes on Bright Star. Most had houses now and farms. Buildings, some tall, up to thirty floors, brick, glass and steel reflected the craftsmanship and architectural genius of the designers. The Narin buildings were colorful and oblong or dome shaped about as tall. Businesses were varied and everywhere as were market places. There was a large government and council hall, new schools, a planetarium, two sports domes where Narin and human athletes competed, science and medical research centers, two large hospitals, parks and more lakes; a museum and opera house had just been completed. Human and Narin cultures could be expressed there, they could sing beautifully. The museum was one of the most promising newer buildings; part of it showcased ancient artifacts both from Narin and human space travel. One new addition was a plaque attached to part of an unmanned human spacecraft, Pioneer 10, depicting humankind. The Narins had found it years earlier as the craft left Earth's solar system in 1987 and entered interstellar space, it had been hit by a meteor. Nothing was displayed from the moon M13 as of yet.

The other part of the museum was a library dedicated to human and Narin books, star charts, scrolls, video documentaries and scientific discoveries.

Several spacecraft bays were now able to house more ships, human and Narin craft protected by a more effective power grid.

The now seven lakes and the expanded ocean provided for recreation and contests. Several watercraft were moored at each of the lakes. Boat racing became a popular sport as did flying enjoyed by humans and Narins. Small flying vehicles and boats were manufactured on Bright

Star and Sanctus and became a contest of technologies as well as abilities in those sports; humans traditionally won in several flying categories.

Ice boating contests were now held on Sanctus due in part to the urging of VE'AR and Jason to incorporate humans into the sport. The Narins had placed a huge freezing unit under their largest lake and would continue the popular sport begun on NARIN'MAR. A contest would be held in a few months as new and faster performing ice boats were constructed. Jason and two of his childhood friends would compete as they tried to bring others into the sport. The Narins on Bright Star might be persuaded to compete on the human team.

Four humans had died of known causes as accidents and ailments. The Narins observed carefully the rituals following human death. RU'AR was the only Narin to have died as a resident of Bright Star. The Narin ceremony acknowledged a creator as did the human ceremonies. The ritual was one of respect and an outpouring of heartfelt feelings and love. She was allowed to be buried beside her husband in a human cemetery instead of in a Narin resting place.

Colonel Sobel had married Angela McCormick in a small ceremony presided over by Pastor Ames who had also presided over the funerals given for humans. He was maturing as a pastor and as an advisor and was actually a comfort to those who sought his council.

There had never been a way to counteract the damage done by the toxin which harmed the Narin's ability to pro-create; Dr. Kindle and other scientists would keep trying.

Marco and Allison had a daughter, Jamie, now three-years old; she looked like Allison, medium length light brown curly hair and a few freckles with grey eyes. She was taught by the Colonel's wife, Angela.

Allison had decided to teach gymnastics, JAS'AR and MY'AR had been enrolled and also mentored the younger students. Jacob was into basketball.

The modes of travel on Bright Star besides walking, were bicycles, motorbikes, hovercraft and riding horses which helped everyone to reach their goals in business, schooling, and recreation.

Marco and Lieutenant Vann from Battalion II co-owned a communications business and had communication towers strategically placed on the outskirts of towns and further away into desolate areas near mountain ranges to accommodate future growth of population and needs. Marco now began to teach the subject and advanced electronics.

There were classes on Narin as a second language attended by humans and another, English as a second language for Narins who preferred to speak the language rather than use telepathy to learn the language.

One evening, Jason, Myra and the children travelled to the ocean with Colonel Sobel and Angela. There was a small mountain range in the distance with trees, some earlier terra forming helped nature along after the residents came. It was a pleasant place to be. The large moon could be seen in the distance even though it was hours before dark. A game of tag football was initiated. Jacob had grown taller and his leg showed no signs of having been lame as he played. All participated in the game.

Later, Myra and Angela had time to talk.

"I can't get over Jacob," Angela said, "and majoring in engineering and science."

"We're proud of him and he's adjusted well to all of us . . . how are you and the Colonel?"

"Very well, he's quite special to me."

"He has mentored Jason and Steven, they have the upmost respect for him, my father certainly does."

There was now yelling and running as the game got wilder. Finally Jason bowed out for a moment, he wasn't wearing shoes.

"Got something in my foot, be right back." He saw a red spot on the ball of his foot, touching it became impossible it was so painful.

"Let me have a look," Angela said, "I was a nurse before I became a teacher."

Jason didn't cry out, but obviously it was very painful.

"It feels like something is in there Jason."

"Looks like I'm in a time-out," he said looking at the Colonel.

"We should get back and get that looked at," the Colonel said.

"No way, I'll have it looked at."

"Promise?" Myra said with a worried look.

"Promise."

They built a small fire and grilled steak. The evening was beautiful.

"Jason, how's the foot?" Angela asked.

"I almost think nothing happened."

"Get it looked at . . . soon. We don't know what micro-organisms might be on our new world."

"I will."

Suddenly the kids ran by screaming at each other.

"You and Angela want kids?" Jason laughed as he asked.

Colonel Sobel thought for a moment, "Maybe."

"They're worth it, all of it. Honestly, a blended child isn't that different from humans. They love to run and play. Boundaries have to be set as with all kids."

"But you were so young when your children were born, you could enjoy their youth and you matured quickly."

"Believe me, I didn't know if I was up to it as a young person, but they matured me into becoming a dad even as I grew up."

"Proud of you Jason."

"I had help," he said looking at Myra.

When they returned home hours later Jason remarked how pleasant the evening had been. As they were walking with the Colonel and Angela suddenly Lieutenant Miller came in their direction, both Jason and the Colonel walked over to him as he signaled to them, both dreading his ravings.

"Listen, something is here on this planet that's going to kill all of us . . ."

The Colonel interrupted but the Lieutenant had more to say, "This is important. There is something in the ground, it enters where it can, lethal to humans . . . it has been here all along. See about your foot Jason." Then he left.

This startled both Jason and the Colonel.

"How did he know about my foot?"

"Let's go have it checked, now."

"Myra, back in a while, kids behave, good to see you Angela."

"No definitive answer," the doctor said. "Something definitely pierced your foot; this scanner doesn't show what." A blood test was then given.

"It doesn't hurt now."

"We'll check it again tomorrow with another device and have the blood test results." There was a pause then, "I hate to tell you both this, but several people have come to my office complaining of searing bites that occurred on different parts of their bodies and just like you we only have ideas. All those bitten are getting very weak and sick."

"This is news to me, why wasn't I informed?" the Colonel asked.

"We thought we could control it, this seemed like a bug situation, not serious."

"When was the first?"

"Alma Pierce, two weeks ago, doesn't know where the bite occurred, but had searing pain for about half an hour. She is hospitalized here as of last Thursday, extreme weakness, flu like symptoms are beginning."

"What about Sanctus?"

"We don't know yet. Should we restrict travel to and from? We can't say."

Colonel Sobel talked with VE'AR, who hadn't sensed the presence of the creatures.

The next day the doctor saw Jason accompanied by the Colonel and VE'AR. The results of the blood test were given. He now used a heat sensing device developed by Narin—human collaboration which revealed the presence of an amoeba type creature that, "Survives well in a sandy environment as well as in water and can enter the soft tissues of the human body easily and will ravage the body in some manner; I'm painting a bleak picture here."

"The Narins?" the Colonel asked as he looked at VE'AR.

"They seem unaffected and the children who are mixed."

Jason was concerned about his family. "So if this thing can't be stopped we humans die, but our Narin blended children as well as the Narins will be spared?"

"It would seem so."

"What should we do?" the Colonel asked.

"Bring every scientist on board for now," the doctor replied.

"We will restrict travel to Sanctus as a precaution," the Colonel told VE'AR.

Colonel Sobel called a meeting the next day of the Council; doctors, scientists representing humans and Narins would speak to the public about this.

This news startled everyone. VE'AR and a Narin scientist spoke later.

"With your permission Colonel and the Council, the science ship will be coming in three days and orbit Bright Star until this matter is solved."

"Agreed," he replied. "We must find all who have been bitten then escort them to our medical facility."

After the meeting VE'AR talked to Jason, "We'll make every effort."

"I know . . . I have a class to teach while I still can."

VE'AR could read him and knew he was devastated.

After his class he stopped by one of the galleys instead of going home, he found ice cream, he bought a half gallon and was about to eat it alone. VE'AR and Jacob came in and joined him. Each got a spoon and shared the ice cream.

"How are you?" VE'AR asked.

"Puzzled, down."

"We will win this . . . this ice cream is very good."

"It is, isn't it Jacob?"

"Yes, it's good."

"Tomorrow there are some tests then I go to the Council Chamber for . . ."

"Your will?"

"Jacob, don't read my mind and don't interrupt or finish my sentences."

"Sorry Dad." Jacob sensed his father's despair and turmoil which he had tried to mask.

Jason hugged him. They finished the ice cream then walked home.

"It seems that our two species have made so much progress together and now we will be exterminated with only markers to indicate we existed."

"Your children, your mates and friends will be a testament so all will remember . . . it won't come to that."

"Jacob, VE'AR and I need to talk, tell your mother I'll be there soon."

Jason and VE'AR walked for a while in the park as they talked.

"We aren't giving up Jason, don't you."

"I am trying VE'AR, but I'm . . . this is going to destroy everyone human. I suppose we deserve this after what the Narin race has been through."

"No, the human race doesn't deserve this and we will fight to preserve all of you, we are connected."

Jason looked at VE'AR saying nothing for a moment, then, "What is the next logical step?"

"It is recommended that every human, all ages, even babies be put in stasis before death. Tomorrow the scientists both Narin and human will inform us . . . the toxin could end all of this killing the amoeba infestation."

Jason was startled at the statement. "That won't happen, why would you say that?"

"It was only a suggestion."

"A bad one VE'AR. There will be a meeting of the Council, only for us on this very thing . . . why we would even vote on this I cannot imagine because we wouldn't use it; Colonel Sobel has sent a warning to Earth about this situation."

"I know. Try to believe our efforts will be successful."

"I will VE'AR . . . come be with us this evening."

"There is much to do Jason, I must decline." He touched Jason's shoulder, "Till tomorrow."

Scientists, doctors, human and Narin and anyone who could come attended the meeting the next day to inform everyone of the findings and recommendations. One scientist began, "There have been several that are dying painfully as an amoeba which seemed to be dormant on this planet, now apparently awakened, enters the human body in some manner causing a painful sore as it enters then ravages a person's insides causing death within three to four weeks. Children of a blended heritage and our Narin partners and friends are not in danger. Flu like symptoms come just before death."

"The Narin science ship is on its way and will remain in orbit. We appreciate the efforts of the Narins on our behalf," the Colonel told them.

Another scientist then spoke, "Stasis seems the only way to give us more time to fight this, the amoeba will then cease to destroy its host until the host becomes active again. We must prepare enough of the chambers, five hundred as quickly as possible and more in case they are needed."

"I suggest all of you get your affairs in order, prepare documents, wills, anything pertinent as soon as possible," the Colonel told them, "and concentrate on helping to build these chambers. There will also be a meeting here tomorrow for the five hundred of us to take a vote on a matter to be discussed . . . let's get going."

Everyone left.

Steven contacted Jason, they met at a coffee shop.

"How's it going?" Steven asked.

"I was infected a week ago, now trying to get my affairs in order, and you?"

"I felt something on my arm as I was working in the hover port. Two days ago I saw the doctor; Shirley hasn't been infected but there is no way to protect her and our unborn child, stasis might be the only way of surviving until there is a solution."

"So you're going to be a father?" Jason smiled. "How is she?"

"Scared, two months into the pregnancy . . . we didn't tell you or Myra or anyone, she asked that as a precaution." Jason understood.

"Sorry you came here?"

There was a hesitation then, "No, neither one of us are sorry we came, it has been a challenge for sure, something you certainly understand."

"Are Myra and the kids holding up?"

"So far. As you heard in the meeting, the Narins and our blended children should be safe; the Narins are doing everything possible to save us."

"I believe that especially after spending time with AR'TYN aboard Breedlove's ship."

"We vote tomorrow."

"There shouldn't be a vote. Killing off the Narins to protect ourselves doesn't make sense."

"Agreed."

"It's been good to have you and Myra as friends. If things work out we'll manage to get into more trouble, crashing onto a planet or finding new friends out there, visiting M13 perhaps."

"Things will work out Steven. Congratulate Shirley. I'm going to file papers at the courthouse then use the afternoon to work on the stasis chambers."

"See you there," Steven said.

The next day a meeting convened with the humans on Bright Star. The human half of the ruling council conducted this meeting.

Colonel Sobel began, "We are dying, none of us will live. There is only hope if our Narin counterparts find a way to destroy this enemy within our planet. If we use the toxin we destroy our Narin friends, mates, children; we might live but at what cost? Our race sent this into space before we were aware of how it had been used harming the Narins."

Jackson Kindle spoke next. "We have had the challenges like no one else from Earth. My son Jason met an alien being who was willing to save our ship. Together they joined humankind to Narin and formed an alliance between two species. The Narin leader, VE'AR, welcomed us, has been a friend helping us through several situations. I cannot imagine why there would even be a vote on the toxin except to show our resolve to not harm our friends."

Others stood up and spoke, all were adamant about not using the toxin.

"Now we vote, a show of hands."

Everyone voted no.

"Then it is unanimous," the Colonel said, "let the record show it. Now we have work to do, this meeting is adjourned." He then met with VE'AR.

"I assume you already know."

"Yes Colonel, all of you made a difficult choice."

"We did the right thing, this was our only choice. The human population on Sanctus should stay on Bright Star in stasis in case any were infected as they travelled here on visits . . . our scientists believe this is a necessary precaution."

"Agreed . . . another matter of concern, AR'TYN is headed to KA'OW in a desperate attempt to converse with the Crystal Entity. Wanda has been placed in stasis as of this morning. He has broken the law by doing this."

"I hope he is successful, we'll discuss the legalities of his actions later. The Crystal might yield information vital to our survival, but he might also become fuel for the Crystal to feed off of . . . let me know."

Jason felt weak that evening but pushed himself to entertain the kids, he knew he was dying but wouldn't give in to it for as long as possible. Myra cooked his favorite foods and plenty of pizza and ice cream to soothe him.

AR'TYN and three other Narins reached KA'OW in an effort to get help and information. He beamed down to the planet alone, only placing himself in danger. He tried to communicate with the Crystal who had instructed him three years ago on returning the children and finding fuel for Bright Star and Earth, but he saw no one. Moments later it did appear giving him a type of greeting. Suddenly there were hundreds of the Entities standing, encircling both AR'TYN and the Crystal. AR'TYN looked around trying not to appear nervous then faced the Crystal who dismissed the others, they departed, the two of them were now alone. AR'TYN related the problem on Bright Star which was killing the humans.

"We need your help . . . you met my wife when I brought you to our home in your crystal form. She is human and is dying as are all humans on Bright Star."

The Crystal knew about the amoeba and gave a solution as well as a suggestion. It then asked about the boy Jacob whose parents died there three years ago. This startled AR'TYN who communicated that he was doing well but had a new father who was dying from the amoeba. "His name is Jason Kindle, he assisted in getting the Entity Children back home to this planet we call KA'OW, The Ancients."

The Crystal remembered him and an incident when he and another aboard a flying vehicle landed there and the ground gave way injuring both and remembered how one of them had stayed in the storage area with AR'TYN as the children were returned. The Crystal communicated more with AR'TYN about a solution to purge Bright Star itself. The planet was to be bathed in a green spectral light that would be emanating from a star in the Ianis constellation. The light would be magnified as it hit the planet, then for ten complete revolutions. The infected, who were in stasis, would be taken into space and exposed to that green spectral light. The Narins should protect themselves as much as possible from that light. Their thoughts were still joined, "We encountered these creatures and defeated them and so will you."

"We appreciate your advice, be well." AR'TYN left but felt there was hope.

In a week much had been done to prepare and retrofit four ships for the journey into space carrying those in stasis chambers and to protect the Narins aboard from the green light. They mourned for their human mates and friends but were motivated more than ever to save mankind whatever the cost even to using the toxin which no human wanted or would have sanctioned. All of the other Narins who wouldn't be aboard any of the four ships and the blended children would be transported to Sanctus until Bright Star was purged. All animals would be left on Bright Star and wouldn't survive.

Another week passed, Jason was no longer able to work. Myra and the children took care of him until he was moved to the hospital. His concern was for them. VE'AR assured him that everyone would be all right. "Until you get well." They shook hands, it was evident that Jason's strength was gone.

"Don't let them clone us."

"I'll be travelling with you."

"For all it means to have you with us, won't you need to be with your people? With Myra?"

"You are my people," VE'AR replied. He left so Myra could tell Jason a last goodbye. He went into a hallway with the children to console them, Jacob was inconsolable; VE'AR turned pale for a few moments. Myra turned pale and sat by her father.

"Is it safe for you, all of you out there?" She asked.

"We Narins are strong and we'll protect ourselves . . . AR'TYN is also going, we must follow exactly the instructions from the Crystal Entity."

"How long before the four ships reach Ianis?"

"Baring trouble, two years." VE'AR then stood up, hugged Myra and left to check on Jason. As he watched the two Narin doctors, "Be careful with this one," he said telepathically.

One of the doctors then spoke, "We know who he is," as if to reassure VE'AR, "and we'll be careful with all of them." Jason was then moved into a stasis chamber.

Within two weeks all four Narin ships departed.

CHAPTER XIII

GALAXY—THE JOURNEY

VE'AR looked around the ship, a forth of it was filled with two-hundred and fifty in stasis chambers. Another ship like it was carrying the second group. Two more ships would escort these larger ones. Four large oval spectral analysis devices were manufactured and attached to the top outer hull of each ship in order to find this particular spectral signature. They were several feet across and half a foot thick, five feet in height protected by a force field. There were scientists aboard each ship. All were committed to this mission no matter how long or how dangerous, everyone had a job to do. Reading and education were encouraged to keep mentally sharp for the long journey.

Several had a human mate in stasis aboard ship. They would also be discussing for four years their interaction with the human world. Some told more than was necessary concerning joining and copulation. VE'AR decided to devote time to discussing matters both verbally and telepathically with Jason; even in stasis Jason would absorb and later remember these lessons. He told him about the origin of the Narin race and about his growing up. He would teach Jason several subjects ranging from the sciences to advanced math and discoveries on different worlds since he loved astronomy. He thought often about Myra and the children. The Narin population aboard compelled him to be with them for the socialization and encouragement they needed and to be forthcoming about Jason, his first human family member.

Scientific discoveries would be one of the secondary focal points of the trip for the crew. Exercise was certainly part of the Narin regiment. There were both men and women aboard. Men were generally the military while women and men were the doctors, scientists, attendants, navigators and pilots.

Travelling into space beyond the Milky Way Galaxy presented many spectacular sights. One was a major solar flare shooting outward from a large yellow sun one hundred times the size of Bright Star's sun. Solar flares were the most energetic of the solar disturbances, this one having erupted as an intensely bright area in a chromosphere plague. The Narin ships were not close enough to be in danger.

Stars and those being formed within a nebula sparkled like jewels. Meteor showers were not as rampant as they were within the Milk Way. A previously unknown comet, newly discovered, brought excitement as it was documented by the Narin astrophysicists. An unknown solar system with twenty orbiting planets and their moons was the next discovery. Then Shear Alfvén Waves appeared, named after a human scientist Hannes Alfvén, who predicted their existence. They were magnetized plasma with special patterns of color; sparkles appeared in the waves proportional to the electric field in the plasma induced by the wave. Then there were the anomalies, the unusual events in space. Each discovery was visually documented so the Narin's human counterparts could enjoy what they had seen once they were awakened from stasis.

Nine months later as their journey continued, there was suddenly an increase in the brightness of a nearby star by tens of thousands of times as it became temporarily unstable undergoing a quick, violent but superficial explosion. The Super Nova blew debris in several directions hitting the Narin ships. A large hole was blown out of the first, there was genuine panic as they attempted to seal the hole and get past the star which engulfed the ships in fiery debris. The stasis chambers were their main concern. The force fields around each were being pushed to their limits. Several minutes were like hours as the crews attempted to seal the hull breaches and get past the nova. One Narin officer, a woman, Lieutenant CH'AR temporarily took the place of the Narin commander when he was injured. Her orders were followed to the letter as she was taking drastic measures to save the ship. Everyone was working frantically as they began to seal the large gaping hole and smaller ones. VE'AR was watching her carefully knowing how capable she was; she was one of the 'AR family, a distant relative. He heard one of the crew remark earlier of her qualifications and being military and unmarried. She was familiar with him not only as Narin leader but his earlier exploits when he proved himself in the military as he rose in rank to general; she had considered him unattainable as a mate as he had chosen to remain unmarried after his wife was murdered.

The other three ships had sustained damage but attempted to protect the more damaged one using their laser weapons as shields out and away from the nova. After they passed the danger they stopped to do major intricate repairs losing only three days on their journey.

She and VE'AR spoke later, "Repairs are almost completed, we are resuming our journey."

"You handled the situation with efficiency."

"I appreciate your words Leader."

"You have time to converse with me? Coffee?"

"Yes, I believe so, humans have come up with some interesting beverages and foods."

They entered a large galley, one of four, they sat. Several of the Narins kept their human facade to honor their loved ones and friends as did VE'AR and Lieutenant CH'AR also out of respect.

"How have you been Leader?"

"Well for the most part, many things have happened. Jason, my son-in-law has united our two species and brought changes for the better."

"You are proud of him."

"Yes, Myra and Jason have three children, blended we call them, the best of both worlds. Many Narins are taking human partners and now have children and think of Bright Star as home. When this mission is over you should visit us."

"A possibility," she said, "Sanctus has proved to be a good choice for an outpost and for getting acquainted with humans; the terra forming was quite a project."

"So you will be stationed there?"

"For the time being it seems."

"Who knows, you might find a reason to stay. There are many challenges out here . . . we are witnessing a major one in the making."

She smiled, he was enjoying her company, she found him interesting to be with. Several minutes later she left.

He would socialize more with the crew then visit Jason as he continued to teach him about different subjects. He told of events that happened as he grew up on NARIN'MAR. There were battles fought against opposing forces who were fanatical and warlike, for revolution against the authorities of peace there. The family of 'AR joined with others to keep order from chaos and banished or executed the others. VE'AR became a general as he had also fought in several of the later skirmishes then the 'ARs returned NARIN'MAR to a rule of peace which had now lasted for two hundred years. Those who were banished were never allowed to return to NARIN'MAR or any planets occupied by the Narin Federation.

CH'AR found VE'AR sitting by Jason's stasis chamber one evening, reading to him.

"I am adding to his education," he told her.

"When he awakens, his head might explode."

"Let's hope not."

She looked around at the others visiting their human partners in stasis. "We're going to do this VE'AR, we're almost half-way to Ianis."

In the months that followed, VE'AR and CH'AR got to know one another better. He told Jason about her and how she piloted the ship through the destructive supernova. "Her commander resumed his duties a month after the incident and gave her a medal for her having saved the ship and many lives . . . something else Jason, she and I are joining tonight."

She came by, they left together for her compartment; they had several liaisons in the months that followed.

Two months went by. They entered a region of space unknown to them. "The very stars seem to have disappeared," one of the officers remarked.

For a month it was like that as if something had covered every star in every direction. Several Narins experienced depression and anxiety during this time and felt there was a presence in the darkness, VE'AR felt it as well.

"Something is out there," a Narin scientist BEN'ZAR remarked, "living in the dark matter. I don't sense hostility at the moment but curiosity."

Then mysteriously all four ships were suddenly stopped which caused more anxiety.

"Why do you think it lives in the dark matter?" Commander AUR'ZIN asked him.

"Because it is dark matter."

No one could comprehend this.

"It isn't hostile? It has stopped our ships. It told you?"

"I felt it," BEN'ZAR said, "communicating with me . . . I don't sense malovence."

VE'AR and AR'TYN agreed with him.

"Now what?" Lieutenant CH'AR asked them.

"Wait."

A day passed, frustration was growing. Three Narins agreed to attempt contacting the Presence. VE'AR was first; so much energy surrounded him at once that he collapsed, he was taken to the medical facility aboard, a more sophisticated sickbay. Then BEN'ZAR suggested to the Presence not to overload their minds which were incapable of processing so much energy and information at once. Then he began receiving information not being overloaded. AR'TYN was next. All were then scanned even VE'AR in sickbay who recovered in a few hours. There were then discussions aboard ship, now a meeting. The Presence read VE'AR's mind and entered Lieutenant CH'AR. She had been chosen because of being Narin, a female, and on VE'AR's mind. She turned and faced them, her eyes had darkened, her speech was different. The Narins there remained calm but knew they couldn't defeat this Entity nor help CH'AR.

An hour had gone by as the Presence asked about the Narin race and about the humans aboard. VE'AR explained that the humans were injured by a small creature and would die if not cured by a green spectral light in a constellation they called Ianis. It then looked over this one ship describing the two species as weak. It revealed that it was without physical form and was as old as time itself. It had created the blackness over the stars to confound the ships into stopping and when that didn't work it stopped the ships. It further conveyed that it had placed information about itself into VE'AR, BEN'ZAR and AR'TYN.

For three days it studied life in its physical form using CH'AR as a host, experiencing interaction and comradery with other beings. Eating, breathing, feeling vulnerable, happy, sad, a range of emotions. It answered many questions for the curious Narins. It would release them soon after one more question; it didn't present the question yet, so everyone assumed it would return later. The Presence then left CH'AR.

VE'AR and CH'AR had planned their liaison after the Entity left for the evening. He was in his compartment waiting for her. She entered saying nothing until she joined with him. VE'AR only now felt the presence of the Entity as he held her. It didn't understand love or being joined until now. He had no choice but to cooperate and protect CH'AR. Two hours later the Entity left them, both CH'AR and VE'AR were exhausted.

Morning came, CH'AR tried to awaken him. He looked at her, finally awake, he pulled her to him and kissed her.

"Are you . . . ?"

"Yes, the Entity came back so suddenly I couldn't warn you. As you see it got the answer and we are unharmed, exhausted, but unharmed."

"To experience what love is, joining, feelings."

"Should we keep this between us?"

"Yes, I think we should." They kissed.

Three months had passed. There was shouting in the navigation room. Stars had been visible since the Entity left them.

"The light," one said as he studied the light penetrating from one of the large spectral indicators, this particular light they had searched for.

Months passed. The two ships with those in stasis then retracted the overhead shielding outer doors and allowed the light in, careful not to expose themselves for long periods of time as the passengers in stasis were given heavy exposure to the light. Three times of exposure then all were checked for any signs of the amoeba.

"Clear," the Narin doctors said.

The ships remained stationary. Each would now become part of a process to direct the green light to Bright Star. Magnification devices were used to focus the light as they formed a path from ship to ship bending the light to reach the planet. This process continued for months then when there was nothing to impede the light on its journey, the ships travelled warp 7 to Sanctus to await the light going warp 1 to reach its target and purge Bright Star of the amoeba infestation.

Two years later they arrived in orbit above Sanctus. Everyone was freed from the stasis chambers.

VE'AR was there when Jason was freed.

"Did we make it?" he asked as a doctor was working over him.

"We did . . . there were a few incidents, nothing we couldn't handle, the green spectral light is on its way to Bright Star; we will remain on Sanctus for the time being. Not one Narin or human was lost."

"That's great news VE'AR . . . my head feels like it's about to explode."

"That will pass, you had assimilated a great deal of knowledge over four years."

Jason laughed, "I am now remembering, but who is Lieutenant CH'AR? You both did what?"

"I'll tell you later, Myra has beamed aboard."

"She's all right?"

"Oh yes, and the children."

Myra found him quickly as he was being taken to rehab, they embraced. "Four years, how can it be that you're back and well again?"

"I missed you even as I slept, VE'AR was there with me, with all of us."

"When I get you home . . ."

He smiled wanting her. "We have many Narins to thank."

"And we will," VE'AR said.

Across the room they saw many Narins with their mates now well again. AR'TYN found Wanda, he held her, there were tears, "You're well again."

"Four years," she said, "but you were travelling with me."

"Yes, it seemed longer."

"How did you figure it out?"

"A visit with the Crystal Entity, I broke the law."

She kissed him again, "I'm glad you broke the law."

"There will be a penalty for this, I don't know how I will be punished."

"Perhaps I will think of something but first I must get my strength back."

He smiled. Their children came aboard, a daughter and a son now about six.

The new residents on Sanctus now began building houses, creating more farms, more children were born, more schools were built. Colonel

Sobel and the governing council from Bright Star were welcomed and temporarily became part of the governing body on Sanctus.

Steven's wife Shirley delivered a healthy baby boy, Mark; the child was in stasis inside his mother for four years. There was a celebration over the birth and over the success of the mission to save mankind.

Basketball and other sports were played in one of three sportoriums where Narins and humans would challenge each other as they interacted in each other's sports.

Everyone had jobs to do. Sanctus was very special to both human and Narins. Many changes were made to add to this recently terra formed world; the Bright Star population still looked forward to their return home.

VE'AR and CH'AR visited with Jason, Myra, Colonel Sobel, and Angela one evening. Telepathically he told Jason that he considered mating CH'AR. No one else was told. They all spoke of the four year trip to save humanity. CH'AR was given high praise for her role as saving the ship hit by the debris from the supernova. She didn't want the praise but accepted it along with a medal from her superiors.

Later, Steven, Jason, the Colonel and VE'AR met for lunch and talked about the new challenges now and when they would return home in two years; everyone saw the visual documentaries of the trip. VE'AR revealed certain information about the Dark Matter Entity.

One of the temporary residents on Sanctus, a human named Malcolm who was also cured by the green spectral light, was about to board a mining ship to search for fuel. As he looked in a mirror preparing himself for the journey, he put on his glasses, his eyes darkened for a moment as he combed his greying hair, then he left for the ship.

Jason remembered VE'AR telling him about the harbingers of evil who battled against peace and order.

"I almost imagine I was there witnessing all of it and you as a young Narin soldier."

"It was a terrible time rivaling Earth's. Our weapons were powerful and destructive. The thoughts that were used against us were devastating much like those of AR'BIN against Myra and yourself. The battles continued for a century . . . death and destruction on NARIN'MAR on an unprecedented scale. Families were torn apart. Finally we got the upper hand."

"You allowed yourself to be captured, tortured, I remember these images."

"So I could gain access to sensitive material. Those who attempted to pull information from my mind had the tables turned as you humans say. I took the essence of their minds and channeled it to those who were fighting to put down the rebellion so every move they would make was known to our side."

"So you didn't expect to be rescued."

"No. Obviously I was."

"These were banished?"

"Yes, or executed, their choice."

"You became a general."

"During the later skirmishes."

"Were all the banished able to reproduce?"

VE'AR wasn't expecting a question like this then, "Only the women who were mated to them and were willing and those who fought beside them could be joined with them, no others."

"Are you curious about what progress they made?"

"Yes, there are the flybys and monitoring devices. They have the capability to leave their worlds which they do time-to-time . . . they don't desire to be reunited with us, just make more powerful weapons to destroy us."

The Dark Matter Entity began studying humankind on Sanctus. VE'AR detected its presence and told Colonel Sobel, Jason and certain others. BEN'ZAR and AR'TYN were also aware of its presence. It was learning from the human host Malcolm who was one of the mining experts sent to investigate a nearby moon. It began contacting those VE'AR knew. Jason was one to be contacted, VE'AR warned him.

"Nothing can stop it," he told Jason and Myra. "It has studied us and our minds are vulnerable to it. So far it hasn't harmed anyone."

"When it was aboard the ship you said it entered Lieutenant CH'AR and left after three days then . . ."

"It returned to her as we joined."

"That was bad timing," Jason said as he looked at Myra, she was in disbelief as she listened.

"It is back to study humanity now, to study you because you and Myra are prevalent in my thoughts and you are human."

"So do we cooperate? What can we do?"

"Nothing, don't fight it . . . it only wants answers and after that I don't know."

Jason was very concerned, "So everything, every memory, every experience it will know."

"Yes."

"How will it react if I ask it to leave Myra and our children alone?"

"No one can say, don't come across as aggressive to it."

Jason looked at VE'AR, "I won't. You'll know if it's in me, right?"

"Yes."

The next day Jason was teaching class, afterward a man approached him, the miner. Jason turned, there was no one else in the classroom except the man who now sat in the first row, his eyes were darkened.

"Teach me," he said.

Jason was nervous, but cordial as he was gathering his papers shoving them into his briefcase as quickly as possible. "What would I teach you? Your knowledge is extensive, we should learn from you."

"VE'AR has told you about me, do I frighten you?"

"To be honest, I don't know. Are you a friend? Do you intend us harm?"

"Neither, I want you to teach me."

"What can I teach you?"

"What it's like to be human. Take me to your mate, to your children."

"I can't do that, you might harm them."

"I won't harm them . . . let's go."

They walked together, VE'AR was aware, he followed.

The Entity turned to him, "They will not be harmed."

VE'AR backed off, Jason glanced at him then proceeded home.

"Jason?" Myra greeted him with a kiss, the kids hugged him.

"This is . . ."

"Malcolm, I am a miner."

She read Jason's thoughts and knew who the miner was. "Come in by all means, dinner is almost ready." She was frightened. "Kids, dinner . . . this is an acquaintance of your Dad, Malcolm."

They all shook his hand, his eyes weren't reflecting the Dark Entity inside. The kids sensed something but Myra told them to stop.

The Entity wanted to see their home. He asked about Curtis the dog and, "You can call me Malcolm."

"Perhaps we should eat first," Jason said. They all sat, they ate.

The Entity used phrases from the mind of the miner, "Great Honey, this is the best, better than sex. What is it you have prepared?"

Myra wanted to laugh, Jason didn't laugh but was amused, the kids said nothing, they smiled.

"Narin steak, potatoes, beans, carrots . . . we grow our vegetables."

"Wow!" The Entity seemed genuinely pleased. "Jason, I would also like that," pointing to a bottle of wine.

"I wouldn't recommend it."

The Entity held the glass until Jason had filled it.

"I've never tasted anything like it."

The miner got very drunk which affected the ability of the Entity to use the body as effectively. Jason then sent the kids to his parents for the night.

An hour passed, by then the miner had overcome the effects of the wine as did the Entity. Jason took him on a tour of the house. He played both human and Narin music. It asked him questions about his home world Earth and why Narins and humans intermarried. Finally the Entity entered Myra and went with Jason to the bedroom. Hours later it again entered Malcolm's body; both Jason and Myra were worn out and slept.

They overslept, both were late for classes, they hugged.

"You all right?" She asked him.

"I am, and you?" he touched her face.

"Tired, but fine . . . is he gone?"

"Yes, hopefully really gone."

Jason met with VE'AR a few minutes as he walked to class.

"We went the distance after it entered Myra, she seemed unharmed. He ate dinner with us, we sent the kids to my parents for the night."

"And you?"

"I'm fine after the initial shock of seeing him in my classroom after the other students left."

"He seemed fixated on how we join which leads me to wonder if he could possibly be considering procreating. I have only a gut feeling that the Entity is male."

"I feel like he is male. Talk later?"

"Meet you at the coffee shop."

As Jason made his way to class he again saw the Entity who was in the body of the miner. He sat several rows up.

"My apologies for being late," he told the students . . . "let's begin chapter five."

The Entity approached him as the second class ended. "No harm to you or your mate was intended."

"We are unharmed but if you put us through that again we will be harmed. What do you hope to find in all this?" He sat with the Entity.

"I realize now what it means to be alone, isolated, and what it would mean to have someone . . . being with others; I want to breathe the air, taste food like that Narin steak. I want children like your children, like the children I see on this world."

VE'AR then entered the room and spoke, "Should I address you as Malcolm?"

"Yes."

"Your children won't be like these children, we are different from you and who would carry your children . . . you are masculine, Jason and I are masculine, our female partners carried our children."

Malcolm stood up, "Then I should look for a female who is willing without doing harm to her, I need to impress the females."

VE'AR and Jason looked at each other then at the Entity.

"And if there is no one willing?" VE'AR asked.

The Entity said nothing more and left.

"VE'AR?"

"I don't know, hopefully it will leave, there is no one who would volunteer."

They left for coffee. Jason called Myra.

Malcolm began to visit hospitals and morgues with permission from Colonel Sobel and an accompanying doctor and guards, questioning human and Narin about injuries and death. One patient, Jennifer, a human, was dying. Malcolm talked with her and afterward he left with the others. He knew about her and that soon she would cease to exist.

He returned that evening. "Don't be frightened." He sat with her. "You don't know who I am or where I come from, but I will show you."

He filled her mind with images of time at its beginning and of meeting the Narins in deep space beyond the Milky Way Galaxy on their way to the green spectral light. "You were in stasis with the others, I was there in the blackness of space, part of the dark matter. I learned about the Narins and about humans and returned aboard one of the ships to Sanctus."

"What are you?"

"Part of the dark matter in space," he told her again. "I have been in this human body since arriving on Sanctus."

"What do you want with me? Is Malcolm your name?"

"Malcolm is the name of my host. I want you to get well and to join with me. I'm not trying to frighten you and it would be your choice."

"How could I join with you?"

"We will find out. First I must do this." She is frightened. He places a hand on her head and several minutes later he leaves her.

The next morning Jennifer is awake and unclear about dreaming or did she experience a visit from an alien entity. The doctors couldn't explain her miraculous recovery. VE'AR, Colonel Sobel, and the doctors asked her questions.

"You understand that Malcolm is the host for the Dark Matter Entity?"

"I'm trying to wrap my mind around it, he was talking to me about joining."

"The Entity is experiencing everything he can, much like a child he is curious. It seems he is the only one of his kind and he is masculine. He wants what we have, a mate and to procreate," VE'AR told her and those who were discussing the situation.

"And what if I refuse?"

"Then we don't have a way to protect you. It's up to you . . . we can try to reason with him," the Colonel told her.

"If I have a clean bill of health release me and I'll talk to him."

Everyone was on edge over this, the Entity sensed it. He found her.

"You are looking better," he said, "you're not sick anymore."

"And I have you to thank for this."

They went to a small sandwich shop followed by two soldiers who were trying not to look aggressive or menacing.

"I suppose they have to come."

"They are only trying to protect me, but they couldn't really because your powers are much greater."

"Have you considered my words?"

"You frighten me."

"That wasn't my intent."

"How could we ever join?"

"I'm still working on that one . . . would you be willing?"

"If I said 'no' what would happen? Would I become sick again? Would you harm these humans and Narins who tried to show you kindness?"

Malcolm stood up, "No, to all of these questions, I don't want to harm anyone."

"Please sit," she said. "As you know I am a nurse, I care for these people and I care for you. I don't know if I can do as you ask. I am flattered that you would want me to join with you. You must know our customs, that we normally have a time to get to know one another before joining. Sometimes the rules are broken and the relationship is ruined before it was even cultivated, like a garden. Walk with me."

She showed him people walking in the large park, many were with their mates, admiring the beautiful gardens.

"This is what you mean by cultivate?"

"Yes, I would like time to get to know you before I can give you my answer."

"I suppose I can wait, I just asked you yesterday. How do I get to know you?"

"I will show you . . . let me talk to the host."

"Why?"

"Because I will be joining with both of you and I need to know that he is all right with this."

"All right." The Entity left Malcolm.

"What is your name?" she asked him.

"Malcolm Gennings and you are Jennifer, you're beautiful."

"Thank you Malcolm. Are you good with this, being the host to an unknown species from space?"

"I never felt like I was anything, I am a miner, but no wife, no kids, no family. An opportunity came to travel here to Bright Star and start over. I was still empty but one day on Sanctus I encountered a being who felt the same, not asking me at first to be the host but I was willing. Together we have a chance at true happiness and fulfillment."

"Am I part of your happiness?"

"Yes . . . I am not being coursed."

Jennifer became convinced of Malcolm's sincerity.

In the meantime VE'AR talked more to CH'AR about the Entity.

"What if she refuses?" she asked.

"Now that is the question."

They were preparing dinner when AR'TYN communicated his need to speak with VE'AR. He came. "Pardon this intrusion."

"Nothing to pardon, will you have this meal with us?" CH'AR asked. VE'AR nodded his approval.

"The warring forces are coming."

"I know, I felt it," VE'AR replied.

"What is happening?" CH'AR asked.

"The forces of anarchy are planning an assault on the Federation of Narin Planets soon."

"What is the next step?" AR'TYN asked.

"A discussion with the Narin—human Council here on Sanctus."

"Will they come here and to Bright Star?"

"I believe so after attacking the Federation."

A meeting was held.

"There are five moons and eight planets where they are located," VE'AR told them at the first meeting.

"We have felt their anger and rage," AR'TYN said.

"How long?" Colonel Sobel asked.

"Probably two years, perhaps sooner. They will attack NARIN'MAR the Federation Headquarters," a Narin Commander SO'TYN told them. "We must prepare a force to protect Sanctus and Bright Star and those of us who will travel to NARIN'MAR must leave in a few months. Commander BA'LOL will join in the defense of both planets with Colonel Sobel."

Jason and Steven attended the meeting with others representing the pilots and engineers and sat anticipating a war as they listened. They would all participate in protecting Sanctus and Bright Star or travel to NARIN'MAR to defend the Narin home world.

News spread fast, then another meeting was convened a week later for anyone who wanted to attend. Malcolm attended with Jennifer.

"Anyone with other special skills besides our regular crews, we can use you," Colonel Sobel announced.

VE'AR and Commander SO'TYN spoke to everyone about the seriousness of the matter.

"Not only to protect NARIN'MAR but our families here and to protect Bright Star."

Malcolm approached Colonel Sobel after the meeting. "I have a special skill."

He took Malcolm to VE'AR. "You'll want to hear this."

"I believe I can help . . . take me to NARIN'MAR."

There was a long discussion, Jason and Steven heard the conversation.

Preparations were made over the next six months. Narins were sent to orbit Bright Star to protect the planet from invasion. They couldn't remain on the surface and be exposed to the approaching green spectral light when it arrived nor could they risk bringing a contaminant, the amoeba back to their ships and to Sanctus. Humans couldn't be near the surface for the same reasons, but were able to protect the planet from orbit as needed. Sanctus was also protected. Malcolm would go to fight the rebels and to protect the Narin Federation as a gesture of goodwill, he didn't know what he could do to help, but he was sure he had a skill that would prove useful. No one really knew his capability, for the most part, only a few knew that he was a Dark Matter Entity.

"I don't know if I can be killed or wounded," he told those who needed answers. "If I am to travel quickly I must be aboard a ship. I can't give you all the answers because I don't know. I've been out there in that same region of space before Ianis was or the other stars and there I remained alone until all of you came in your ship." This was a theme he often repeated.

"What about Jennifer?" the Colonel asked.

"We are cultivating," came the reply.

Everyone gave Malcolm a strange look.

Chief Engineer Henry, Jason, Chief Engineer Ovilla and the other engineers and mechanics had prepared several ships and retrofitted them with the newer ion engines and weapons that put the human cruisers and warships on an equal footing with the Narin rebel ships; the force fields were sufficient. Those who would pilot the ships were trained by the best which included Steven who actually coordinated how they were trained in mock flights. A Narin Commander SO'TYN also trained those Narins and humans who would be part of the Narin crews and flying Narin ships as needed. Jason was one of those given extra training as he would be piloting one of four rescue ships; the downloads into his mind of information about every ship he had flown wasn't enough without evasive pilot strategy and how and when to use weapons, as defense would become necessary. He was also trained in a Narin war cruiser should it become necessary to fly one.

Three months later they were now enroute to NARIN'MAR. Malcolm was aboard one of the Narin vessels for the trip which would last a year or longer. He was asked many questions. VE'AR, BEN'ZAR and AR'TYN were given knowledge about the Entity earlier while approaching Ianis, but now they asked for more details about the universe and the Entity itself. Jason beamed aboard briefly to listen.

"I can warp space. As you know dark matter is like gravity in that it holds planets, stars and galaxies together. Twenty-three percent, in human terms, of the whole universe consists of dark matter, but I have never been able to communicate with any other source of dark matter . . . why was I alone?"

"No one can answer your question, we haven't the knowledge to do so," BEN'ZAR told him.

"The fact that you're willing to help us speaks of your courage," Jason said.

"I hope I can help all of you. It's better that Jennifer stayed behind, she'll be safe . . . I miss her already. Would I be considered an anomaly?" he asked VE'AR.

"Because you are a Dark Matter Entity and we have never met an Entity of dark matter, then the answer would be 'yes', an unusual and previously unknown life form," VE'AR told him.

"Since NARIN'MAR is about to face attack very soon, who are these anarchists?"

"Those who oppose peace and won't stop until they are at war with destruction and upheaval as their goal. Many of us fought them and banished or executed them. The banishment gave them another chance to redeem themselves but after two-hundred years of peace, they are ready to take our home planet and the other worlds of our Federation of peace."

Malcolm was learning very quickly about war and death, he was determined to assist these Narins and humans who had been kind to him.

Eleven months had passed. They arrived in orbit over NARIN'MAR, all twenty ships of both human and Narin ready to join the Narin Federation fleet.

"It's beautiful," Malcolm said.

"We are on several planets but NARIN'MAR is our origin," Commander SO'TYN told him.

VE'AR and representatives from each ship met with the Narin Council comprising the Federation, Malcolm was with them. Each planet and moon was identified by a signature wave picked up by a monitor on each of the twenty ships; those signatures of the planets and moons of the anarchists were also clearly identified as were their ships.

AN'ZAR a Narin admiral and commander who was coordinating the defense efforts and would be leading the Federation defense force explained the strategy that would be used to defeat the enemy. His ship was a prototype that brought Jason back to NARIN'MAR after his Earth experience to stop Dr. Weed. Admiral AN'ZAR's ship had remained in orbit and temporarily cloaked as were the twenty-five others in the Narin fleet.

"Malcolm, this is our strategy. If you can help us or make suggestions or anyone else, do so now. Rest if you can, we meet in a few hours, be well." Lieutenant CH'AR's words were the last they would hear in the meeting.

"I won't know until we encounter the enemy what I can actually do," he told VE'AR.

The evening hours passed quickly as there was great anxiety among those who would be putting their lives on the line. The preparations were made. Jason and Steven attended a last briefing and met the Narins and humans who would be flying the ships as well as their crews, engineers, among others and the doctors who would be aboard the rescue ships; Jason would pilot one of the four. They were quite large and had a compliment of laser cannons and were the most vulnerable due to size and frequent stops. Steven's ship was more of an attack cruiser, large, heavily armed and faster; the cloaking devices would be more of a hindrance to the ships' force fields and would be deactivated as the battle began.

Colonel Sobel, who was commander of defense operations with Narin Commander BA'LOL was making preparations to engage the enemy. The forces remained in orbit around Bright Star and Sanctus, which was also protected by ground forces as well.

The time had come, enemy ships had now begun an attack on NARIN'MAR. A day of fighting had seen several casualties even with the power grid in place and the extensive defense system. Several ships on both sides sustained damage; the Narin craft with photon engines of matter, antimatter annihilation sent dangerous amounts of gamma rays into space when the engines were targeted and a glow like lightening lit up the sky. The human craft with their ion engines were not as lethal when hit. There were more casualties over the next several hours.

Malcolm was in a smaller cruiser flown by a Narin as he observed the carnage. He then asked to be released and left Malcolm's body which remained aboard. He entered space behind the first line of the enemy fleet then began to grow exponentially and quickly. He threw off their ships' navigational abilities and quickly moved to a smaller enemy vessel covering it and crushing it by a gravitational force he possessed then on to another vessel, larger, like a blanket he covered the larger ship and within minutes destroyed it. The enemy began to lose focus as they had encountered something they couldn't see that was literally able to disengage their navigational instruments and disintegrate their ships.

The Narin—human forces had hoped that Malcolm wouldn't be vulnerable to the weapons as they fired on the enemy who fired with deadly accuracy. There were reports of attacks on other planets of the Federation which were being defended by the inhabitants as best they could until those of the Federation force could assist. The force fields of the ships were being severely tested.

The power grid surrounding NARIN'MAR was beginning to weaken. Malcolm related a thought to VE'AR, even out of the human host he was communicating.

"Pull back."

The ships did. Malcolm came toward the enemy fleet again and took out the most lethal one. He was tiring but tried to cover this one as he did the others. The force field around this one was stronger and the ship was so large that he couldn't totally surround it but covered the aft part and began to siphon off its power as he began to fracture that section crushing it and killing all aboard. The enemy hesitated to withdraw but feared their own fate was in the hands of those possessing a new super weapon, not realizing that a dark matter entity was what was killing them.

The fighting continued into days. As Jason continued the rescue of the wounded and they were brought aboard his ship, he and Steven communicated; unknown to Jason an enemy ship had followed.

"It's on your tail Jason, coming on fast."

They attempted to outmaneuver the smaller cruiser then fired the aft laser cannons. It fired back knocking out their shields.

"Steven, I think this is it, our shields just went, the rebel ship is headed straight for us, we can't . . ."

"Hang in there Jason, I'm coming . . . Jason?"

The transmission abruptly ended as the rebel ship blocked the transmission and was about to fire. Suddenly the rebel ship was hit by a laser blast from a considerable distance away, its weapons disabled.

"It won't fire on you again," a voice said.

"Steven?"

"That would be me."

"Where are you?"

"Later, get going."

The Rebel forces retreated for the moment planning a new strategy. The Entity had returned to the one ship where the host was. VE'AR and the human—Narin commander met with him aboard VE'AR's ship.

"You turned the tide Malcolm," VE'AR told him.

"I haven't anything left to fight with until I can regenerate, I don't know what else will deter them."

Several suggestions were made as he regenerated.

Malcolm and his Narin pilot then allowed themselves to be captured by the Rebels, information was leaked that he had developed a super weapon, the information was from an unknown source. The enemy took them aboard a larger rebel ship. They mentally tortured both, Malcolm got the worst of it. They were taken in the fast ship to their home world, SETTIS, for further interrogation. VE'AR agreed with the decision for Malcolm to go out of desperation not wanting him or the Narin pilot to be tortured but the plan might save thousands of lives. It would take a week to reach SETTIS.

The battle to destroy the Narin Federation continued to grow more intense since they knew of the capture of the creator of the super weapon which had been used against them. When they arrived at the Rebel home world, Malcolm and the Narin pilot were quickly taken for further interrogation.

"There is no weapon," Malcolm told them as he was tortured.

"Then we will find out what you do know."

Malcolm asked them why they were determined to oppose those who pursued peace, even to massacre; he and the pilot were punished for the question.

"I will tell you what I know, but you must allow the pilot to leave."

"No," one replied.

"All right then, bring your leaders to hear this, the ones in charge."

"What will we hear?"

"The truth of how your ships were destroyed."

Several came minutes later.

"Take the Narin pilot out of here," he said pointing to a door. They did as he asked.

"Now where is the weapon?" one asked angrily.

"You're looking at it."

"You?" the Rebel commander laughed. "You're nothing."

Suddenly all exits were locked down as Malcolm, the host was literally covered by the Entity for his protection.

"I am a Dark Matter Entity, Malcolm, I am going to destroy your world and all of you."

All were in disbelief as the Entity began to fill the large room, growing quickly. Several minutes later all entrances were then opened revealing the deaths of all inside. Those outside the room were afraid to confront him and offered no resistance. He communicated with the Narin pilot who had been freed; he found a ship and stayed in orbit until the Entity could join him. Malcolm, the host was left on the ship as the Entity travelled into the atmosphere above the planet then stretched as far as he could covering a wide portion of it and destroying the areas he covered; he did this several times. The power grid went off-line, weapons fire didn't seem to deter the repeated assaults. A few hours passed before he joined the Narin pilot and entered the host again. They would reach NARIN'MAR in a week.

Distress signals were sent to the Rebel forces, the war had ended. The enemy now terrified by reports of their home world having been crushed in several large areas that were lifeless now, retreated even as they were bombarding NARIN'MAR and about to gain the upper hand. Those Rebel ships enroute to Bright Star and Sanctus with the intent of carrying the rebellion there and all out war were recalled.

Malcolm was heralded as a hero. There was a celebration. He wasn't comfortable with his new status and a medal for bravery for him and the Narin pilot. All those who assisted in the war effort, the pilots, engineers, mechanics, medical personnel and others who helped save the Federation were also honored and received commendations.

Loss of life, both human and Narin, was tragic but minimal. Two of the other Federation planets had been attacked leaving more devastation than on NARIN'MAR. VE'AR had contacted the Narin Commander on Sanctus to relay the news to Colonel Sobel.

Now everyone had gotten to know Malcolm.

"This could put you in danger even if they believe that you invented a weapon, not what you are," VE'AR told him.

"Then I must return to Sanctus and talk to someone."

"Would that be Jennifer?" Jason asked.

"Yes."

With the war having ended, the Federation celebrated the heroes again. Everyone got to see NARIN'MAR and its beauty even after the assault on the planet. Jason, VE'AR, BEN'ZAR and Steven met up with SA'MAR the Narin astrophysicist who travelled to Earth with Jason to stop Dr. Weed. They saw the hospital where Myra regenerated and the school where he taught Narin children and adults.

"How did you feel being the only human here?" Steven asked Jason.

"Nervous at first but mostly my mind was on Myra and I had VE'AR to reassure me; everyone went out of their way to make me feel welcome."

Several Narins came to see Jason again asking how he was and about Myra. They welcomed their Leader, VE'AR.

"No gum wrappers in the park SA'MAR if you travel to Earth again," Jason said.

He laughed, "No, not on Earth."

VE'AR knew about the incident. Steven knew about Jason joining the Resistance to stop Dr. Weed but not about the gum wrapper incident.

Especially meaningful to the Narins from Bright Star and Sanctus was getting reacquainted with their families on NARIN'MAR as did CH'AR. She and VE'AR were mated in a Narin ceremony. Jason and a few humans were allowed to attend with Narin friends.

Four days passed, it was time to leave. All would take with them a feeling of goodwill between humans and Narins. The memory of seeing this beautiful planet would last forever; several would return to see more of it as they could.

It would take over a year for all the ships to reach Sanctus and Bright Star as they travelled in a convoy. Bright Star was just now being purged as the spectral green light had finally arrived from Ianis.

There was concern for Malcolm, for his well-being.

"How far now?" he kept asking like a child.

Both Narins and humans suggested activities to occupy his time. Everyone was patient with him as they answered, also asking him more about his existence in that region of space. He knew nothing about the Travellers or the moon M13.

"I will make a suggestion," VE'AR said, "if Jennifer agrees to join with you, perhaps a small moon would make a suitable home."

CH'AR walked in, "That sounds plausible." She hugged VE'AR then sat by him, he smiled.

"Narin women cast their spells," he said.

It was evident that Malcolm wanted Jennifer as a companion as he listened.

Months went by. The ships arrived at Sanctus. Colonel Sobel, his Second, Commander BA'LOL and several of the military and civilians were there to greet them before they left for Bright Star. There was a meeting and another celebration. Myra and Jason found each other, embraced, excited about the Federation's victory over the Rebels and VE'AR mating CH'AR. Malcolm found Jennifer, she kissed him, Steven found Shirley.

Colonel Sobel praised all for their service. "We will have our own celebration when everyone gets settled again," he said, "and all the details."

"Malcolm was there fighting with us, every step," Jason said.

"He turned the tide," VE'AR told the Colonel.

Jennifer heard this, "Really?" She touched his hand.

"They gave me a medal." He showed her. "The others who fought also got medals or commendations."

"We're proud of you Malcolm," the Colonel told him, "and we will celebrate soon."

"I'm proud of you too," Jennifer said.

After hesitating for a moment, "There is something I must ask you."

"Let's go home first Malcolm," she said. "They provided an apartment for me on Sanctus so things will seem different until we are home in a few days."

Colonel Sobel, Jason, and Myra escorted Jennifer and Malcolm home with a gift basket filled with cards and notes from grateful Narins and humans. Jennifer made everyone eat some of the tempting treats and beverages that were also part of the gift basket.

"I must ask you something Jennifer," Malcolm said.

"I should leave now." The Colonel stood up and shook Malcolm's hand.

"We'll stay for a while longer Colonel," Jason said. "I would like another cup of tea."

The Colonel was relieved that Myra and Jason would be there for moral support for Jennifer.

"Can we sit on your patio?" Myra asked.

"Well certainly."

Then with privacy Malcolm asked his question, "Would you consent to be with me?"

"Where would we live?"

"A nearby moon, not far."

"I want to live on Bright Star, to be with people."

"Malcolm, my host and I would agree to that, but what will we do if we can't live there?"

Just then Jason and Myra walked back inside, "We didn't purposely eavesdrop on your conversation, but you should ask the Council tomorrow. Thank you for the meal," Myra and Jason told her.

"We'll talk tomorrow," Jennifer said.

They left feeling like Jennifer would be safe.

She and Malcolm walked to the bedroom. An hour passed, they were laughing.

"It seems we have a way to make this work," she said.

They worked out details of where to live with the consent of the Council. There was a vote to allow them to live on Bright Star on a distant mountain range. They married. They were given a hovercraft to travel to and from places as needed. Several residents would travel there to help them start a farm and build them a home. Scientists would construct research buildings a distance away to study the universe as seen from Bright Star and asked Malcolm to help in describing that area of space and beyond as they created new star charts. They would also be discrete as they studied the Entity and family. Radio telescopes would be built strategically dotting the open land but only one of these would be near the two residents, it would be called the Malcolm Radio Observatory which he could visit anytime as he talked to the scientists.

The Narins in the meantime would continue research on how to preserve their friends and human mates for longer lifespans and the investigation of M13.

~ The Story Continues ~

CHAPTER XIV

DEFINITIONS

Photon Engines: Matter, anti-matter engines (a photon is a particle of electromagnetic radiation). A photon rocket engine would be powered by controlled annihilation of equal amounts of matter and anti-matter. Dangerous because of gamma rays produced by the annihilation of matter in launching the ship which would cause gamma rays and damage Earth. A two-stage chemical nuclear propulsion system would be necessary to move the spaceship far enough from Earth so it could be launched without causing damage.

Ion Engines: On October 24, 1998 a Delta Rocket lifted off from Cape Canaveral bearing a spacecraft, the DSI Probe (Deep Space 1), propelled by the Glenn Ion Thruster Solar Electric Propulsion (also known as Ion Propulsion). This system was developed and managed by Glenn's on Board Propulsion Branch. Ion propulsion uses electrically charged gas as the propellant instead of chemicals like liquid hydrogen and oxygen and uses a solar array that focused sunlight for extra power, no shielding to protect it. On December 18, 2001, NASA sent final commands to DSI which now remains in orbit around our sun.

Electric Plasma Engines: Are propelling the next generation of space probes to the outer solar system; NASA proposes 123,000 MPH plasma engine. Protons fuse with boron nuclei.

Proton (not Photon):	has a unit of positive electrical charge equal and opposite to that of the electron.
Traveling Wave Thermoacoustic Electric Generator:	An article in <u>Science Daily</u>, September 17, 2004 tells of a University of California scientist at Los Alamos National Laboratory and researchers from Northrop Grumman Space Technology have developed a method for generating electrical power for deep-space travel using sound waves. The Traveling—Wave Thermoacoustic Electric Generator has the potential to power space probes to the farthest reaches of the universe. The Traveling—Wave Engine/Linear Alternator System is similar to the current thermoelectric generators in that it uses heat from the decay of a radioactive fuel to generate electricity, but is more than twice as efficient. Los Alamos National Laboratory is operated by the University of California for the National Nuclear Security Administration (NNSA) of the U. S. Department of Energy and Works in partnership with NNSA's Sandia and Lawrence Livermore National Laboratories to support NASA in its mission.
Shear Alfvén Waves:	The fourth state of matter is plasma (hot ionized gas that is electrically conductive). The Hubble space telescope has sent back vivid images from space of ionized gas clouds (interstellar plasma), new 3-D images of Shear Alfvén Waves which are delighting scientists. Plasmas support a large variety of waves. Some of these are light and sound waves. One of the fundamental waves in magnetized plasma is the Shear Alfvén Wave, named after Nobel Prize winning scientist Hannes Alfvén who predicted their existence.

When they were first studied, it was discovered that their creation gives rise to exotic spacial patterns, all of them Shear Alfvén Waves. These waves are important in a wide variety of physical environments. They play a central role in the stability of the magnetic confinement devices used in fusion research, give rise to Aurora formation in planets and are thought to contribute to heating and ion acceleration in the solar corona. Shear Waves can also cause particle acceleration over considerable distances in interstellar space. Sparkles in the wave are proportional to the electric field in the plasma induced by the wave.

Solar Plage: Bright enhanced patches in the chromosphere of the sun surround the photospheric sunspot groups in spectroheliograms. Hotter and more dense than the normal chromosphere. They are larger than the active region of sunspots below them and always appear before the spots form. Life span is about forty to fifty days.

Super Novas and Novas: Most spectacular of the eruptive stars signaled by a rapid rise in brightness amounting to tens of thousands of times in a few hours. A slow decline in light for a year might persist until the star settles down.

Eruptive Star: A class of stars which undergo a violent superficial explosion because of a temporary instability. The most spectacular of the eruptive stars are the novas and supernovas.

Dying Star: Can become a white dwarf, black hole or a neutron star pulsar. Earth's sun will eventually become a white dwarf. A star's final state depends on whether degeneracy pressure can halt the crush of gravity. A white dwarf is supported by electron degeneracy pressure. A Neutron star is supported by neutron degeneracy pressure. If neutron degeneracy pressure can't halt the collapse, the core becomes a black hole. A dying star with too little mass to form a black hole becomes a neutron star. Some of these neutron stars are pulsars emitting powerful radio waves at regular intervals. A pulsar is a rotating neutron star with magnetic fields.

A black hole is a place where gravity has crushed matter into oblivion creating a hole in the universe from where nothing can escape, not even light. We can't see black holes directly but know they are present by their influence on their surroundings. The study of x-ray binaries shows that some of these binary systems may have black holes rather than neutron stars. The x-ray behavior of black hole systems differs from that of neutron stars because a neutron star has a surface and a black hole doesn't.

White dwarfs, neutron stars and black holes can all have close stellar companions from which they accrete matter.

Asteroid: Relatively small, rocky objects that revolve around the sun often referred to as minor planets or planetoids. Most are found in a region of the solar system known as the asteroid belt midway between the orbits of Mars and Jupiter.

<u>Meteor:</u>	Bright streak in the sky resulting from a small piece of interplanetary debris entering Earth's atmosphere and heating earth molecules which emit light. Smaller meteoroids are mainly the rocky remains of broken up comets.
<u>Kuniper Belt:</u>	A region in our solar system where most short-period comets are thought to originate outside the orbit of Neptune.
<u>Outer Space:</u>	Is everything beyond the Karman Line which is sixty-two miles above the Earth's surface. Deep space is 2.7 degrees Kelvin (space is cold). Astrophysists usually quote degrees in Kelvin.
<u>Prograde Orbits:</u>	Eastward motion for rotation, normal.
<u>Retrograde Orbits:</u>	There are periods when a planet's eastward motion (relative to the stars) stops and the planet appears to move westward in the sky for a month or two before reversing direction and continuing on its eastward journey.
<u>Solar Flare:</u>	A sudden and violent explosion of solar energy erupting as an intensely bright area in a chromosphere plage. A flare outburst rises from energy suddenly released in the chromosphere. This outburst is possibly triggered by the collapse of the local magnetic field in the plage. A major flare is the most energetic solar disturbance. Ultraviolet and x-ray radiations arrive at earth, disrupt radio communications and cause auroras in the magnetosphere.
<u>Prominence:</u>	A bright gas cloud arching outward from the sun. Can look like a loop, spray or surge shooting tens of thousands of miles off the sun's surface.

Dark Matter:	Matter that cannot be observed because it doesn't emit electromagnetic radiation. It has a gravitational influence in galaxy clusters and galactic halos as well as the warping of space, measured by gravitational lensing. 23% of the universe consists of dark matter. It is gravity like in that gravity holds planets, stars and galaxies together.
Dark Energy:	73% of the universe consists of dark energy. Makes objects repel like anti-gravity and makes the universe expand faster. Dark energy tugs on the fabric of space and time.
Revolution:	Earth revolves around the sun every 365 days.
Rotation:	Earth rotates on its axis every 24 hours.
Electromagnetic Radiation:	A form of energy that travels through space as waves of electric and magnetic fields. Commonly called radiation or light. It spans the range from short wavelength gamma rays to long wavelength radio waves. The radiation our eyes can detect is visible light.
Milky Way Galaxy:	Is Earth's galaxy. Has between 100 billion and 200 billion stars, has a 3-4 million—solar—mass black hole at the center which is not currently active but could be if it received fresh fuel say from a star coming to close. Diameter of disk is 100,000 LY (light years).
Light Year (LY):	The distance light travels in a year 186,000 miles per second or six trillion miles.
Parsec:	3.26 (LY) light years.
Black Hole:	One place to find black holes is in binary systems where the gas streams from a visible companion (component) of the binary to the black hole.

The center of a black hole is where gravity crushes all matter to an infinitely tiny and infinitely dense point called a singularity which is the point at which all the mass that created the black hole resides. A singularity is a black hole's heart. Nothing can ever emerge from the event horizon. Black holes emit no light. One state of a dying star.

Accretion Disk: A flat disk created by matter spiraling down onto the surface of a neutron star or black hole. Sometimes the matter originated on the surface of a companion star in a binary-star system. Binary-star systems which consist of two stars in orbit about a common center of mass, are held together by their mutual gravitational attraction. Some stars are members of triple, quadruple or even more complex systems. The accretion disk as a swirling flattened disk of matter can shoot out matter in opposite directions from a black hole or a neutron star.

Andromeda Galaxy: Our nearest galaxy 2.5 million light years (LY) away.

Pulsar: A neutron star is believed to be collapsed cores of supernova that have turned into superdense, rapidly rotating neutron stars.

Non-Static Universe: Our universe is moving and changing unlike in a static universe.

Kelvin Temperature: Used in astrophysics. Uses absolute zero as its starting point -273.15°c. the temperature at which all thermal atomic and molecular motion ceases. No object can have a temperature below that value. All thermal motion ceases at O Kelvins, abbreviate (OK). Water freezes at 273 Kelvins. Water boils at 373K.

Hydrogen: Is the main component of the universe.

<u>Earth's Atmosphere:</u>	Is 78.1% nitrogen, 20.9% oxygen, 1% water vapor which includes carbon dioxide and other gases. Air weights 14.7 PSI at the surface.
<u>Sun:</u>	Earth's star. Thermonuclear fusion occurs as the sun converts hydrogen into helium. Takes 200 million years to orbit around the Milky Way's nucleus. Will become a white dwarf when it has burned up the hydrogen in about seven billion years. It is the category of a yellow sun.
<u>Earth:</u>	Earth has a 24 hour rotation period and revolves around the sun every 365 days. Earth's circumference is 40,030 kilometers. Earth and our solar system is in the Cygnus Orion Arm of the Milky Way Galaxy. Orbital speed is 29.79 kmls.
<u>Proxima Centauri:</u>	Is the closest star to Earth after our sun. This star is a member of a triple star system, three separate stars orbiting one another bound together by gravity. These are known as the Alpha Centauri Complex.
<u>Comet:</u>	The nucleus is a mixture of ice, dust and rock. The coma is huge cloud of gas spanning 50,000 km.
<u>Stellar Atmospheres:</u>	Hydrogen is the most abundant element in stellar atmospheres and in space.

Atmospheres:	Gravity holds Earth's atmosphere in place. Heat, the rapid random motion of the molecules in a gas along with gravity keep the atmosphere buoyant. The sun supplies heat to Earth's atmosphere and the rapid movement of heated molecules produces pressure which opposes the force of gravity, preventing our atmosphere from collapsing under its own weight. An important measure of the strength of a body's gravity is the body's escape speed, the speed needed for any object to escape forever from its surface. This speed increases with increased mass or decreased radius of the parent body (often a moon or planet).

To determine whether a planet will retain an atmosphere, the planet's escape speed must be compared with the molecular speed which is the average speed of the gas particles making up the planet's atmosphere. This speed depends not only on the temperature of the gas, but also on the mass of the individual molecules—the hotter the gas or the smaller the molecular mass, the higher is the average speed of the molecules. Earth's gravity has more influence than the heat of our atmosphere and is able to retain its nitrogen-oxygen atmosphere. |
| Runaway Greenhouse Effect: | A process in which the heating of a planet leads to an increase in its atmosphere's ability to retain heat and thus to further heating, causing extreme changes in the temperature of the surface and the composition of the atmosphere. |
| Light: | Is an electromagnetic wave produced by accelerating charged particles. Light waves have a particle nature. |

Photometry:	The measure of brightness.
Interferometry:	The main disadvantage of radio astronomy compared to optical astronomy is its relatively poor angular resolution. Sometimes radio astronomers can overcome this limitation with interferometry. Radio telescopes are used in tandem to observe the same object at the same wavelength and at the same time (many separate radio telescopes are working together as a team).
Spectroscopy:	The study of the way in which atoms absorb and emit electromagnetic radiation. Spectroscopy allows astronomers to determine the chemical composition of stars. Stars get their greatly diverse spectral appearance mainly from their varied temperatures not from differences in their elements.
Spectrometer:	Instrument used to produce detailed spectra of stars. Usually, a spectrograph records a spectrum on a photographic plate, or more recently, in electronic form on a computer.
Spectral Class:	Classification scheme based on the strength of stellar spectral lines, which is an indication of the temperature of a star.
Spectrograph:	Usually a spectrograph records a spectrum on a CCD detector (a charged coupled device) for computer analysis. The optical telescope can be equipped to analyze celestial light by means of a spectrograph. This instrument disperses the composite light into its wavelengths so we can analyze the elements in the celestial body.

<u>Spectroscope:</u>	Instrument to view a light source so that it is split into its component colors. In many large instruments the prism is replaced by a device called a diffraction grating, consisting of a sheet of transparent material with numerous closely spaced parallel lines ruled on it. The spacing between the lines is typically a few microns, comparable to the wavelength of visible light. The spaces act as many tiny openings and light is diffracted as it passes through the grating (or is reflected from it depending on the design of the device). The different wavelengths of electromagnetic radiation are diffracted by different amounts on encountering the grating, the effect is to split a beam of light into its component colors. Large spectrometers work in tandem with optical telescopes, light collected by the primary mirror.
<u>Luminosity:</u>	A star's luminosity is the total amount of power (energy per second) it radiates into space which can be stated in watts.
<u>Brightness:</u>	Measurement of brightness is called photometry. The apparent brightness of any star in our sky as the amount of light reaching us per unit area. Apparent brightness is the amount of starlight reaching earth (energy per second per square meter).
<u>Electromagnetic Spectrum:</u>	Complete range of light as characterized by wavelength frequency or energy. The entire range of wavelengths for electromagnetic radiation consisting of gamma rays, x-rays, ultraviolet, visible light, infrared, microwave and radio waves (from short to long wavelengths)

Radio Telescope: Designed to detect and collect radiation at radio wavelengths. Radio astronomy studies celestial objects by examining radio waves. Radio telescopes are used to observe electromagnetic radiations longer than about one millimeter from celestial sources to one-hundred meters. Light waves and radio waves are both forms of electromagnetic radiation. One is visible (light), the other is not (radio waves). Radio telescopes have a large horseshoe shaped mount supporting a huge carved metal dish that serves as the collecting area. The dish captures incoming radio waves and reflects them to the focus, where a receiver detects the signals and channels them to a computer. The detecting instruments are placed at the prime focus. Radio detectors normally only register a narrow band of wavelengths at any one time. To observe radiation at another radio frequency, the equipment must be returned to pick-up the radiation. Cosmic radio sources are extremely faint. These telescopes can observe twenty-four hours a day. Observations can often be made through cloudy skies. Even the longest wavelength radio waves can be detected during rain or snow storms.

CREDITS

Science Daily   September 17, 2004 (on computer) Generating Power for Deep Space Travel

Science Daily   November 8, 2010 (on computer) Shear Alfvén Waves

Astronomy Today   2008 Edition Textbook, Chaisson & McMillan

National Radio Astronomy (NARO)   In Socorro, NM helped answer questions about radio Astronomy and give tours.